INDIANAPOLIS

Three Grindhouse Novellas
by
Alec Cizak
Scotch Rutherford
and
Andrew Miller

Foreword by
Rex Weiner

Contents:

FOREWORD

You could say I first learned L.A. from the point of view of a corpse. It was 1981, and I'd been to Los Angeles before, but Disneyland doesn't count and Mickey Mouse can go fuck himself. If you really want to know LA, as I later came to understand it, you've got to take the wheel in a city always rushing to be born when it's not too busy dying.

The city sideswiped me early on when my high school sweetheart ran away from our little upstate New York burg to L.A. with a close friend's husband. It was the early '70s, the two of them following their dreams to the Hotel Wilcox, a rundown Hollywood flophouse on the corner of Wilcox and Selma, where the small-town runaways were found DOA of a double OD. It's now an upscale hipster hang with a rooftop bar. Probably has a nice view.

Cut to October, 1981, a sweltering Santa Ana condition in the City of Angels: I arrived from New York City under contract to Columbia Pictures to write a screenplay based on my original stories about a "punk rock detective" named Ford Fairlane. Escaping a bankrupt Gotham, a stalled writing career, and a failed relationship, I was taking a long shot in a newly unfolding decade. Sorta glam, sorta punk, with its own Ronnie Reagan in the White House, LA gave me second chance—and more cash in my pocket than I'd ever imagined would be mine. Riding around in my producer's Ferrari, blasting X's "Johnny Hit And Run Paulene," banging the hottest chicks and snorting the best coke movie money could buy, I'd say the world was my motherfucking oyster.

For research purposes, I was often accompanied in jaunts across the city by Donny and Ray, two plainclothes detectives from Sheriff's Homicide, assigned by the studio, and paid under the table, to show the new guy around. My two cops had a field day cruising all over town busting my balls with the nastiest, grossest shit they could throw at me. They regarded it as "light duty."

One afternoon on a visit to the city morgue, after pointing out the world's saddest corner where dead babies were stacked like cordwood, they led me over to the "canoe factory." This was where bodies on slabs undergoing examination by the county coroner showed up-thrust rib cages vaguely suggesting something Hiawatha might've paddled across a tranquil lake. Passing a nude cadaver with a blonde bush and a bullet hole in her chest—a Sunset Strip hooker shot point-blank by her pimp—one of my cop pals grabbed my hand and clapped it onto the dead woman's icy breast. "Nice tits, eh?" Donny said. Then he looked over at Ray. "Your turn," he said.

Those guys were a barrel of laughs.

I was supposed to ride around with them for a couple of weeks but those weeks turned into a lifetime trip, until Ray passed away. I still count Don as one of my closest friends, now retired and memory mostly sketchy. I like to drive out to the ranch where he lives with his wife in the high desert, shoot guns, drink too much whisky for his own good (and mine), and talk a lot of crazy shit.

The same kind of crazy shit is what you'll find in this formidable anthology, I promise you, and then some. Assembled by Alec Cizak, today's foremost crime fiction outlaw triple-threat writer/editor/publisher, he is joined by notorious *Switchblade Magazine* editor Scotch Rutherford, and their prolific crime writer crony Andrew Miller. Together they deliver a scabrous tribute to LA in the Eighties that gives "edgy" an even finer, bloodier, demented edge, while uncannily capturing a time and a place, from Oki-Dog to Musso & Frank.

Call it Grindhouse, Transgressive, Nuevo Noir, or whatever—if you're easily disturbed by murder, cannibalism ("fresh cutlets in the freezer"), incest, graphic sex ("He had his pickle in her business"), flying "on the wings of Kukulán" back in time to LA's darkest era, you couldn't do better than Cizak and his partners in this shocking (and often laugh-out-loud in spite of yourself) literary outrage. I've met them all and I swear, they're sweet guys in real life. On the printed page, they're absolutely terrifying.

Your turn.

Rex Weiner
December 2021
Los Angeles, CA

by
Alec Cizak

From the Hank Shepherd Show, June 3, 1979:

Hank: Welcome back. You're listening to the Hank Shepherd Show on KABC, 790 AM. All Talk, All the Time. I am, of course, the one, the only, Reverend Hank Shepherd. Wherever there's a spiritual crisis, I'm the man for the job. This hour brought to you by Schlitz beer. Whatever you've got planned, make it great, make it Schlitz... I spent the last segment talking your ear off about some of these so-called comedians that have been sprouting up around the country lately. I can remember when Lenny Bruce was considered vulgar. Good Lord and Mother Mary, what would Lenny think of the filth coming from his cohorts these days? Hey, Mr. Carlin, there's a reason you can't say those words on television—we don't want to hear them! It's like these degenerates from the big cities who think the people out in the country don't have a say in how we run things around here. Last time I checked, this is a democracy and, frankly, I feel we're having one point of view dictated to us by the entertainment industry and it's not the point of view this country was founded on. No sir. We're headed to the phone lines. Let's go to Carol, in Santa Monica—

Carol: What culture are you trying to get back to, Reverend Shepherd? Mowing down students at universities for protesting a brutal, violent, corrupt foreign policy? Attacking black people in the South for wanting to be treated with half an ounce of dignity?

Hank: So, I'm guessing you're one of the meatheads responsible for the dolt we got in the White House right now. Look, lady, the level of permissiveness in this nation has gotten absurd. The Loews theater at the mall in my neighborhood, they actually show X-rated movies now. Caligula. You heard of this one? Wall to wall, hardcore pornography. I thought it was going to be a historical picture. My wife and I walked out after the first hour and a half. I'm telling you, if we don't put the clamps down, we're going to have complete anarchy.

Carol: What you call permissiveness, sane people call equal rights.

Hank: How dare you refer to the influx of psychotic behavior as sane. Only in a sick, filthy, degenerate world would we even entertain the notion that showing an X-rated film in the same theater as Disney's superb science fiction film, The Black Hole, a movie I took my nephews to, is in any way appropriate. What if a child wanders into the wrong theater by mistake?

Carol: He'll see something natural. What's wrong with that?

Hank: You haven't seen this Caligula picture, have you?

Jerry couldn't remember his last name. Lost it somewhere between basic training and Saigon. Sometimes he caught a glimpse, a trace of memory from combat. A man he didn't recognize, shouting in a language he never bothered to learn, emerging from a hole in the ground. He didn't think twice, he shot the man with his army-issued M-16. Took multiple showers to scrub all the blood and bone fragments from his body. He found the needle on leave in Thailand. Hooker he'd spent the night with introduced him. Said it would take him to other planets, help him avoid thinking about all the shit he'd seen, all the shit he would see, before his tour finished. He plunged the junk into his vein and stopped giving a goddamn about anything. When it became obvious he couldn't hold a job back in the states, his wife checked him in to the VA hospital in Brentwood. His mother and his brothers thought it cruel, threatened to sue her. He told them not to. Orderlies filled him with Thorazine every day. Existence dwindled to the easiest tasks—Open eyes, take drugs, allow nurses to shove food in his mouth, take drugs, eat again, close eyes, over and over until darkness wrapped its arms around him for a final embrace. Simple.

By that time, he no longer identified as Jerry. He called himself J-Unit 83. Claimed angels named him during a vision he had in the hospital. These angels looked like children with large, gray heads and black, almond-shaped eyes. They slipped through cracks of light that materialized in thin air. They told him they were the true servants of God. Invited him to join their crusade. "Spring me from this loony bin," he said, "and I'm yours." He got his walking papers within a week. "Guess I owe them motherfuckers," he said to the clouds, the first time he stepped onto a cracked, crumbling Los Angeles sidewalk in the new decade—the wild, free 1970s. The city looked nothing like it had in '68, when he went into the service. Those days, he could still smell the gold at Wilshire and Western, still see the ghosts of Fatty Arbuckle and Douglas Fairbanks cruising for starlets outside the Ambassador and the Brown Derby.

Now he roamed Hollywood Boulevard and the Sunset Strip every night. Pushed a shopping cart filled with items he believed God wanted him to have. Why else had they been left in the street? He recovered a red telephone from a wire-mesh trashcan outside the Roxy nightclub. Such a work of technology, just sitting there, waiting for him—a sure sign from God. Using duct tape off a roll he pulled from a dumpster behind the Chinese Theater, he secured the phone to his right, upper-arm. It became his personal line to the angels, whom he now recognized as the Lords of the Galaxy.

On a scorching June night in 1979, J-Unit encountered Matthew Roberts for the first time. Matthew was a lanky white guy stumbling through the neon-coated haze loitering like a demon over Hollywood and Highland. Any time a smoking-hot hooker bumped into him, he shielded his eyes, like he thought getting a peek at some fine pussy might kill him. He reminded J-Unit of the frail peckerwoods who'd pissed their pants in the jungle when shit got crucial. Peckerwoods like Don Corya, who walked around camp with his chest huffed like he was Atlas. First firefight the kid saw, he hid behind J-Unit until the platoon wiped out the enemy. He begged J-Unit not to snitch on him for being yellow. J-Unit collected half the kid's paychecks for six straight months.

Matthew Roberts was buttoned up in a plain dress shirt and plaid pants and a heavy sports jacket. The peckerwood looked like he'd just stepped off a bus from Shithole, Alabama. He carried himself like he belonged on one of them talk shows with those famous honkeys who bullshitted about poverty and freedom and laughed at jokes that weren't funny. The peckerwood carried a Bible under his left arm and twitched to the right when he walked, like someone had stuck a cattle prod up his ass and he'd never gotten over it. The tin-tones of an AM station crackled from a small transistor radio in his shirt pocket.

The peckerwood pointed at the phone in J-Unit's hand, flashed him a condescending smile—the same expression J-Unit witnessed every time he asked a tourist for spare change. They'd pat down their clothes, as though they randomly put money in them and simply forgot about it until right then. Sometimes they dug out a few nickels and dimes, sometimes they'd give him a handful of pennies, as though that shit was worth something in nineteen-*goddamn*-seventy-nine. The ones who were more comfortable with their greed, they shrugged and said they had nothing. All of them, no matter what they coughed up, offered the same, stupid-ass grin people wore when confronted with a slice of reality they'd been, for the most part, spared.

"The fuck you looking so jolly for?" J-Unit said to the peckerwood.

"Oh, no." The peckerwood shook his head. "I'm sensing a lot of stress here."

"No shit, Sherlock." J-Unit had been talking to angels before the peckerwood strolled over. He told them he'd call back and hung up. "I'm trying to negotiate a peace treaty between motherfuckers from the star system known as Horace. You ever took on some shit like that?" Before the peckerwood could answer, J-Unit said, "I didn't think so. You don't look like the kind of motherfucker'd get a hard on counting a bitch's pubic hair. You sure as shit don't look like no kind of diplomat." He tried to get away.

"I feel your pain, brother," said the peckerwood.

"The fuck you calling *brother*?"

"We're all brothers and sisters in God's family."

The voice of some fake, racist-ass preacher struggled from the tiny speaker on the peckerwood's radio.

"You going to talk to me about God?" What he would have done to get that radio, get something super high tech to use to communicate with the Lords of the Galaxy.

The peckerwood turned the volume on the radio down and brought his Bible to his chest, embraced it like a child holding a doll for security. It had a nice, leather cover. The pages looked like they'd been rifled through many, many times. "I'm so glad you asked that."

"You don't know shit about God."

"I beg to differ." He grabbed J-Unit's shoulder.

J-Unit stared at the peckerwood until he removed his hand. "Do something like that again, motherfucker," he said. "I triple-goddamn-dog dare you."

The peckerwood put his hands out, emulated the Rabbi on the cross. "So sorry, brother."

Brother. *Again*. Did this dumbass not understand that J-Unit 83 represented a higher form of life that no hairless monkey could possibly be related to? He said so out loud, he said, "Listen, you pale little primate, don't you ever think we're on the same plane of existence. I come from the loins of the cosmos. You're barely out of the swamp, you hear me?"

"Oh, no, no, no," said the peckerwood. "Evolution is *Satan*'s theory." He slurred the 's,' as though maybe he'd gotten drunk, for just a moment, thinking about evil. Peckerwoods were like that—acting like they stood on the highest peaks when they knew damn well they frolicked in blood-soaked rivers in the valley any time they thought nobody was looking.

"*Shit*," J-Unit said. "Evolution is *all* part of God's plan. You can't see the intelligence there, you need to put in for a new set of wits, 'cause you've been bamboozled."

Neon lights from the tourist shops cut rainbows through the haze. A harsh green aura the color of NyQuil surrounded the peckerwood. Looked like the devil had pissed on him. J-Unit picked up the receiver on his arm and dialed. "I think I got something," he said into the phone. Then he listened to the angels' instructions. When he finished with them, he said to the peckerwood, "They could use you at the temple."

"Excuse me?"

"They say I should bring you to the temple. Motherfuckers there, they got a thing for pencil-dicks like yourself."

The peckerwood said, "I've got a better idea." He produced a business card from his inside jacket pocket. "Name's Matthew Roberts." He held the card out for a moment. When J-Unit refused to take it, he put it back where it came from. "Anyway, I'm looking for lost, hungry souls." He stared at him for a moment too long, reminded J-Unit of the Thai girls he fucked in Bangkok, how they held onto him afterwards, acting like he didn't have someplace else to be. The shit made him nervous. He thought about throwing the peckerwood into the street, letting a bus turn him into jelly. The peckerwood snapped out of his gaze and said, "I look into your eyes, brother, and I see someone who's missing the Lord's nutrition."

"I do get hungry sometimes," said J-Unit. "The angels usually provide what I need."

"Amen, bro—Amen, ah, what's your name?"

J-Unit said nothing.

"Well, my church is on Fountain and Fairfax. West Hollywood. Right down the street from the Chateau Marmont." He paused, as though he expected J-Unit to know what the fuck he was talking about. "We meet every night at six," he said. "There's a kitchen for, you know, people like...*you*."

The peckerwood had been right about one thing—J-Unit had not eaten since that morning, when he found a bite from an Egg McMuffin outside the McDonald's off Highland. Some tourists stood in line at the Hollywood Theater to watch that damn *Star Wars* movie, gawked at him like they'd never seen a motherfucker eat. "You got some change you could give me?" he said to the peckerwood.

Matthew Roberts searched his pockets. Took less than ten seconds pretending to look for money. "I'd rather give you the best change there is—Jesus Christ."

"Get the fuck out of here." J-Unit shoved the peckerwood into a glass display window filled with plastic Charlie Chaplin and Marilyn Monroe statues. He pushed his shopping cart over Matthew's feet and hustled down Highland toward Sunset. He glanced back and saw a rat the size of a rabbit leap onto the sidewalk from the street, its spine twisting in directions familiar only to those who'd been to the seventh dimension and back. The rodent hissed at Matthew Roberts, its black eyes shining under a broken streetlamp.

"They going to get him," J-Unit said to himself. "Them motherfuckers is on the way."

From the Hank Shepherd Show, June 3, 1979:

Hank: Hey friends, you're listening to the Hank Shepherd Show on KABC, 970 AM. The Hank Shepherd Show is brought to you by Smith & Wesson. It's an unsure world out there, let Smith & Wesson make things a little more secure where you live. Smith & Wesson, because a bullet speaks louder than votes… Hey friends, I want to talk about Hollywood for just a moment, if you'll indulge me. And you will. I'm in charge of this show. Thank God. And I mean that, literally. Thank. God. Have you seen the tripe they're putting out these days? For every good, wholesome film like Star Wars, we're assaulted by a dozen pieces of crap like Texas Chainsaw Massacre, or the absolute worst of them all, Last House on the Left. Have you seen this garbage? The sleaze-maestros responsible for that one claim it was inspired by an Ingmar Bergman film. This is a movie that has the audacity to suggest slaughtering the murderers of your children is somehow just as immoral as the murderers themselves. It's that relativism garbage they've been pushing at the universities for the last two decades, telling young folks there's no such thing as right or wrong. Sweet Jesus. And the justification for this garbage, this Last House on the Left, is that it was inspired by some European socialist named Ingmar Bergman? Sounds like a good reason to ban anything by Ingmar Bergman from here on. While we're at it, why not ban anything from Europe? Good Lord, almighty. One scene in this movie Last House on the Left, it shows a young, decent white woman shot in the head. What kind of society are we building where shock hucksters are allowed to pollute the minds of our youth with images of people being shot, point blank, in the head? What's next? Movies depicting torture for pure entertainment? Let's go to the phones. We got Ted, from Long Beach—

Ted: I think you're talking about b-pictures, Hank. Those movies you mentioned, they don't really come from Hollywood.

Hank: Well, Hollywood is synonymous with film, so you'll forgive my occasional technical gaff.

Ted: It's an important distinction, though. Hollywood films serve to reinforce the status quo.

Hank: Friends, the status quo in 1979 is decadent, depraved, and needs to be eradicated.

Aton Miller put his hand on his wife Eva's knee. Her black skirt stopped just below her waist. He couldn't take his eyes off her thighs. Meaty in all the right places. Thank God she'd never wanted to be an actress. Hollywood compelled actresses to starve themselves to meet some sick pervert's notion of sexy. "I want to eat you right here," he said to her.

She brushed her hand across his face. "Calm down, baby." She'd worn Fendi. Her skin smelled like a spice sent from another planet. "What are you in the mood for tonight?" she said.

His eyes focused on a homeless man in a brown, soot-stained suit. The grease and dirt on his face identified him as a street person. The tie and button-down shirt made him more interesting than the usual hooker or dope fiend. This man had been something at one point. Not like the starlets and fairies who came to Hollywood to be in the movies and quickly learned it was an invite-only affair. He squinted, thought he recognized the man. He pointed him out to his wife. "Seems like I know that fellow."

"Holy cow," she said. "That's Bill Baxter."

Her husband drew his head back. "*No.*"

"Look at him. That's the same suit he wore when Dick Zeitman fired him."

Aton pulled their Town Car to the curb. Rolling down the window, he snapped his fingers at the man in the suit and said, "Bill?"

The homeless man searched a wire trashcan by a bench so polluted with graffiti its original color could not be discerned. The sign announcing Bus Stop had a swastika spray-painted over the letters. The stench of urine dominated unpleasant odors drifting into the car.

Aton and his wife stepped outside. He tapped the man on his shoulder. "Bill? It's me, Aton Miller." He wanted to wash his hand as soon as he felt the moist, sticky, unwashed fabric of the man's clothes.

The man stopped sifting through old newspapers and cardboard cartons of stale and rotten food. "Aton? Vicious Pictures?"

"Buddy!" Aton opened his arms for a hug, the standard greeting amongst producers. Even the has-beens, the washed-ups, the kicked out for transgressions the Dens of Babylon couldn't tolerate, yes, even the men sentenced to homelessness were forever treated to this phony ritual.

Bill Baxter didn't move.

Eva said, "What are you doing out here?"

"Are you stupid?" said Bill. "You don't know what happened after *The Erotic Adventures of Helen Keller* tanked?"

"You should never have crossed over to hardcore porn," said Aton. "I know the receipts are good, but they don't let you in the front door once you've exploited the back door."

"Are you kidding?" He directed their attention to the Pussycat Theater, across the street. "They've been selling out *Deep Throat* for seven years now."

Aton couldn't break his heart, tell him only the mafia profited off smut pictures. The money may have gone into cash registers in Los Angeles, but it was counted and divvied in New York. "You should have stayed with Richard," he said. "King International pretty much owns the drive-ins these days."

"That prick let me go. You know that. Everybody in this filthy town knows that. They didn't want me producing a fuck-flick they shouldn't have stopped giving me the time of day. Hypocrites, every last one of them. You see *Last Tango in Paris*? That's pornography, people, *that's* pornography." He stepped away from them. Tripped over the trashcan.

Aton grabbed him by his shoulder and helped him to his feet. "I could always use a veteran at Vicious Pictures. This knife movie, *Halloween*, it's been knocking them over from here to Boston. Super simple, buddy. Put a freak in a mask, have him chase some girls with big tits, sit back and let the dollars flow like the River Jordan. We're ready to make our own version. I figure the appeal is the sex before the murders. They don't really show any skin or violence in *Halloween*, though. Big mistake, I say. Get some blood on that screen, hire some girls willing to show the full bush, oh, buddy, we'll swim in the green. Box office petrol, baby, I'm talking millions on the dollar."

"I hate that horror shit." Bill Baxter tried to leave again.

Eva put her hand out like a traffic officer. She spoke in her rational, diplomatic tone, the one she employed to squeeze extra cash from executives too stingy to fund reshoots *they themselves* had ordered. "Bill, you're a producer. You shouldn't be living off trash."

"Just dinner and a conversation, Bill," said Aton. "You don't have to commit to anything."

"Why do you care?"

"You told me what I needed to know when I started in this town. I owe you." Aton put his arm around his wife.

Bill Baxter laughed. "You two look just like Gomez and Morticia Addams."

"Thank you," said Eva.

From the Hank Shepherd Show, June 3, 1979:

Hank: You're listening to the Hank Shepherd Show on KABC, 970 AM. Hey friends, are you worried your rations might run out when the apocalypse comes and you've retreated to your shelter or your cabin or wherever you plan to go? Grim's Baked Beans is the answer. Grim's is made with the finest preservatives. Stock your shelves with Grim's Baked Beans, guaranteed to stay fresh for decades to come… Now, I want to get back to what I was talking about before the break. My son, he's in kindergarten, he comes home the other day and tells me about the alphabet pictures his teacher's put up over the blackboard. Says each letter has a picture of someone doing a job that begins with that letter. So, for instance, next to the letter J, there's a picture of a guy sweeping the floor. You know, a janitor. I say, that's interesting. Then he tells me all the respectable jobs, like 'd' for doctor, or ' l' for lawyer, they got pictures of women, and all the jobs nobody wants to do, they got pictures of men. So I pay a visit to his teacher and I ask her what the heck she's thinking, putting these terrible ideas into my boy's head. Well, she shows up for a parent-teacher conference in a sundress I could see straight through once I focused and took a good look. She doesn't wear a bra and, my friends, the air-conditioning was working well that day and her chest is just pointing right at me, like maybe I'd forget why I showed up in the first place. She turns out to be, surprise-surprise, one of these uppity feminist gals. She tells me boys don't need encouragement. She gives me the usual this-and-that about patriarchy and schmatriarchy, like maybe I haven't heard this routine before, like maybe I live on a foreign planet or something. She says girls need to be encouraged now. I explained to her that she was righting a wrong with another wrong. She called me a barbarian, called me a knuckle dragger, a mouth breather, whatever the heck that means, said she was sure glad she had my boy under

her influence on account of the fact that I'm such a myso-myso
something, I don't even remember. She was just making up words,
calling me names, like that constituted a mature argument. So much
for an intelligent exchange with someone on the left...

Matthew Roberts handed out the last of his business
cards for his church. Standing by the Pussycat Theater, he
wished the patrons going in and exiting a blessed day. If
any of the perverts cursed him, he told them, "Jesus loves
you." Flashed his Bible in their faces. Some nights he got
punched in the mouth. He turned the other cheek, as the
church ordained. Stuffed his hands in his pockets and
squeezed until his knuckles turned to ivory. On the
evening he met J-Unit 83, the devil took control of his
body around midnight.

It started in his crotch, as always. *Even the word is*
dirty—crotch. One mini-skirt-clad prostitute after another
traipsed past him, some offering their services, some
calling him names ("Hey, Bible Boy," or, more often,
"Aren't you on the wrong side of the street, sweetie?").
Oh, how they made his blood *boil.* They'd rub their
breasts in front of him, lick their lips. Some of them
would lift their skirts and pat themselves on their naughty
parts. They'd laugh, ask him why he blushed. He'd engage
them in conversation about Jesus. They usually stomped
off the moment they realized he had no interest in renting
their bodies.

The night he met J-Unit 83, a woman in a bleach-
blonde curly wig approached him. She looked British, like
women he'd seen in a sinful movie called *A Clockwork*
Orange. "Evening, honey," she said. Her breasts ballooned
in her tiny, leather bra. A slit ran up the side of her pink
mini-skirt. She had bruises inside her thighs. Somehow,
that made the devil stronger, made The Voice louder—

Open that whore like a bag of potato chips!

"Have you heard about Jesus?" Matthew turned down the radio in his pocket. Neither he nor his hero, Reverend Hank Shepherd, could convince him, at that point, that he didn't want to take the woman to an alley and save her. *Yes, yes, save her. She's making your naughty bits move. She's not supposed to do that! Save her! Save her!*

"Why don't we step into my office? I'll show you some real old-time religion." The woman flicked her tongue at him like a lizard.

Oh, wouldn't you just love to bite that slimy thing in half?

Matthew adjusted his collar. His underarms dripped from the summer heat. Satan's breath on his neck smelled like popcorn and perfume. "Okay," he said, trying to sound weaker than he felt.

The prostitute took his hand. "Come on, honey." Her palm was sweaty and sticky. She led him to Orange Street. They walked down an alley behind a disco that had been converted to a punk rock club called *Shrub's*. One evil form of music traded for another. And the people inside had the audacity to call themselves progressive. When disco had been king, lanky men who liked to show their chests loitered near the door. The new clientele, the punks, dressed like they were tougher, but when they spoke, they didn't seem different from the disco crowd at all. A street lamp at the far end cast a violet light on the brick buildings. Had things been any less evil when they'd been built in the 1920s, when Hollywood kept its pagan leanings to itself? The prostitute stopped, put her hand on his arm and said, "Ten for a tuggy. Twenty-five for a whistle. Fifty for a dive. Seventy-five if you like it raw."

"Oh," said Matthew, "let's make it raw."

Yeah, baby, grind inside that squishy hole until it bleeds!

The woman unzipped the closed side of her skirt and slid it down her legs. No panties. She didn't shave that awful clump of hair just above her sopping, slippery lips. Hadn't she gotten the memo? All whores shaved their naughty parts to avoid crabs. Matthew turned his head, offended by the smell from between her thighs. She climbed out of the skirt and laid it on a closed, metal trashcan. The lid looked like the punk rockers had slammed it against the walls a few times. She squealed and jumped toward Matthew when a black rat poked its snout from behind the garbage can and ran to the mouth of the alley. The damned beast looked like a miniature werewolf, its eyes glowing in the purple light.

"Jesus," said the prostitute.

"Amen." Matthew put his Bible on the ground. He helped the prostitute unhook her bra and dropped it onto her skirt. He shoved his crotch into her back. "Please hurry."

She snaked her hand into his pants and stroked him. Her fingers were so sticky he thought they'd rip the skin off his naughty part. When he didn't respond, when his naughty part stayed limp, the woman said, "What's wrong?"

He shoved her fingers out of the way and yanked his naughty part until it behaved.

The woman bent over the trashcan she'd placed her clothes on. She spread her legs and pulled him inside her. She pushed back against his thrusts, rocked the lid on the trashcan to a steady rhythm.

"Oh God." Matthew slid in and out of her, increased the pace until his thighs smacked her skin loud enough to echo off the walls around them. As he climaxed, he slapped her ass, digging his fingernails into her hips, making her shriek.

They remained attached while they caught their breath.

Just look at how this used, wasted creature has betrayed your purity!

He picked up the woman's bra and wrapped it around her throat. "Whore," he whispered.

She brought her hands high to stop the attack. Matthew yanked her head back and strangled her. The bra straps dug into her skin until she bled. When she stopped moving, he let her drop to the trashcan, which spilled with her weight and knocked over a rubber can next to it.

He waited, as he always did, for God to tell him he had done the right thing. It didn't happen. As usual. He scraped his Bible off the ground and ran away from his latest judgment.

Bill Baxter had accepted the drink from Eva and passed out when the glass was still half full. She and Aton dragged his body into their kitchen and hoisted him onto the giant, stainless steel counter in the center of the room. *Claire De Lune* seasoned the mood from a radio near the sink as they laid plastic around the counter to catch stray fragments.

Once upon a time, Bill Baxter had been chubby, carried a paunch signifying his success as a movie producer. He knew how to work a bar in L.A., let the women know he'd manufactured hits and made people famous. Despite his hefty stature, he'd go home with whomever he wanted. Rumor had it he'd kept track of his conquests, wrote the names of the wanna-be starlets he bedded on the inside of his closet in his bungalow in Malibu. Living on the streets had shrunk him so much he resembled a concentration camp survivor. His round cheeks had scrunched inward, making his face look like a thin layer of skin stretched across a skull. His sharp, beady eyes, once nestled inside thick, meaty lids, had become saucers, the eyes of a bug.

"You think he'll provide enough meat?" Aton asked as he watched his wife strip off Bill Baxter's suit and tie. He smacked Bill Baxter's jaw, producing a hollow sound.

She said, "Sweetheart, we're doing your old friend a favor. Nobody's going to work with him ever again. He produced *actual* porn, for Christ's sake. I mean, *you* made a mistake, but you'll recover. You even mention Bill Baxter in a meeting, they'll laugh you out the door."

"I suppose." He opened a cabinet near the sink. As he took out a hacksaw, he said to his wife, "Get naked, sweetheart." He ran his fingers along the teeth of the saw.

Aton and Eva removed their clothes. Eva folded them and placed them on top of the refrigerator. "I'm so hungry." She caressed her husband as he carved into Bill Baxter's right shoulder. Blood splattered and bone splinters tossed and turned. The arm detached from the rest of the body with a swift crunch. Eva put it into the sink to be washed. Aton repeated the process for the other arm. He cut off the left leg and, as he went to work on the right leg, Bill Baxter awoke.

He rolled over, no doubt expecting to balance on his arm. The remaining weight on the opposite side of his body forced him back. He rocked a bit, like a Weeble-Wobble. Then he screamed. His voice struggled over blood gurgling through his throat.

Eva, busy rinsing the severed limbs, shook her head. "Oh, dear. That won't do."

Aton grabbed Bill Baxter's lower jaw and forced it open. "Easy, now." He wedged the hacksaw into the hinges holding Bill Baxter's skull together and ground through it until the jaw slid onto Bill Baxter's chest. "This is going to be hell to clean," Aton said to his wife. He ripped Bill Baxter's lower jaw from a patch of blood it had gotten stuck to and tossed it into the sink.

Tendons and bone fragments whipped and cracked as Bill Baxter tried to protest. Tears cut paths down the sides of his bloodstained face. Every time his lungs heaved, red, translucent bubbles popped and boiled around the gap where his jaw had been. Aton turned him over and sliced into his back. "Come here, baby," he said to his wife.

"I'm busy," she said.

"I have a gift for you."

Eva scrubbed her hands clean.

Aton carved out a foot of Bill Baxter's spine. He licked the blood and torn tissue off it. He approached his wife and got on his knees. "Here, my dear," he said.

She opened her thighs. She played with her husband's hair while he slid Bill Baxter's spine between her legs. She swayed, like a girl working a hula-hoop, faster and faster, until her knees buckled and she collapsed. Aton flipped the spine fragment into the sink and entered his wife. They made love to the sounds of Debussy and Bill Baxter's harsh, unattractive death rattle.

From the Hank Shepherd Show, June 3, 1979:

Hank: Your radio dial is set to AM 970, KABC. You're getting an ear-full of inspiration on the Hank Shepherd Show. Friends, I started to talk about this before the break and I don't want to move on until I get this out of my system. So I drive across Hollywood Boulevard and I see these movie theaters showing smut. Porn films. I'm curious, you know? Are these movies anything like this Caligula garbage? Turns out, they're all the same. No differentiation whatsoever. I mean, I thought Hollywood was the land of imagination, dreams. Is everybody having the same, insipid, vulgar dream? You ever watched one of these things? I mean, really, REALLY watched one? Purely for research purposes, I attended a screening of Deep Throat. I know you've heard of this one. The corrupt, mainstream media has been all over it, acting like it's some profound cultural event. Yeah, right. Maybe during the fall of Rome this sort of smut could be called meaningful. Goodness gracious. Close ups of genitals locked together in throbbing heat. This Linda Lovelace, you seen her? She's not even that attractive. I'm looking around me at this theater, the Pussycat Theater, of course, talk about lack of imagination….Anyway, there's people fornicating right there in the movie theater, grown men humiliating themselves in public. It was like watching a live performance of National Geographic, only humans were doing it instead of animals. Tell me how that's not disgusting. Sex is a closed-door activity, isn't it? Otherwise, are we any different from the animals? Let's take a call. Herman from Orange County, how are you, my friend?

Herman: Hank, don't you think it's time to take action ourselves? Our politicians aren't doing a damn thing to stop this downward slide. Cops sure as hell have no power. Was a time you could rely on the cops to keep the degenerates in line. Was a time politicians would put sleaze where it belonged—behind bars. You know what I'd like to see? I'd like to see somebody hunt these smut producers like predators, shoot them in their fat faces. You think Hollywood would change its tune if some of these slime balls started getting gunned down?

Hank: I understand your frustration, Herman, but are you prepared to go to jail for life over the killing of someone who's basically lower than a rat?

Herman: If that's what it takes.

Matthew Roberts turned off his radio. He washed his hands with a hose left on the front lawn of his apartment building. He dried them on his pants and entered the code for the door. The lobby smelled like body odor. He thought of the prostitute he'd saved earlier. It made him nauseous. A young couple he didn't recognize rode on the old-fashioned cage elevator with him. The girl's bellbottoms hugged her hips so tight they might as well have been skin. She left the top half of her frilly, vanilla blouse open. Her pendulous breasts begged for his attention. The boy had big, bushy sideburns covering his sharp cheekbones. Beautiful skin, like a surfer. Matthew faced forward. He told himself the kids didn't even exist, that he'd only imagined them. They got off on the floor before his. The boy had bathed in Old Spice. Matthew held his breath. When the girl passed him on her way out, she grimaced. He heard her laugh as the doors closed.

Do we need to save all of them?

He straightened his clothes as he stepped off the elevator on his floor and found the key to the door of his apartment. His wife, Linda Hanson-Roberts, sat at the kitchen table, typing her latest Christian manifesto. As he walked in and greeted her, she tossed two valiums down her throat. She chased them with a glass of gin. "Honey." She didn't look him in the eye when she spoke to him.

Save her! Save her!

Matthew leaned over and kissed her forehead. How soon before he could duck into the bathroom and scrub his lips with soap and water? Her skin tasted like wet leather. Not at all like the young girls on Hollywood Boulevard. The wrinkles above her brows grinned. The devil's grin. Linda reminded him more and more of his mother. That hadn't been the case when they'd met ten years earlier. Unlike his mother, Martha Roberts, his wife made it clear she would punch him right back if he ever thought of raising a hand to her. How different growing up with a weak woman had been. Whenever his father, Dale Roberts, a truck driver, came home from the road, he spent most of his time beating his wife. Sometimes with a belt, sometimes with a wooden spoon. Usually with his fists. He'd curl his hands into weapons and the gouges and scars on his knuckles would announce themselves like war medals. Little Matthew Roberts threatened him once—

First came the laughter. Then the derision. His father, who looked like Hoss Cartwright from *Bonanza* and always reeked of Old Spice, had said, "You puny faggot. You can't even take your sister. How the fuck you expect to trade blows with a *real* man?" Then the shellacking. His dad's forearms eclipsed Little Matthew's face. The old man clobbered him until he folded himself on the floor near their tacky, flower-patterned couch and sobbed.

Matthew's sister Camille bullied him as well. She provided an early counterpoint to his spineless mother. After school, she'd knock him over and sit on his chest. She was a big girl, inflated to balloon proportions on a diet of Twinkies and donuts. She rarely showered and she always wore shorts, rubbing her flabby, cheese-like thighs against him. She'd pin his arms down with her feet and straddle him. She'd flick at his eyes and his temples with her fingers. "What's the matter, shitface?" she'd say. "You going to wet your panties?"

His sister went to trade school. Studied engines so she could be a mechanic for a race car team. Her dream: Work the pits at the Indy 500. She had posters of Bill Vukovich and Mauri Rose on her bedroom walls. She brought home her first girlfriend, a lipstick number named Deanna Camp, and Dale Roberts promised he'd dice his daughter with a machete if he ever saw her or any of her "dyke-bitch muff-buddies" again. Camille ran away for good, removing one of Matthew's problems.

The night Dale Roberts killed himself, taking time to first choke his wife to death, Matthew hid in his bedroom. Little Richard shrieked "You Keep-a-Knocking" into his headphones while his mother begged for mercy. The walls shook from his mother being thrown into them. Matthew dismissed the rumbling as a thunderstorm. He couldn't ignore the gunshot. Poking his head out when the ruckus stopped, he saw his dad's army-issued .45 near his bedroom door. Enough blood splattered onto the handle to glue it to their dirty, shag carpeting.

One of the investigating officers took more interest in Matthew than he thought appropriate, even at seventeen. He brushed his long, blond hair from his eyes, twice, and asked if he could do anything for him. The way he spoke reminded Matthew of girls at school who'd pretended to be concerned about him and then claimed they'd forgotten the promises they'd made to him. So he decided to find God before any more perverts found him. A Lutheran minister explained the evils of the Catholic Church. Young Matthew denounced his baptism and communion with the Roman cult and became a *real* Christian.

Linda asked him where he'd been.

"Where do I always go?" He addressed the window overlooking an alley off Franklin, rather than his wife.

"Whatever." She continued typing.

"You coming to bed?"

She ignored him.

He poured himself a glass of water. God hated Matthew's wife more than anyone else. Aware of her strength, he didn't needle Matthew too much about saving her. If The Voice did speak up, it usually said something like, *Any woman that tough must be in line with the devil.*

On their honeymoon night, Matthew had his usual problems getting aroused. His wife laughed at him, accused him of being broken in some way. "I told you we should have tried this before we got married," she said.

"Why?" he'd asked.

She explained that sometimes two people match outside the bedroom, but not inside. Then she revealed she'd shared her body with several men before they had met. One of them, she admitted, had been a negro. She confessed she didn't believe she'd ever feel passion with another man after that. "He opened me so wide," she'd said, "no mortal can possibly please me now."

Matthew's hand raised in the dark. He paused, midair. His wife had donned a Medusa-stare. She said, "Do it, limp boy. I double-dog dare you."

When he brought his hand down, Linda sneered. "That's right, buddy. I'll cut your balls off with a chainsaw, you ever even *think* about hitting me."

For five years they tried to make the sex work. Linda refused to get a divorce. Said it would shame her and her family. She hyphenated her name, instead. They slept in separate beds. Matthew couldn't be sure, but it seemed like his wife should have at least *tried* to take a lover by then. She toured the west coast, promoting her books, lecturing at Christian high schools and colleges. Certainly, somewhere on the road, she might have found a man who got aroused without effort.

Aton helped Eva wrap the extra pieces of meat in butcher's paper. He cleaned the table and floor around it while his wife stored the fresh cutlets in their freezer. They'd constructed the counter in the kitchen so it could tilt and their nightly carcass could slide into an industrial-sized trash bag. He wrapped a tie-on clip around it, checked it for leaks, and slung it over his shoulder. "Headed to basement, darling."

Eva sipped from a glass of apple wine. "Don't be long." She shook a pan on the stove, a pan with Bill Baxter's kidney sizzling amidst garlic and onions. Aton had begged for tomatoes, but she insisted Bill Baxter's humiliated blood provided enough juice.

After looking through the peephole in their front door, Aton ducked into the corridor. Despite no one being around, he acted casual, just in case someone emerged from another apartment. The faded blue carpet in the hallway, complete with oriental designs, cushioned his heavy footsteps. The building looked like it had been decorated in the 1920s and the owners, who charged an arm and a leg for rent, had invested the money necessary to maintain the art-deco, old Hollywood feel. Aton expected Myrna Loy to step out in a satin nightgown trailing behind her. He tip-toed to the elevator, drew back the outer cage, and rode it to the basement. It rumbled and clattered, having particular trouble at each landing, acting as though it might get stuck. Finally, it set down in the basement with a metallic thud.

The incinerator, a massive steel oven at the far end of the bottom floor, produced a low hiss. Made him think of hell. Hollywood taught him to disregard all organized religion. The stains of influence from his youth, however, didn't wash so easily. These post-slaughter moments were always the same—He knew eating another human showed the highest form of respect, but he could not shake the guilt he felt when ridding the remains in the fire. Similar to his adolescent understanding of masturbation. He'd worried he might be doing something *bad*. Mostly because of the whispers he heard at church, or the lectures from adults, who told him there were specific times and places to relieve urges. Alone with a *Playboy* magazine, or in the shower, thinking of Jenny Purliss, the girl in algebra class with tits the size of bowling balls, these did *not* constitute "appropriate" times. When he asked his preacher if there ever were an instance God wouldn't mind him masturbating, the old man said, "God will *always* be unimpressed by a man who can't control his passions."

When he turned the corner and entered the room with the incinerator, he ceased wallowing in his guilt. One of his neighbors, at least, he assumed it was a legitimate resident of the building, stood by the square door to the oven, shoving newspapers into it.

"Hello, neighbor." Aton noticed the newspapers being destroyed by the other man were various editions of the *Hollywood Express*, an independent rag sold in street corner boxes along the Strip and the Boulevard. Pictures of alleged call girls graced the covers. Inside, want ads filled every page with phone numbers. Giant names announced each ad—*Blair! Janessa! Stefania!* Aton had been told by several reliable sources that the girls in the *Hollywood Express* were drag queens.

The man burning the newspapers glanced at him and said, "Going to be a while, brother." Sweat drenched his broad forehead. His white, button down shirt had massive stains under the arms. As he crumpled the papers and tossed them in, his hands shook.

Aton dropped the trash bag. "Might I help?" He wanted to call the guy a Nazi. What harm did the *Hollywood Express* cause him? These poor schmucks in need of temporary affection wouldn't be able to find a companion. They'd pick up a girl or boy off the streets. Cheaper, yes. The chance of catching something horrible like herpes, no doubt, much greater. The neighbor was probably some do-gooder, some holdover from the prehistoric days, when Jews and blacks and women were told to shut up while a cluster of limp-dicked white men fucked the world from the safety of their desks in high rise buildings. Then he told himself to stop. He knew nothing about this man. Judging him, as he had just done, made him just as evil.

The other man stared at him. A bit too long. He couldn't read his eyes. Had he done something terrible as well? Could he get violent? Aton grabbed the trash bag again, held it like a sling, in case the man attacked him. Finally, the stranger extended his hand. "Where are my manners?" As they shook, he told him his name.

"Matthew Roberts?" said Aton, "Nice to meet you. Name's Aton."

"Oh." Matthew nodded. "I'm on the fifth floor. Five-twenty."

"Seven-seventeen." Aton set the trash bag on the other side of the hatch on the incinerator. "Well," he said, "let's get this stuff in the fire."

"Good idea, brother." Matthew snapped his fingers and stepped aside so Aton could grab an armful of newspapers.

As Aton tossed them into the incinerator, he said, "You don't mind my asking, what's the deal here?"

"How's that, brother?"

"I mean, you know, how'd you come to have so many of these? Don't you just need one?"

Harsh, orange light danced in the dark of Matthew Roberts's pepper grain eyes. "Why would I, or anyone else, need these at all?"

Aton laughed. "Well, there you go. So why do you even have them?"

Leaning in, Matthew said, "I take them off the street as soon as the delivery drivers put them in the boxes." He nodded, suddenly projecting confidence, like he'd saved someone from drowning and felt no need to be humble.

Aton moved back. "Why?"

Matthew opened a newspaper and held it in front of Aton's face. He let his fingers caress the pictures of transvestites. "These are *sinners*. I'm doing what I can to salvage their souls. By removing their platform, I'm eliminating their customers. If they have no customers, maybe they'll rethink their life choices."

"Okay." Aton put his hand out to push the paper away from him. Disappointed his initial judgment had been correct, he sunk his head and grabbed another pile of papers and crammed them through the hatch. He repeated the gesture, faster and faster, so as to get away from the Nazi. As he loaded the last of them into the incinerator, Matthew stopped him.

"Brother," he said. "If I didn't know better, I'd say you got some blood on your hands."

At first, Aton thought the man read his mind, knew what he'd done, what he'd been doing every night for a few years now. As though searching for a miracle, he brought his arms up and realized he had not thoroughly cleaned his fingers. "Oh," he said. "The wife and I are cooking some raw meat tonight. Fresh from the shop, you know? Kitchen's a mess." He waved his hands apart, as if illustrating a giant splatter flooding outwards and up imaginary walls.

"I see." Matthew did not look convinced. "Let's get your garbage in there, why don't we?" He clapped once, directed Aton to give him room.

Picking up the bag by himself, Aton said, "It's no problem." He shoved it into the incinerator. Bill Baxter's carcass popped like a string of firecrackers.

"My goodness, brother. What you got in there?" Matthew grinned.

Aton considered punching him and stuffing *him* into the incinerator. "Trash. No different than your newspapers, right?"

Eva tugged on her skirt. She checked herself in her compact mirror every other minute while she waited. Her script sat on her lap in a bland, vanilla cover. She'd written it without her husband's knowledge. Gone to the library on Western and 8th Street to research and then used their rental typewriters in the basement while Aton attended meetings in Century City, desperately trying to get his career back on track. Her appointment with Carol Hill, likewise, had been arranged behind Aton's back. Not that she felt she'd betrayed him. If she could put the deal together, she'd bring him on as co-producer. Hopefully, he wouldn't be a prick and resist. So many guys in the business still believed not being in charge constituted an affront to their masculinity.

"Carol will see you now." The assistant working at the desk rolled his finger like a talk show host introducing his next guest. He wore bright colors and a fly-away collar far too extravagant for 1979. Must not have heard about the death of disco.

Eva knew Carol had been twiddling her thumbs for the past twenty minutes. Sitting at her desk playing with whatever executive toys she'd purchased at Brookstone on her last trip to New York. In Hollywood, no one ever saw you on time. Just another illusion—if everyone were as busy as they claimed to be, the town would produce ten times as many movies per year.

The office smelled like lemons. Plants hung from the ceiling. Eva whistled as she sat in a high-backed leather chair on the other side of the desk. Carol had produced a string of hits for Columbia in the early seventies with her husband, David Woppit. They'd discovered the New York director Milton Trestle, helped him put together the sleeper hit of 1975, *The Rogues of Central Park*. When Dave divorced her, she tried to go out on her own. To Eva's knowledge, none of her projects had made it past preproduction before falling apart. She no doubt survived on fees paid up front by lowly independent filmmakers looking for something resembling a name to attach to their projects.

"So good to see you," said Carol. "Lance tells me you've written a script."

Nice. Straight to business. Not like male producers, who did everything they could to get in your pants before explaining why the idea of a woman producing a film was, to them, nonsense. Eva put the screenplay on the desk. "It's about Rosa Luxembourg. Socialist in Germany. Assassinated. Awesome chick. Like Jesus, you hear me? Highly influential on the Frankfurt School, the folks we can thank for not having to spend our lives barefoot and pregnant, know what I mean? Isn't it about time we girls had a Jesus figure? Shouldn't *this* be the gospel of the Age of Aquarius?"

"Terrific." Carol motioned for Eva to slide the script across her desk. It snagged, for a moment, on a line of steel balls suspended from tiny wires. Carol flipped through it the way all producers did—her eyes rolled down page one, page twenty, page sixty, and then she skimmed the last few. "What's the title, again?"

"*Rosa.*"

"We'll have to change that."

"Because of *The Rose?*"

Carol snapped her fingers. "Bingo."

"That's not an issue for me." She knew there'd be compromises. Working with a woman, hopefully, would minimize them.

"Good, good." Carol ran her pinky along the edge of her desk, back and forth, back and forth. "What's Aton's stake in this?"

Dammit. She had to go there already? As though Eva had somehow been born from Aton's flesh and bones and therefore could not possibly be her own, individual self. Carol had yet to crawl from the shadows created by the men in the industry. She still thought like them. "Well, as you know, he's making b-pictures and doesn't seem interested in moving past that."

Shaking her head, Carol said, "That man had promise. Real promise, I tell you."

"He's a great producer, Carol. And you know that, don't you? We don't need to look at the first part of his resume, do we? We don't need to review how he was already standing on two feet when you and I were dolled-up innocents just off the bus."

"Sure, sure. Thing is, I can round up some money for a project with *your* name on it, but Aton's name will sink it. You'll have to produce this without him."

Sounded tempting. But she loved Aton, wanted to help him get out of the drive-ins and all-night theaters. "It's been five years, Carol. He made *one* film with Harvey

Novak and, technically, it wasn't even a porno. Just a bunch of fat, hairy guys rubbing their peckers against Rene Bond's vagina. No penetration, you know?"

"I know, I know. But sex is going out of style. Like people have had too much of it, or something. That damn space movie has got everybody scrambling to please the hayseeds in the Midwest. I mean, talk about fascist film. You must have recognized *Triumph of the Will* in the end of *Star Wars*?"

Eva looked at the floor. "Aton refuses to watch that movie. Or anything by Spielberg. Calls him and Lucas hacks. He insists *Close Encounters* is a narrow-minded rip off of *2001*."

"Yeah, well, Spielberg's on his way out," said Carol. "Word I've heard is this crap he's working on, *1941*? It's going to tank his career. I mean, really, making a joke out of World War II? It's insensitive. We need to develop some new rules about what you can and can't make jokes about, you know?" She slapped her desk. "Enough of that. Let's get back to your picture. You said this woman Rosa was a socialist?"

Eva nodded.

"No good, no good."

"Excuse me?"

"We're selling bullshit to blue-collar schmucks in Cleveland. These animals equate socialism with Satanism. They get word we're not even trying to hide our politics in subtext, they'll crucify us. They'll give all their money to bums like your husband who still think it's okay to ring the register on the slopes of a naïve young woman's breasts."

"So? Let's educate them."

Carol Hill scrunched her face. She looked like she was constipated. Her cheeks turned red and expanded until she exploded with laughter. "We're not teachers, Eva, you know that. We're making entertainment. Nothing more.

We slip the occasional afterschool special message in there about getting along with colored people and we cash our checks. Simple, darling, simple."

Eva wondered how that could possibly be different from profiting off close ups of tits and ass. She wished she'd brought Aton, then chastised herself for being weak. "All right, we can figure out ways around the socialism. Bury it, somehow."

"Sure, sure." Carol clapped her hands. "Now we're cooking, sister."

From the Hank Shepherd Show, June 5, 1979:

Hank: Hank Shepherd here. Listen, times are tough, you're working all the time, you got one of these modern wives at home, doesn't like to cook. What's a working man to do for food? Friends, BigMan instant dinners will get you through this Cultural Marxist storm we're enduring. One entire pound of food on a microwave-ready tray. Just pop it in the old microwave, nuke it for five minutes, and wham bam thank you modern ma'am, you've got yourself a meat and potatoes supper your own mother couldn't duplicate if she tried... We're talking about the entertainment business, as usual. Aside from the commies on college campuses, these degenerates in Hollywood are the biggest peddlers of communist filth in the country. Now, I can't help but notice the girls I see struggling to make it in the movie business are these petite, blonde princesses from the Midwest. Why does Hollywood attract these innocent girls? More importantly, how does the movie business work so fast to corrupt them? One moment they want to be Marilyn Monroe, then, after a month or so in Hollywood, they become Marilyn Chambers. Can you just imagine being a mother or father back in some poor, blue-collar cesspool in Nebraska or Minnesota, thinking your daughter is off in Hollywood working to become an actress and then, one day, you get word from your perverted friend who goes to porno theaters that he saw your little girl taking it in all three directions from a ghastly variety of degenerate men—black,

Jewish, Chicano, whatever the filth-mongers in this town use to degrade the God-fearing soil in this country...

She couldn't have been more than nineteen. Strolling Hollywood Boulevard between Highland and Vine. High heeled boots. Fishnet stockings. Baby fat bubbling from her hips and thighs. Young, perky boobs spilling out of a low-cut halter top. She wore an ankle bracelet with shiny stars and crescent moons around it, reflecting the lights of Hollywood like a disco ball. Twitched her butt like a slow-moving Hippopotamus to tempt the weakest mortals.

Put your hands on that child!

Matthew Roberts followed her for a block. *Craved* the opportunity to save her. He stepped around broken booze bottles and discarded hamburger wrappers. He would lure her into the devil's private church with comforting talk of Jesus. Whether she wanted it or not, he would strip her of her Earthly clothes and save her like both their lives depended on it. Just as he reached into his jacket for a business card to give her, a Town Car pulled over near the girl and the driver rolled down his tinted window. The driver looked like a mortician, dressed in a fine, black suit and bow tie. Matthew didn't recognize the man at first, just listened as the pervert propositioned the whore:

"Hey there." His voice sounded familiar. Had he heard it on the radio?

"Hey there, yourself," said the girl.

"Anybody ever tell you that you look just like a movie star?"

"All the time, mister."

Someone opened the back door while the driver said, "Want to star in a private little picture for me? I'm listed in *Variety*, in case you were wondering."

The girl stopped. Lord have mercy. There should have been age requirements to move to Los Angeles. Young people were just too stupid to know better. Constantly getting roped into cults or performing in pornographic pictures. The girl said, "Really?" She touched her chin, like a five-year-old trying to charm her father into buying her a pony. Like she actually believed a legitimate filmmaker would prowl Hollywood Boulevard for talent.

The driver said, "Why don't you come back to my place for a screen test? If it makes you feel better, my wife, Eva," he nodded to the woman in the passenger seat who'd opened the back door, "she'll be there, too."

The man's wife looked even more morbid than him. She'd smothered her face with pale makeup, giving her the appearance of a corpse.

"No funny stuff?" said the girl.

From inside the car, the woman said, "Don't you think you've paid your dues, honey?"

"We're going to take you places you've never dreamt of," said the driver.

The girl nodded between the front and the back of the car, probably thinking she was fooling them into believing she was careful and cautious. Then she just about leapt through the opened door and slammed it.

Matthew realized where he'd heard the driver's voice before—his neighbor. The man who'd been so nosy about the *Hollywood Express* newspapers. Married? Picking up a hooker? Did he think God wouldn't notice his filthy soul?

Are you saving the right people?

Matthew moved on, sought another lost child to bring to the Light. The devil assured him they were out in numbers. Cool, summer night like that, the whores littered Hollywood and Sunset and Highland like termites in an abandoned farmhouse. He spied a hooker who didn't even look legal. She wore a feather boa around her neck, way too much blue shade on her eyelids. Like she had no sense about make-up whatsoever. He approached her, held out his card for her. "Are you friends with Jesus?"

When the girl spoke, she sounded like she'd been smoking cigarettes for too long, her voice on the verge of collapsing to a permanent whisper. "Have you met *my* friend?" She tossed her skirt over her rear, allowing any and all a gander at her leopard-print panties. Her butt didn't look like a normal girl, however. Flat and dimpled, as though it had been violated so many times it had deflated.

What a whore.

"Want to be a gentleman? Want to push my stool in?" She licked her lips and winked while she ran her fingers between her pancake cheeks.

Matthew could have sworn Satan's tail had curled up in the front of her panties, waiting to swat weaker souls with temptation. This girl *begged* to be saved. The Voice said so. *God* said so. At least, if God had ever spoken to Matthew, he surely would have agreed. "Where do we go?" he said to the whore.

The girl nodded toward Franklin. "I got a room at the Galaxy Inn." She took his hand and led him through the crowds of sinners on Hollywood Boulevard. Strangers glanced at her and smirked at Matthew. Did they know what he intended to do? Did they need to be saved as well? The whore's fingers were rough, hard, like she'd worked construction at some point. And they were *big*, especially for a girl her age. Alarmed, he asked her, "How old are you?"

"What does it matter?" Her voice deepened.

"I need to know."

"How old do you want me to be?" Now she sounded, of all people, like his father, Dale Roberts.

He considered her question as they veered off Highland, onto Franklin, across from the Capitol Records building. "Are you under eighteen?" He'd always wanted to save a minor. Seemed to him a girl that young would go to heaven, no questions asked.

"Sure."

"Are you under sixteen?"

"Sure."

"Are you under fourteen?"

"Whatever you want." She licked her lips again and said, "*Daddy.*"

They walked through the motel parking lot. The oval, neon sign out front had lost half its light bulbs. Stars and planets revolved around fancy letters spelling out the word Galaxy, reminding him of science fiction magazines his dad used to wrap around disgusting girlie rags he kept in the bathroom. Semi trucks loitered in the parking lot. No lobby, just a slim booth near the stairs to the second floor with a ragged woman hacking on a cigarette while she read what appeared to be a romance novel. Rats fought each other near a dumpster for empty McDonald's boxes. The working bulbs in the neon sign made the building glow a sick shade of orange. Matthew felt nauseous, like he'd been flushed down a toilet in hell. He put his hands between the girl's legs as she opened the door to her room. The devil had done grand work on her. He'd given her a penis instead of a vagina.

From the Hank Shepherd Show, June 5, 1979:

Hank: Hey friends, you're listening to Hank Shepherd on KABC, 970 on your AM dial. Friends, it's summertime and even in the jungles of the city, we need to cool down every so often. When I'm parched, I reach for Country Flavor Lemonade. Tastes like Grandma made it right there on the back porch. When you're sipping it, you'll be able to close your eyes and see that gorgeous countryside, free of all the soot and smog and animals of the city. Country Flavor Lemonade, takes you away from the hassles of the day... Okay. So I'm researching for my show and I catch this flick at the Las Palmas Theater called My Sister, My Love. Anybody out there witnessed this imported garbage? I mean, why is it that degenerate films made in America are called pornography while the very same subject matter stuffed in a movie from Europe is called a 'foreign film' and treated like some kind of intellectual royalty? Here's a movie that asks the audience to sympathize with two sisters engaged in an incestuous lesbian affair. Friends, I don't know where to begin with this one. Sure, we get the proverbial cry from the perverted bleeding hearts that two people of the same gender having sex is perfectly normal, that nothing has gone wrong there genetically or psychologically. But sisters? This is being called entertainment, my friends. Graphic displays of a woman slurping between the legs of her sister! I mean, I'm getting more and more callers pushing for a violent solution to this problem. These suggestions usually involve active use of our Second Amendment rights. I can't condone that sort of thing, not on the air, but I have to wonder, who will be The One? Who will save our culture from the rodents?

J-Unit 83 had been gathering scraps of newspapers from mesh trash barrels near Ivar. He found a nice mix of the *Los Angeles Times* and the *Hollywood Express*. Difficult to tell which one was smuttier. No matter. They were both propaganda sheets designed to comfort and profit off the peckerwoods. An angel had instructed him to assemble different pages from different tabloids, to combine what he'd rounded up into one, *new* publication. The angel had claimed a secret code would reveal itself, one that would help him thwart a developing conflict between the CIA and minor aquatic gods from the moon called Io.

He stuffed a batch of articles on the failures of the Carter administration in the Middle East into a utility pocket in his jacket. The writers claimed Carter's maneuvers with Iran had been incompetent and something drastic would take place in that country real soon. J-Unit grunted, knew damn well where the peckerwoods were headed—full on conflict with the entire region. "Wouldn't be too surprised," he said to the night air, "if they don't start sending some PLO shit over here, start fucking with the peckerwoods' bank accounts, get them the only place they know pain." He imagined they'd strike in a primitive manner, like a car bomb outside an embassy, or a hijacked plane, flown into an important financial building. He smelled a familiar scent. The stench of ancient decay barely masked by a tidal wave of designer cologne. Behind him, two men cleared their throats. They struggled to remember where to put their hands when pretending they actually understood the human body. They wore tuxedos and overcoats entirely unnecessary in the summer heat. Though they looked like normal, rich people, they were aliens. They'd come from the Temple of the Rat, which convened weekly between Highland and Orange. J-Unit didn't mind recruiting for them, but he refused to stick around and watch the rituals. The angels told him the Temple of the Rat engaged in sacrificial activities beyond human imagination. He'd seen the ushers load blood-soaked cloth bags into the backs of trucks behind the temple. How they disposed of them, who knew? Even the Lords of the Galaxy couldn't track their movements. The angels let J-Unit know these rites represented the highest orders of evil. They implored him to cooperate with them so they wouldn't suspect he was working for the other side. "What you motherfuckers want?" he said to the imposters.

"We need to feed the beast," said one.

"By Thursday," said the other.

They promised him a stack of dollar bills, as though he might still be oblivious to the all-seeing eye on the dirty paper. The flimsy, green rectangles they forced normal people to worship had been imported from the planet Linkranf, the tenth, hidden major body revolving around the sun. "Dumb motherfuckers," he said when they were gone. "Can't even address me by a slave name."

The *Los Angeles Times* had run an article exposing a plot by far-right Christian leaders across the country to appropriate the Republican Party and run a candidate in 1980 who would help them overturn the Supreme Court's most disastrous ruling—*Roe v. Wade*. While it represented one of the few times the liberal propaganda rag had gotten something correct, the general public couldn't be allowed to read it. In addition to emptying any newspaper boxes carrying it, Matthew Roberts bought as many as he could from newsstands around Hollywood. He was busy tossing them into the incinerator when his neighbor stepped into the room. Matthew stared into the fire and said to the man, "Saw you earlier, brother."

His neighbor had another giant trash bag in his hands. What in the world could he have been doing in his apartment to generate so much garbage? "That so?" said the man. He nodded toward the stack of newspapers. "What are we burning tonight? Paperback editions of *McCarthy's Guide to the Salem Witch Trials*?" He laughed, as though he'd actually said something funny.

Matthew pointed at the trash bag. "Couldn't help but wonder the same thing, brother."

"This?" His neighbor kicked it, chuckled as it toppled over. Whatever he'd stacked inside it collapsed like a child's building blocks. "Nothing important."

Matthew continued throwing the *LA Times* into the fire. He showed the front page to his neighbor before flinging it into the flames. "Even the mainstream media," he said, "has taken up transcription of the devil's tongue."

"What the hell does that mean?" His neighbor's face twisted into a grimace.

"You're not a religious man, are you?" He struggled to remember his neighbor's name. "Abel, was it?"

"*Aton.*"

"Are you friends with Jesus, brother?"

"Not really," said Aton. "I work in the movie business. We're not a pious bunch, in case you hadn't noticed."

"Oh," said Matthew, "you better believe it, brother. With all due respect, you guys are the *worst*. The very worst." He stopped for a moment, said, "I apologize for being so honest. It's a casualty of my calling."

"Not a problem," said Aton. "I'm used to hayseeds criticizing my work."

Matthew ignored the comment. "So this incinerator," he said, "must look like home to you."

"Eventually," said Aton.

"What?" Matthew stopped tossing the newspapers.

"I imagine my wife'll have me cremated when the time comes."

"Your wife?" said Matthew. "Is she like you?"

"She must be, a little," said Aton. "Used to be a unit production manager. I suspect she'll want to start producing her own pictures. She's a modern woman, you know? Thinks there's something wrong with her if she can't do everything men can." He picked up the trash bag and carried it to the door to the incinerator. "You mind if I pitch this in here? I have other things to do tonight."

"I guess." Matthew wanted to tell him how rude he was, cutting in front of him. He realized he'd never deal with people like his pushy neighbor once he got to heaven. The saved knew how to wait their turn. His neighbor struggled with the bag. Matthew leaned over to help him shove it into the fire. Whatever was in the bag was a mix of soft, fleshy goo and hard, bone-like material.

"Thanks so much," said Aton. "And if I were you, I'd get used to an America without God. The majority in this country, I'm pretty sure, enjoys freedom." He moved closer and said, "With all due respect to *you*, the Puritan age ended before the Revolution. You should get that through your thick skull."

Matthew turned to see if the trash bag had disappeared in the flames yet. At the base of the ash pile it produced, something shiny poked from the dust. He squinted. Crescent moons and stars—the bracelet on the sinful young girl's ankle from Hollywood Boulevard. He reached into the incinerator and grabbed for it. It hissed and steamed into his palm until he dropped it and fell backward, holding his hand and thanking God for the first *true* sign he'd been doing good work his whole life.

Aton and Eva prepared the starlet's liver. What had her name been? Laticia? Larissa? Some trailer trash mutilation of a normal name she would have had to change had she the talent to make it in the business. Aton couldn't remember. Visions of pushing his Bible-thumping neighbor into the incinerator crowded his thoughts. He wouldn't even cook the bastard. Puritan blood tasted like shit. He'd discovered that the hard way, having once roasted a nun. He forced himself to enjoy the red wine and raw spinach he'd prepared for the evening's meal. Eva said the starlet's flesh tasted so innocent, she wanted to make love.

"Don't know if I have the energy." Aton had already had sex with the starlet's headless body while they were cutting her up. He'd come inside her neck, where he'd thrust his penis just before climaxing.

His wife pouted. "But I didn't get *mine*."

He sighed, wiped his mouth, used a toothpick to clear the tender meat from between his teeth, and said, "All right, my love."

After dinner, they stepped into their standup shower for a second time that night. Aton ran his hands over his wife's body with a reverence one might have for a priceless artifact that would crumble at the *hint* of carelessness. She hummed in his ear as his fingers traced across her hips, between her thighs, and inside her. He hoisted her onto the bench along the back wall and entered her from behind. They whispered to each other as steam fogged the glass around them. To keep from finishing too soon, Aton thought of the old days, before they'd gone on the trip it seemed impossible to return from—

They'd met on the set of *Wacky Wally Walrus*, a stop-motion animation children's film he'd produced for CBS. He interviewed Eva for a production assistant position. Her experience as a junior high teacher, wrangling hormonal pre-teens at King-Drew Middle School, suggested she might make a good assistant director. He asked her to have dinner with him at Musso and Frank's. She convinced him she could handle UPM duties. While they ate breakfast in bed the following morning, he gave her the job. And she executed it so well the film came in one week under schedule and seven thousand under budget. When the movie grabbed the majority shares the Saturday night it aired, Aton Miller and Eva Rodiguero became the power couple of the year. They produced two films for Disney that flopped and found themselves working for the Roger Cormans and AIPs of the world, making drive-in schlock for teenagers smoking grass and humping under summer skies.

While shooting *The Farmer's Niece* in Alabama for Harvey Novak, Aton learned about the Temple of the Rat, a group of filmmakers who rented the Masonic temple on Hollywood Boulevard for what they described as "highly spiritual rituals." The first gathering Aton and Eva attended, they witnessed the sacrifice of a sixteen-year-old starlet from Avon, Indiana. The fathers of the temple sliced the girl from her neck to her vagina with a gold-plated bone saw. They grilled her lungs, her heart, and her liver on an imperial Hibachi located in the center of the temple and served her to the audience. They promised eating a human complimented sex like nothing else. After the feast, the fathers instructed the audience to disrobe and an orgy blossomed over the lake of blood gathering in the middle of the room.

From the Hank Shepherd Show, June 7, 1979:

Hank: You're listening to the Hank Shepherd Show on 970AM, KABC. I'm your portal into the soulless vortex of American popular culture. Take my hand, friend, let me lead you through the darkness. Boy-girl-boy-girl, please. The scum suckers in Hollywood may not remember what happened to Greece and Rome, but I sure do. I was just looking through the latest edition of the New York Times. I know what you're thinking—Why in creation would Hank Shepherd poison his eyes with phony news? Friends, you got to know what the enemy's thinking. The devil guides the hands of the so-called men who have besmirched the Fourth Estate. We must pay attention to their transgressions. So I'm reading an article about Studio 54, one of these disco places the hip and the cool go to snort cocaine and fornicate in public. Apparently, a recent example of debauchery at this joint included the raping of a goat. Yes, folks, you heard me proper. Somebody decided to violate the sphincter of a farm animal. Now, I know this happens. I've seen pictures of it in smut magazines. There are sick puppies out there who have sex with animals. And why shouldn't they? The only natural union between humans, that of a man and his lawfully wedded wife, has been so thoroughly mocked and degraded by the leftists in the universities and mass media, who can blame some lonely loser for deciding the only way he's going to be happy is by poking his business in an animal? (Pause, laughter) I just don't know, friends, I just don't know. Let's see, we got Ana, from Palo Alto. Ana, you're on the Hank Shepherd Show—

Ana: Thanks for having me, Hank. Like, I'm a long-time listener, first time caller.

Hank: Glad to hear it. Go ahead.

Ana: You know, like, I listen to some of the women my age talk about their husbands and I just think, gosh, it's no wonder society is falling to pieces. I remember when I was a little girl, growing up in Anaheim in the 1950s, divorce was totally a terrible thing. If somebody's parents got a divorce, we shunned them. The parents were shunned and their kids were shunned. The community at large understood the best way to protect the institution of marriage was to make sure anyone who profaned it paid a dear, social price. I mean, like, we couldn't call those women witches and throw them in a lake, but we could make life very, very difficult for them.

Hank: I hear you, Ana. You have a lovely voice, by the way. What's the point you're getting at?

Ana: Thank you, Hank. That, like, totally means a lot, coming from you. To get on with it, I think when we finally get this pinko commie poofter out of the White House, why don't we encourage the next president to make divorce illegal? Like, bring back something resembling common sense to our legislative culture.

Hank: We'd have to make sure the president is Christian. I mean, a real Christian, not like this phony, Jimmy Carter, who smokes pot with Willie Nelson and whose wife sluts around with the publisher of a leading smut magazine.

Ana: You read my mind, Hank. We need, like, a savior in the White House.

Linda went on tour, leaving Matthew to save souls without having to look at her ugly face when he got home. *Liberation*, The Voice called it. She would be gone for three weeks, telling young women to make better decisions so abortion would never even become an issue for them. She sure had some oddball concepts of how to share the gospel. It wasn't up to society to tell whores not to spread their legs for just any old bum who took them to dinner and a show, according to her. No, only *women* should determine what happens to their bodies. She'd suggested, several times, that God might be a woman. Matthew wondered why he couldn't bring himself to save *her*. Of course, her book sales paid the bills, allowed him to do his work without the interference of an Earthly, mundane nine-to-five job.

He set out when the sun vanished over the ocean, just past Santa Monica. He listened to Hank Shepherd as he made his way down Hollywood Boulevard, carrying a fresh stack of business cards and his Bible. The streetlamps and neon struggled to cut different-colored beams through an especially thick smog. He approached a woman who looked and smelled homeless. She was seated on a bench next to the upper torso of a male mannequin. As he introduced himself, he eyed the mannequin. It didn't have a head or legs. Just a chest and arms.

"Evening, sister," he said. "Can I talk to you about Jesus?"

The woman scooted to the side. "Please do."

Matthew rarely met anyone who showed interest. Could he keep the conversation going for longer than a minute? The woman, saggy and silver, must have been in her sixties. She dressed as though she were a silent movie star—gaudy hat and pearl necklace, like Betty Davis, or Mae West, or one of those other harlots from the golden age. She introduced herself—"Name's Ellen." She'd moved to L.A. from New York forty years ago. "Soon as I stepped off the bus," she said, "some jerk in a suit told me I was already over the hill. I was nineteen, for Pete's sake." The woman put an end to Matthew's fear of having anything to say—she talked and talked and talked. "Oh sure, I went on auditions, slept with producers, writers, directors, you name it." She said she'd been desperate and posed for a calendar in a bathing suit. That got her blacklisted. When she couldn't find waitressing jobs anymore, she answered phones for a living. Never prepared for retirement. Now, she lived on the streets.

Matthew regretted having approached her in the first place. His mind wandered to the souls he'd saved the previous two nights. Both had been women without vaginas. Tiny or no breasts.

"Have you met Thornton?" The woman picked up the mannequin and offered its plastic hand to Matthew. The last two fingers had broken off. "Thornton used to be an actor as well."

When Matthew shook the mannequin's hand, the woman let go. The torso slid onto his lap. He ran his fingers in the lines of the mannequin's square, sculpted chest.

The woman said, "Oh, dearie." She smiled and waved her hand up and down like a fairy. "You're one of *those*, eh?" She covered her mouth. "Nothing to be ashamed of, sweetie. Most of the men in Hollywood have a little sugar in their tanks."

Sweat tickled the sides of his face. He threw the mannequin at the woman, causing both its arms to fly out of their sockets. "Shut your filthy mouth!" He stood and stormed off. He looked back at the woman. She repaired the mannequin's arms and ballroom danced with it. "She's not a whore," he said. "She's a *bitch*." Like his sister, Camille. He'd never gotten revenge on her. Never settled the score with his mother, who did nothing to protect him from his father. What he wanted to do, right then, was break the homeless woman's neck without first seeding her.

That would teach her.

From the Hank Shepherd Show, June 7, 1979:

Hank: The Hank Shepherd Show is brought to you by Kaiser Ammunition. You find the targets, we'll provide the bullets... Nothing but targets running around our big cities these days, eh friends? Our Founding Fathers gave us paradise, but I'll tell you, our recent fathers have a lot to answer for. Were they tired after World War II? Does that explain how they let the country get away from them? Why didn't they keep their feet on the throats of women and minorities? How could they have let the monstrosity of the 1960s even happen? Your son comes home with long hair, says he smokes dope, says he doesn't have the stones to fight in Vietnam, what do you do? You punch him in his spoiled-rotten face, you remind him who the freaking boss is. Sorry for my language, friends. Your wife says she wants a job? Smack her in the mouth until she gets her little behind back in the kitchen, apologizes, and fixes you a drink. Don't you people read your Julius Evola? Corruption of the woman leads to loss of memory and loss of memory leads to destruction of culture. Don't believe me? Take a stroll down Hollywood Boulevard.

"**We**'re making a goddamn knife picture," said Aton. "Who the hell wants to watch a movie about a commie kraut? A *kraut*, for Christ's sake, Eva. This is Hollywood. Krauts are the fucking devil. You hear a Kraut off-screen, you already know who the bad guy in the movie is. Didn't you see *Marathon Man*? Hollywood's declared permanent war on Germany and you want to make a movie that depicts them as anything *but* Nazis? Have you lost your mind?" He paced for nearly an hour. Mumbled, over and over, "She wrote a script behind my back?" As though Eva weren't actually in the room.

"I'm trying to make a deal," she said. "I'm trying to get you on as co-producer."

"*You're* going to help *me*?" He laughed.

He'd never belittled her so. Then again, she'd never asked to create her own project. "I understand working for me might make you feel threatened," she said.

"Don't give me that *shit*," he said. "Don't hand me that fast food processed, Phil Donahue, pop-culture, pseudo-feminist *bullshit*. You know as well as I do, I'm the most progressive-thinking son of a bitch in Hollywood."

Now she had a chuckle. "And you want to make a knife picture? Tits with zits screaming their pubes off? It's no different than porn."

"What we do for profit and what we do for society," he said, "is totally different."

She said what she'd hoped to avoid saying—"We can get away from the sleazebags at the temple."

"Sleazebags?" he said. "Those are the most powerful people in the business."

"Just because they make money," she said, "doesn't mean they're *good*. Besides..." she paused, prepared to drive in a dagger. "And besides, honey, they haven't done jackshit to help you. They could have taken some meetings with you after the Novak picture."

He got on his knees, stroked her thighs. "Don't we have it set here? We're not in the spotlight. We don't have to live like the schmucks in the rest of the country, the slaves who break their backs for someone else's profit. Doesn't that make you happy?"

She shook her body away from him. "I'm not proud of what we've done."

And he walked away, head slumped like a scolded child. He'd hidden in his study until dinnertime.

Now, in the car, he let the radio fill the air, prohibit conversation. He'd tuned to KABC, the talk radio station on the AM dial. Shushed her so he could listen to the Nazi, Hank Shepherd. That asshole had actually encouraged a listener to slaughter what he called "the purveyors of filth" in Hollywood.

"There." Aton pointed to a woman on a bus stop bench. She wore a flapper dress that looked like it had been dragged through the muddy fields of World War I. She'd smeared makeup on her face, looked more like a clown than a 1930s glamour goddess. She cuddled with the top half of a headless mannequin. She smiled, but Eva saw past it. A relic driven insane by the Hollywood machine. Had she ever been someone? *Anyone* at all? Possibly. Maybe she played Rita Hayworth's best friend in a 1940s picture and failed to make an impression. Maybe she didn't even get that far. And when her time passed— and time for women in Hollywood passed quickly—what skills did she have? The unlucky ones ended up here, on the streets, talking to imaginary friends. The smart ones killed themselves as soon as they realized their window had closed. They prayed the scant bit of work they'd done would be referred to by the opportunist news media as "genius" out of deference for their brief, tragic lives.

"Let's find someone younger," said Eva.

"Old meat seasons better, you know that." Aton pulled the car over. "You act like the rules can just change, just like that." He snapped his fingers in her face. "That's not how the world works." Then he got out.

Eva rolled down her window and listened.

"Greetings, sweetheart," Aton said to the woman on the bench.

"Young man," said the woman. Even in the relative dark of night, Eva could see the woman blush. She fanned herself, as though Aton had already asked her to bed.

He offered her his hand. "You look familiar," he said. "You look like someone whose name I should know. Someone whose name should still grace every marquee from here to Iowa and beyond."

The woman scoffed at the compliment. "No, no," she said, "not me. Never, never little old me."

"I find that hard to believe." Aton turned back to the car. "Eva, darling, don't we know this beautiful specimen?"

Eva stared through him. In the hills, the brand-new Hollywood sign glowed. They'd replaced it the year before and everyone pretended all the damage done to the image of the business itself had been wiped away with that gesture. The more they scrubbed the sign, kept it white, the dirtier the streets of Hollywood became; The radical on the radio, that Hank Shepherd jackass, he was right about the decadence. But Eva believed it had nothing to do with Biblical morality or anything like that. The quality of the films themselves had degenerated. For all the criticism of the old studio system, the writers and directors back then had to be clever when dealing with adult subjects. You could put *Double Indemnity* on the television with children in the room and they'd have no idea what was going on. That took *real* talent. Those were *real* adult films. Now, the business had seen what big-budget drive-in schlock like *Jaws* and *Star Wars* could do for everyone's bank accounts. Serious movies for adults would become a thing of the past very soon. Then again, who the hell was she kidding? She'd already agreed to downplay the socialism in her script. And she risked everything going to bat for her husband, a man who had no bigger aspirations than to cash in on the *Halloween* craze, a fad she predicted would die before the decade turned.

The back door opened. Aton stood beside it, pointing to the car. "Come on, my love," he said to the woman. "Your star has not burned out yet, I shall see to that."

"Do you mind if Thornton comes with us?" The woman hoisted the mannequin in her arms. "He's an excellent dancer. Better than Gene Kelly. Believe me, handsome, I was on the set for *Singing in the Rain*. Kelly was nothing special. Most of his magic occurred through editing."

"But of course, my lady." Aton helped the woman and her half, headless mannequin into the car. When he got in the driver's side, he said, "Eva, this descendant of Aphrodite is Ellen. Ellen, my wife, Eva."

The woman smelled, as they all did, like ancient urine and dried feces. She smiled at Eva and said, "Charmed, dearie."

Eva didn't look at her as she shook her soft, fragile hand.

From the Hank Shepherd Show, June 7, 1979:

Hank: Welcome back to the Hank Shepherd Show. I'm your host, Hank Shepherd. We've been talking about movies that mix sex and violence to the point where seeing a murder on screen becomes arousing. I got a caller from Simi Valley, wants to argue with my interpretation of Halloween, the movie everybody and their mother insist is some kind of masterpiece of horror. Debbie, you've got the stage.

Debbie: Yeah, first time caller here. I don't normally listen to your show.

Hank: Thank you so much for saying so. We'll take that into consideration when listening to your opinions.

Debbie: Look, I just don't agree with your reading of this movie.

Hank: What part?

Debbie: All of it. You say Halloween is liberal propaganda?

Hank: It was made by a bunch of hippies. A bunch of spoiled hippies, I should say. The director went to USC. You know what us working class folks call USC? University of Spoiled Children.

Debbie: The film is completely reactionary.

Hank: Let's hear it, Debbie.

Debbie: Michael Myers is the conservative order, punishing the hedonistic youth, particularly women, who are promiscuous. It's a backlash against feminism.

Hank: How I wish it were, Debbie, how I wish it were. Don't you see the film is critical of Michael Myers? I'm on board that he represents common sense, before the civil rights movement of the 1960s, hence, his shock and horror as a child, seeing his slutty sister making out with her goofball boyfriend. His crime is punishing a woman for not being pure. So they put him away and he escapes nearly twenty years later and he's referred to as pure evil. He's gunned down by a psychologist. Let's not pretend for a moment we don't know what role psychoanalysis has played in the war against what Nixon called the Silent Majority.

Debbie: Even if that's true, what do you make of the end of the movie, where the killer demonstrates he can't be stopped, even with bullets—that this reactionary force is just going to keep coming back until it gets what it wants?

Hank: (Silence).

Matthew had to flee from Hollywood. The filth around him had become too much. He walked south for a few blocks, then headed west on Santa Monica. Hookers and dope dealers loitered on both sides of the street. Like animals, in packs. Predators. Sinners. They stood in clumps in the center of the sidewalk, forcing good people to make an effort to get around them. If Matthew said, "Excuse me," the whore or pimp or whatever lingered in his way glared at him. Some refused to move. The black guys lowered their shoulders and tried to ram him off his feet. Mexican women cooked hot dogs on shopping carts converted to grills. They smelled great, but Matthew would never eat food prepared by someone he didn't know. At least the Mexicans feared God, even if they still believed in the medieval cult of Catholicism. And they smiled, demonstrated the lost art of humanity. Matthew thought them the most pious until one woman dressed in a yellow *Star Wars* shirt and shorts inching a bit too high between her thighs held a sausage out on a fork and said, "You like big meat, yes?" He could have smacked her. Now some lady who didn't even know English was making accusations? Would he have to save the whole darn city? He spotted his church in the distance. A house of God, certainly, would zap all the evil words women spoke to him.

The farther west he walked, the more he noticed the people on the street staring at him. Like they knew him. They were the most evil women first—the ones who had been born with penises. Winking at him, licking their mouths just like the normal females in Hollywood. Oh, he'd save them, all right. And then there were just men. Men in leather pants, the crotches and rear ends cut out. Who had raised these cretins? Who had told them dressing like that in public was acceptable?

When he reached Fairfax, a boy approached him. Maybe sixteen, maybe younger. He wore a tight, blue vest, showing his bare chest, and shorts so skimpy they'd make the whore Daisy Duke, from the otherwise wholesome television show *Dukes of Hazard*, blush. The boy had an unlit cigarette between his moist, red lips.

"Mister?" Such a soft, sweet voice. He could have sung in a choir if he'd wanted to. His wild eyes throbbed in sync with Matthew's racing heart. When he smiled, giving him that same, all-knowing grin everyone west of La Brea gave him, Matthew considered strangling him.

"Mister?" the boy said again.

"What?" Matthew clenched his fists.

"Got a light?" He rolled the cigarette between his lips with his tongue.

"I don't smoke."

"You sure about that?" The boy grinned.

Matthew stepped backward and nearly fell into the street. The boy grabbed his arm and pulled him to the sidewalk. He didn't let go right away. "You look stressed," he said. "You look like you need some counseling or something."

He did. He needed to talk to Jesus. "I'm trying to go to my church."

"Where is it?"

Matthew pulled a card from his pocket and handed it to him.

"Oh," said the boy. "This is where my AA meetings are."

"Do you want to join me?" said Matthew. "Meet my friend, Jesus?"

The boy blushed. "I'd love to." He introduced himself as Benjamin. "Just call me Ben, though," he said.

Matthew would save the boy in God's house. Surely *that* would get His attention.

J-Unit 83 got a call from the angels. The appropriate candidate for the Temple of the Rat, they said, would be marked with cosmic symbols. "Shit," he said. "Like you need to tell me that."

Matthew hadn't saved the boy. In fact, the boy claimed he'd saved him. The boy had placed his hand on his back and Matthew hadn't stopped him. They stepped inside the church that way. Luckily, the chapel had been empty. Their light footsteps echoed in tiny pings against the stone walls and ornate columns supporting the pointed ceiling. They knelt in wooden pews halfway to the altar. The boy had noticed the bandage around Matthew's hand.

"How'd you hurt yourself?" he said.

Matthew shrugged. He unwrapped the wound. Two stars and a crescent moon had been branded into his palm when he'd tried to grab the bracelet in the incinerator. "Doesn't feel too bad, now."

The boy took his hand, lowered his head toward it. He kissed the stars and the moon. Matthew thought he might break his neck. When the boy looked up at him, he said, "You're not running away, are you?"

Matthew tried to stand. The boy grabbed his wrist with one hand and beat him to the ground with the other. He removed Matthew's pants and judged him the way Matthew judged others. It had been painful and exhausting and not pleasant in any way. He worried his naughty bits would tingle, but they didn't. He didn't get aroused. As the boy saved him, Matthew remembered, for the first time in his adult life, the very *worst* thing his father had ever done to him. Then the boy left, laughing, zipping his fly, showing the carved Jesus on a cross, mounted high over the altar, a middle finger.

"Fuck you, faggot," said the boy.

Matthew didn't know exactly to whom he'd been talking. He felt like he'd sat on the toilet and passed something the size of a brick. When he pulled up his pants, drops of blood streaked down his legs. "Oh God," he said. "Oh God, oh God, oh God." He tightened his belt and limped out of the building, looking only at his shoes, as though he were sneaking away from the scene of a crime he would never admit to having witnessed.

When the cool, June Gloom air hit him, he said out loud, to The Voice, "Where are you?" He should have judged the boy and saved him on the streets, the same as he did the whores in Hollywood. He wondered how he'd let himself get tricked in the first place.

The woman with the mannequin. She'd suggested he might be a tuity-fruity, the kind of person Hank Shepherd insisted needed to be eradicated, along with the other Hollywood trash. All of this, in fact, could be blamed on *women.* His wife refused to sleep with him. The hookers on Hollywood Boulevard mocked him when they failed to arouse him. And now, *now,* this old bitty, this homeless garbage, she had the audacity to suggest the problem was *his?* What in creation could a psychotic woman who hung out with a mannequin possibly know about…*anything?* He made his way back to Hollywood Boulevard, plowing through the crowds of people trying to own the sidewalks and ignored their threats and protests.

On Vine, beneath a billboard advertising the Hank Shepherd Show, complete with a photo of the Reverend in a cowboy hat, looking like the new John Wayne, Matthew found a pawnshop. Musical instruments and typewriters filled the windows. Inside, jewelry and weapons occupied display cases set up in a u-pattern. A skinny man with dark skin greeted him as he entered. He'd slicked his black hair into a ducktail, like he'd decided the 1950s had returned. An old crooner played on a small stereo system in the corner by the cash register. Maybe Frank Sinatra or Dean Martin.

"Hello, brother." Matthew perused the store's selection of firearms. He tapped the glass over the handguns. "What can I get for a hundred bucks?"

The salesman smacked his hands together. "What's your situation?"

"Self-defense."

"Good, good," said the salesman. "What are you trying to protect yourself against?"

"Rodents."

"Oh, buddy, you don't need a real gun to take out some rats."

"I was being figurative," said Matthew. "There's someone trying to hurt me, trying to make me do things I don't want to do."

The salesman opened the case and pulled out a small, silver pistol. It looked like a toy. "Twenty-two," he said. "Five shots. Get the barrel right up on your target and squeeze the trigger."

Matthew said he'd take it. "Will you accept fifty bucks?"

"We don't negotiate here," said the salesman. "But I'll give you five cartridges for it. On the house." When he took Matthew's money, he said, "After you defend yourself, drop the pistol and run like hell."

From the Hank Shepherd Show, June 7, 1979:

Hank: Welcome back to the Hank Shepherd Show. We were talking about east coast liberals earlier, trying to decide if they're any more tolerable than the leftist trash ruining southern California. The filmmakers from the east coast, I will say, seem to be more intelligent than the flakes out here. As much as I despise the sleaze that is New York City, I can't help but feel like the movie Taxi Driver provides the perfect blueprint for the way we can take this country back. I've talked to cabbageheads who describe the main character Travis Bickle as a villain. A villain! Can you believe it? Let's consider what this so-called villain does—He tries to take out a phony, establishment politician, gets thwarted by the nosy federal agents protecting the scummy politician, so he decides to do the next best thing: He cuts down some pimps and gangsters holding a thirteen-year-old girl hostage, whoring her out. I've actually heard whacko feminists claim he's somehow stepping on the girl's rights to do what she wants with her body. Holy snot, folks, a thirteen-year-old child? Being used as a prostitute? And the guy who saves her is somehow bad? Johnny, get your gun. We've got work to do.

They didn't make love that night. They drugged the woman, tossed her mannequin in the hallway by the front door, chopped the old bitty into pieces, and cooked her. All of her, at once. Eva complained when they ate dinner. Said the meat came off the bones too easily.

"Because it's tender, baby," said Aton. "You know that. Old meat is naturally seasoned. It doesn't crisp as easy as the meat we had last night."

Jesus, why was she being such a bitch? She'd written a script behind his back, taken a meeting with a producer, what was next? Would she cut off his balls and put them in a goddamn Mason jar? Eva had brains, talent. He understood that. But if she could do the things he had previously done, what purpose would she have for him? The studios shut him out because of the damn Novak picture. Word trickling down to the smaller companies was that drive-ins and sleaze-houses were going to be extinct within a decade. Something about home video. He didn't want to believe it. How the hell would Johnny Paycheck out there in middle America support a family *and* a piece of machinery as complex as a Betamax? What if it were true? Even his friends in the valley, the ones who produced porn and didn't give a shit what the codgers in Hollywood thought, even they talked about this video boom, called it the future of the industry. Suppose Eva did get him on board for her commie film, what then? Would she control his career at that point?

Insane.

After two helpings of the old woman, Eva finally relaxed. She said, "This *is* good."

"Of course," he said. Didn't she remember the autumn feasts at the temple? When the leaders rounded up ancient, decaying bums from Hollywood Boulevard and served them to the congregation with Tabasco? Senior citizens tasted better than pork ribs. Everyone knew that.

"You don't have to be an ass about it." She cut off a piece of meat, dipped it into a small bowl of Korean barbecue sauce, and slowly sucked the juices until she had no choice but to chew. She closed her eyes, looked just like she did during sex.

Aton sighed, set down his fork. "Okay," he said. "I'll work for you on the Rosa Parks picture."

"If I can get you on," she said.

"Jesus..."

"Calm down," she said. "You have to make amends, you know that. You went outside the system. That makes people suspicious." She said she needed a shower. Said she wanted to be alone.

Aton bagged the old woman's bones. He tried to put the half, headless mannequin in with them, but it wouldn't fit.

From the Hank Shepherd Show, June 7, 1979:

Hank: Now, I have to be careful. The lefties will beat down my door, claiming I'm promoting violence. These hypocrites actually have the nerve to suggest those of us on the right are fascists. All the while, they've taken over the media, the schools, the White House, pushing their sleazeball agenda on the rest of us. Hey, liberals, I'm happy just being with my wife, is that okay? Can you stop calling me names because I go to church, because I pray when life gets me down? I don't use drugs, like you filthy degenerates, I don't screw around like an animal with no self-control. Good grief, we need an avatar, don't we? Someone with our interests at heart, someone who knows how this country is supposed to be run.

Matthew Roberts wept as he burned the latest edition of *Hollywood Express*. He felt the gun in his pants every time he reached for a fresh batch of papers and shoved them into the incinerator. He'd searched an hour for the old woman and the mannequin. He went to the bench where she'd made the offensive remark earlier. No sign of her. Just a few rats nibbling at a bag of popcorn someone tossed on the ground. He asked the other bums and whores nearby where she might have gone. They accused him of being a cop. He could have shot them, if he'd wanted to. He'd put his hand in his pocket, curled his fingers around the twenty-two, and visualized aiming it at their faces and pumping the trigger until magic flew from the barrel and saved his victims without the yuckiness of physical contact.

His brain scrambled the moment his neighbor, the producer, the murderer, walked into the room with his usual trash bag in one hand and the half-mannequin in the other. Matthew recognized the chest, the loose, dangling arms.

"Evening," said the neighbor. What was his name again? Some movie person. He didn't say excuse me, just bumped Matthew to the side and threw the bag in. "This thing's plastic," he said, holding up the mannequin. "You don't want to breathe any of the fumes." And then he shoved the torso into the fire. He ran into Matthew again as he turned to leave.

"Hey," said Matthew. "I know you're too good for Jesus Christ, but is absence of faith in a higher power any kind of reason to abandon all the niceties of a civilized society?"

"Go fuck yourself," said his neighbor.

Later, Matthew would try to remember sliding the twenty-two from his pocket, running toward his neighbor, pulling the trigger again and again, the *pops* from the gun sounding like God's applause, seeing the neighbor's face fracture, watching bone fragments and blood splash against the charred walls like the muck of a modern art painting. The toxic, black smoke from the burning mannequin streaming from the open incinerator made it seem like a dream, something hallucinated while sitting in the dentist's chair, sucking laughing gas and pretending there's no such thing as pain.

From the Hank Shepherd Show, June 7, 1979:

Hank: Friends, we got a serious situation here. We have an anonymous caller on the line. I don't normally take these calls, I mean, you never know when a left-wing socialist will try to ambush you in public, see if they can get you to say something they think is offensive, even though normal folks can see through it. This fellow calls himself a man of God, though. Sounds like he's in a pickle. Caller, go ahead—

Anonymous: Hank? I did what you said.

Hank: You decided you'll vote Republican in 1980?

Anonymous: No, brother. I killed a sleazy Hollywood producer.

Hank: (Pause) Friend, I'd suggest you hang up right now and never, ever call me again.

J-Unit had taken to grabbing people, searching them for the mark. They screamed, cussed at him. He pushed up their sleeves, raised women's skirts, looking for something, *anything* cosmic. The angels had assured him the chosen one would be obvious. For the first time since leaving the VA, he felt like giving up. He spotted a peckerwood on the corner of Hollywood and Highland talking on a dirty pay phone. Dumbass must not have known the CIA had been listening in on that booth since the late 1960s. The peckerwood finished his conversation and stepped out into the street. He looked around like he was lost. He approached J-Unit without being prompted. His voice shook. "Hey, brother," he said.

"I ain't your motherfucking brother," said J-Unit.

The peckerwood's white, button-down shirt had been soaked. Had it rained earlier? J-Unit couldn't remember. Whatever the peckerwood had done, it'd made him nervous enough to sweat through his clothes. He reached into his jacket and pulled out a business card. "You met Jesus?"

And J-Unit saw it—the mark. Two stars and a crescent moon, burned into the peckerwood's palm. *Of course.* This dumb honkey didn't seem to know the first thing about being human. He'd be perfect for the imposters in the temple. J-Unit took the business card and stuffed it in a pocket with half a hamburger he'd been saving for when he finished his quest.

"My name's Matthew," said the peckerwood. As though J-Unit might give a shit. Then the peckerwood said, "I'd love to take you to my church."

"How about you come to *my* church?" said J-Unit.

When she saw the cops through the peephole, she considered not answering the door. She scanned the front hallway. No blood on the floor, no bone fragments. Aton always made the apartment spic-and-span before lugging the remains to the incinerator. A quality she wished she could highlight when pitching his participation to Carol Hill.

"Who is it?" She tried not to sound nervous.

"Police," said one of them.

She opened the door and let them in. Impossible to tell them apart. Buzz cuts, good form, like they'd come to Hollywood to be actors, to be the next Steve McQueen, found they had no talent, couldn't fuck their way into porn, got angry, and decided to take out their frustration on ordinary people by hiding behind badges and getting away with murder. She knew what *she* did wouldn't score any points in the court of morality. Cops, on the other hand, like preachers, pretended to be pious while engaging in evil. The officers standing in her doorway looked so much like Nazis, she named them Hitler One and Hitler Two.

"Eva Miller?" Hitler Two had a mole on his cheek and squinted in one eye when he spoke, like he thought he was Robert De Niro.

"Of course," she said.

"You should come with us."

Hitler One, who had a plain face, like Robert Redford in the lone *Twilight Zone* episode he appeared in, glanced at her exposed belly. "Might want to cover yourself." The smirk on his face suggested he'd confused her for a go-go dancer or a hooker. Fucking pig.

She closed her robe. "What's the problem?"

They led her to the basement. When she stepped off the elevator, she sensed she knew what would be around the corner. Somehow, Aton had met trouble. Had he gotten caught? Had he ratted her out? Would she be able to control herself? She imagined him standing there, grinning like a jackass. Maybe he'd try to pin everything on her. Just as she'd taken steps to break out on her own. Fucking men, all of them. Fucking goddamn pigs, all of them.

The cops cleared a path between other police, some in uniform, some in suits. Two medics rounded the corner into the furnace room, pushing a stretcher. Eva's throat dried. Then she enjoyed a rush of relief she would claim, for the rest of her life, she felt guilty about. Aton hadn't gotten busted. He'd died. Somehow.

The cops directed her to follow the medics. She stepped into the incinerator room. The air smelled like burnt plastic. Without gathering the gravity of the scene, she watched the medics lift Aton's nearly headless corpse onto the stretcher. A police officer had traced chalk around his body. Yellow cards with numbers on them had been placed throughout the room. A small pistol lay near the door to the inferno.

Hitler One said, "That your husband?"

She nodded.

"Yeah," said the cop, "we just wanted to make sure."

What Eva would never admit to anyone for the rest of her life? When she saw her husband had been murdered, she thought, Now I can get my movie made the proper way. And if she had told anyone, they would have patted her on the back and said, in that voice people use when they want to console someone they know is a monster, *Don't blame yourself.*

The homeless black man with the telephone tied to his arm had handed him over to some men in dark robes. They smoked cigarettes in the alley behind the Masonic temple on Hollywood Boulevard. Matthew assumed they worshipped Satan. Why else would they dress that way? The black man had said, "He got the shit you're looking for." Then he threw Matthew against a wall, reached into Matthew's shirt pocket, and grabbed his transistor radio. "This is all I want in return," he said.

The men in robes surrounded him. They removed their hoods. Each wore a John Wayne Halloween mask, the kind with a plastic cowboy hat attached and a red bandana tied around the neck. They poked their cigarettes through slits cut for their mouths. "You funny, pilgrim?" said one of them.

Matthew got to his feet and hobbled away. Another man in a John Wayne mask picked up a brick and threw it at his head. He fell to the ground, woozy, worried he might fade. The men in robes tossed their cigarettes in a dumpster. "Let's get him ready," said a different John Wayne. Their bony hands, covered in loose, ancient veins, like cables holding them together, and their creepy, twig-like fingers clasped Matthew's body. They struggled to lift him and carry him into the temple. He turned his head side to side, took in the spotless kitchen, the immaculate hallways with checkerboard patterns on the floor and occult columns arranged in esoteric patterns. He sniffed the air in the dining area, expecting to get a whiff of roasted goat or some equally inappropriate animal. "You fellows Masons?" he said.

The men in robes laughed.

"I know what you guys have been up to." He'd read tons of anti-Masonic literature at church. Supposedly they worshipped a demon named Baphomet. Even the satanic Catholic church would have nothing to do with them.

"Masons have no power, pilgrim," said one of them. He raised his hood and lifted his John Wayne mask just long enough to show Matthew his real face. It was the reverend from the radio. Hank Shepherd. His hero. He said, "*We're* in charge of this country."

The old men huffed and grunted as they carried him into the actual temple. Plush, leather seats lined one side in rows, like a movie theater. People in ruby robes occupied them. Matthew assumed they all wore the same John Wayne mask underneath. The men carrying him tossed him onto a massive Hibachi in the center of the room. Lit candles surrounded him. The overhead lights dimmed and the congregation stood. They hummed as double-doors opened and a lone man in a ruby robe entered. He put his hands out, like Jesus, and the congregation hushed. His voice seemed familiar. An actor's voice. High-pitched, a little dotty, like he might be on the verge of dementia. He turned to the audience surrounding him. "Brothers," he said, "thank you for making this special session. The gods have informed me we must step up the sacrifices if we're to take back the White House." He addressed the men who'd brought in Matthew. "Is the degenerate ready?"

They stepped out of the way as the man with the high voice approached the grill.

Matthew sat up. "I demand you let me go," he said, not sure who'd actually heed his command. He wished he hadn't wasted his ammunition on his neighbor. He wished, even more, he hadn't tossed the gun when he'd fled his apartment building.

The lone figure lifted his hood. The eyes in his John Wayne mask seemed darker than the others. He motioned with his hands for Matthew to calm down. "It'll be over soon, son," he said. "All of this, this filth and degenerate behavior, we'll make it vanish, I promise you that." He removed his John Wayne mask.

Matthew struggled to figure out who he was; the slick, quaffed hair, dyed black, like all over-the-hill actors who couldn't accept their age, the tilted head, shaking with each word he spoke. What movies had he starred in before Hollywood spit him out? He remembered a monkey picture, *Bedtime for Bonzo*. "Let the rats be satisfied," said the former governor of California. He opened his ruby robe. The rest of the congregation did the same.

Grabbing his mouth to keep from throwing up, Matthew's world spun as rats, previously concealed by the robes, clinging to the bodies of the congregation, swarmed onto the table and gnawed and clawed and tore at his flesh with their tiny teeth. Then he noticed the people in the room were not people at all. They had gray skin and heads too big for their bodies. Their eyes, large, almond-shaped, shone black as the darkness Matthew surrendered to.

From the Hank Shepherd Show, June 9, 1979:

Hank: Friends, you got to drink your milk. But how do you know you're getting quality, wholesome, white milk? Fresh from the farms of Wisconsin, Pure Dairy whole milk guarantees the purity of their product. You can't find Pure Dairy at just any grocery store, no friends, only the finest supermarkets carry it and though it might hit your wallet a bit harder, you can take comfort knowing you're consuming a product only the privileged and decent can afford... Now let's get back to the show. Friends, we got a treat tonight. Christian self-help author Linda Hanson joins us on the phone lines to talk about the future of America and how we can take control of it.

Linda: I wouldn't get too comfortable, Hank.

Hank: Excuse me?

Linda: I'm not here to cozy up to your barbaric, old-world view of higher-than-thou morality. I know what men like you do behind the scenes. You're holier than no one.

Hank: (Nervous laugh) Linda, don't we play on the same team?

Linda: Hank Shepherd, you ought to be ashamed of yourself. Why, I doubt you even know what it means to be Christian. Judging all these lost souls in Hollywood. It's our job to bring them in from the storm, to save them from hell, not condemn them before the Lord even has His say.

Hank: Well...

Linda: Well, nothing, you cheap snake oil hustler. If we want America to embrace Christianity again, we're going to have to be Christian about it. Not Spanish Inquisition Christian, not Salem

Witch Trials Christian, but healing the blind, the sick, the poor, the kind of Christian that inspired the words on Lady Liberty there in New York City.

Hank: Linda, if I didn't know better, I'd say you were a liberal.

Linda: Maybe I am, Hank. Maybe Christian women and liberal women don't have that many differences after all. Women protect life. Men are the ones who start the wars, who make weapons that destroy. And you have the audacity to call abortion murder? Reverend Shepherd, before you decide you have what it takes to lead the people of this country, take a long, hard look at yourself in the mirror. You might be exactly what destroys this nation.

She tried to stay clean. Lasted less than six months. Eva lost her cool the night Ronald Reagan announced his candidacy for president. November. The decorations for Christmas had been strung along Hollywood Boulevard. Always struck Eva as surreal. She'd drive down Hollywood chuckling at the sunshine bouncing off the silver snowflakes and tinsel stretched from broken lamp post to broken lamp post. Some of the street actors at the Chinese Theater traded in their Charlie Chaplin costumes for Santa outfits. Two of the three Marilyn Monroes became sexy elves. Probably earned more money than usual, showing a whole lot more of their tits and asses.

Eva's project transformed as well. Carol Hill turned her Rosa Luxembourg movie into a teenage sex romp set in post-World War I Germany. Called it *Rosa's Park*, the park being a reference to her vagina. "We got to cash in on the *Animal House* craze," she'd said. So much for feminist statements. Maybe if Aton had lived, he might have been able to throw some muscle around, insist the story remain serious.

Then that decrepit old fart, Ronald Reagan, the fucking hypocrite responsible for bilking the Screen

Actors Guild out of a ton of money, told the world he wanted to be in charge of America. It seemed like Ward Cleaver, stepping out of a black and white sitcom, insisting the kids had been bad for the previous decade and needed a spanking. "You asked for it," Eva sang to herself in the Town Car, "you got it, Toyota..."

She realized what she really wanted. Fresh meat. She'd tried to go all the way to the other side—tried to be a vegetarian. Good Christ. Eating at the Green House on Sunset seemed no different than hanging out with the Manson family, or that whacko from Indiana who'd killed his followers with Kool-Aid. Come to think of it, wasn't Charlie Manson from Indiana? What the fuck was wrong with that place? Whatever. The waitress at the Green House had glazed-over eyes. She'd given Eva a pamphlet about some church on Franklin that preached the gospel of science instead of Jesus. So, Eva went back to eating animals. Like normal people. Beef and pork didn't do it. Didn't give her the strength she needed to stand up to idiots like Carol Hill.

Meanwhile, nothing else changed on the Boulevard. Christmas didn't magically make the homeless go away. Didn't convince the hookers and dope fiends to take their lives in a new direction. Eva wondered if progress might not be a dream, one that could never come true. People entered your life and left, but did you really become someone else as a result? Christ, she needed a fix. A real fix. The skinny bums and whores and junkies wouldn't do it. She needed something solid. Something big.

She slowed at Hollywood and Highland, spotted a black man who looked like he could have played middle linebacker for the L.A. Rams. He'd wrapped himself in tinfoil, like an alien or something from *Star Wars*. He pushed a shopping cart filled with broken electronics. For some reason, he'd taped a red phone to his upper arm.

"Hey," she said, rolling down the window on the Town Car.

"What you need?"

"I think you know what I need."

He rolled his eyes. "Where you want to go, then?"

"How about back to my place?"

"You ain't going to try and tell me you've never done this before, are you?"

Eva smiled. "No." She watched a small, transistor radio drop from the man's pocket onto the sidewalk as he climbed into the car. She decided not to tell him about it. She said, "I'll bet you a million dollars I'm the *last* honest person you'll ever meet."

From the Linda Hanson Show, November 5, 1980

Linda: You're listening to 90.7 on your FM dial, KPFK, progressive radio for the new age. I'm Linda Hanson. I thank you for having us in your life. I'm joined today by maverick Hollywood producer Carol Hill. Carol is one of a very small group of women producers in Hollywood and she's here to talk about how the entertainment industry might help combat the fascist monster Middle America just elected president. Carol, so good to have you.

Carol: Thanks for having me on your show, Linda.

Linda: Carol, what are some changes we might see in the movie industry, should more women like you take the reigns?

Carol: Well, Linda, we need to change minds, that's for sure. Ronald Reagan is, literally, Hitler. The fact that he was able to steal the presidency in 1980, over ten years after the beginning of the civil rights movement, means there are a lot of angry white people who need to be educated, who need to be brought into the 20th century before the 21st century arrives and kicks them in their pathetic butts.

Linda: I hear you, Carol. I used to be married to one of those knuckle-draggers.

Carol: Glad you've liberated yourself.

Linda: Thank you. Let's get back to the plan, Carol.

Carol: Well, my theory is this—in order to change minds, you first change the way people speak. Have you seen this movie Airplane?

Linda: I'm afraid I missed that one.

Carol: Well, there's a scene where Barbara Billingsley speaks Black American English and calls it 'jive.' It's like this zombie, crawling out of the black and white past, mocking Black American English, if you can believe it. And the audience, they just laugh and laugh and laugh. We need to get to a point where anyone who laughs at any humor directed at women or minorities is made to feel ashamed of themselves.

Linda: Interesting. How do you propose we make this happen?

Carol: Glad you asked, Linda. I just wrapped production on one of these raunchy teen comedies. It's called Rosa's Park. It's actually about Rosa Luxembourg, a socialist. But, you know, America's not ready to embrace socialism, so we had to hide the real message of the movie as much as possible. But here's the thing—I studied up on Rosa Luxembourg and Marxism and it led me to an interesting period in recent Chinese history. So Mao, as you know, first tried to create collectives in Chinese society. This didn't quite work. But then came drastic measures to enforce Maoist thinking—the Chinese Cultural Revolution. During this glorious period, anyone who disagreed with Mao was publicly shamed, humiliated, and suspected enemies often killed themselves as they lost what the Chinese call 'face.'

Linda: I'm familiar with the Cultural Revolution. What does that have to do with the United States?

Carol: Well, I'm getting there. I've been talking with some of my sisters in the business, and we feel the election of Ronald Reagan is nothing less than the manifestation of one of these horror movies with serial killers avenging perceived wrongs from the past. So, for instance, this insanely grotesque movie Friday the 13th, it begins with a slaughter in the 1950s, then jumps to the present, where the killer from the 1950s returns and hacks up hedonistic young people enjoying the fruits of the civil rights movement.

Linda: I'm not sure I'm following you, Carol.

Carol: We need to be those final girls who kill the killer. We need to be Jamie Lee Curtis. We can't let things go back to the 1950s. We tried the nice way, now we need to be a little more strategic. The first step is controlling language. When you control language, you control thought. When you control thought, you control the population.

Linda: So, you're talking about subverting the language?

Carol: Exactly. In Mao's Cultural Revolution, if someone was deemed an enemy of the state, he was considered 'politically incorrect.' That's the key, right there. Create an environment in the United States where speech is controlled through, heck, let's just steal the term—political correctness.

Linda: That's a tall order.

Carol: It's not as complicated as it seems. Morality in the United States needs to be shifted. The greatest sin shall be racism. You scare the population into adopting politically correct language by calling anyone who doesn't go along with it a racist. Once we have the okey-dokeys in Tennessee worrying about whether or not they're being politically correct, we'll know we've taken the country back.

THE

ROACH KING

OF

PARADISE

by
Scotch Rutherford

JOHNNY BLADE

White hot letters glowed like pale flesh under neon, burnt into the blood red sign. Cue the word *Paradise,* lost in type atop of the signpost. It couldn't be read past 500 feet in either direction. The word *Motel* loomed like havoc against the shape of L.A. Stacked in caps with an arrow pointing downward and astray. Ten laps around the block and he saw only the sign in toxic green any time he closed his eyes. The sky had long since bled out below Sunset. A dark blue hue washed over the boulevard. But Jason Doherty couldn't cool it down.

It probably didn't help he had Molly Hatchet's "Flirtin' With Disaster" on the box. He switched it to AM. He twisted the radio dial to the right and found the voice of reason:

Hank: "Welcome back. It's June third. Nineteen hundred and eighty in the year of our Lord. You're listening to the Hank Shepherd Show on KABC, 790AM. All Talk, All the Time. This segment brought to you by Beretta. Since 1526. 450 years. One Passion. We're talking to Pauline Kael who writes for the New Yorker. Pauline, you had some choice things to say about the movie Hardcore. I thought George C. Scott was fantastic."

Pauline: "I'm sure you did, Hank. He was like a Calvinist John Wayne. At least with Taxi Driver, the protagonist, Travis Bickle, had a fear and hatred of sex so feverishly sensual that we experienced his tensions, his explosiveness. But in Hardcore Jake feels no lust, so there's no enticement—and no contest."

Hank: "Well, Pauline. I left the theater full of hope. There's no greater threat to human decency in the modern age, than pornography. Beyond that, all I'll say is this. To quote the immortal Travis Bickle: someday a real rain will come and wash all the scum off the streets. Speaking of immorality. I read about the new Jack Smight film. Jack Smight of course of Airport fame. It's called Loving Couples."

Pauline: "With Shirley MacLaine and James Coburn…"

Hank: "Correct. I guess it's going to be a romantic comedy of sorts. I can't imagine it's going to be at all funny. The whole film is about infidelity. And I have to tell you Pauline. Infidelity might just be the biggest threat to the nuclear family in this modern age…"

Jason killed the radio dial. He decided to brood in silence. Just three vouchers away from making his way into IATSE local 80. He'd been working seven days a week for the past 9 months. True grit, sacrifice and line or two of marching dust. It had been the one night he'd decided to take off. He'd wanted to surprise her. Show her he cared. Of course, he showed her that every day. But to really show her. Take her out on the town. The way he had before they'd left Jersey nine months ago.

She'd been taking acting classes at a small theater over on Santa Monica. He'd had to park two blocks away. Walking up, when he'd turned the corner, his heart dropped as if lodged in his throat. He'd watched her get into the passenger side of her acting coach's car. He'd followed them here. He'd decided to let them get comfortable. No need to bust in before they'd gotten into character.

"Room Thirteen," Sekhar handed her the room key. He surmised the woman: At least thirty-five with a little spare padding between her wide hips and her enormous breasts. "Sorry, it's all we've got."

As usual, the two of them hung out in the lobby—Sekhar behind the front desk, and Pancho Arvizu, motel security, leaning up against it. Only tonight Pancho had brought along his little cousin, Esteban.

The woman took the key. Cracked a smile. "Someone's gonna get lucky."

"Muy Hermosa. What's your name?" Pancho said.

"Peaches," she said.

Pancho ogled her double D's. "Of course it is."

"Melocotones," said the young kid. Dressed like a tiny vato gangster, he slumped out on the sofa next to the doorway. His fingers spread wide, with his palms facing ten inches above his chest. He flexed his digits like they were squeezing a jumbo pair of tits.

"Si, si. *Melocotones*," Peaches said, with a giggle. She grinned at the little boy staring at her chest. She asked Pancho. "How old is he?"

"He's eleven."

"*Once?*" Peaches cocked an eyebrow at the little boy.

"Si," Esteban said.

"Mira, Estaban," Peaches said, and whipped out her right tit, letting it hang over her tube top. "You want to see the matching set, it'll cost you fifty bucks. Fifty more if you wanna squeeze 'em." She stuffed her tit back into the tube top, turned back to Pancho. Gesturing to the kid she said, "He's gonna start collecting magazines any day now."

"Órale. I still got mine," Pancho said. "Big stack."

"Well, let me know when the little man's ready," She winked. "Or if you get lonely."

Pancho nodded. "Chido, nena,"

"Night little man." Oncoming headlights backlit Peaches. "He's cute."

"*Don't you love her madly? Wanna be her daddy...*" Pancho sang after her.

Both men and the kid checked out the rear view, when she walked out the door.

Jason Doherty made his final lap along the palm-lined street before bounding into the aqua neon-shaded lot. 1950s Motel sign dusting the pavement in crimson light. The building itself, horseshoe-shaped stucco. Above it: 1116 and the word Paradise. Its reflection glowed like Vegas in the black clear coat of his '77 El Camino SS. A trace of powder clung to the bottom of a Ziploc bag. He poured it onto his left knuckle. He pressed down on his right nostril and inhaled with the other. He slammed shut the driver's side door. It reverberated throughout the lot. It didn't give him pause. He'd seen plenty motels like this one in Absecon, when he'd been a runner back in A.C. He knew the look of an hourly motel. He avoided eye contact with the chubby hooker on her way to room number 13.

Long before he'd joined IATSE local 52 in Manhattan, he'd gotten an early education in locksmithing—an invaluable skill when it came to taking down scores. Got him a four-year scholarship to Rahway. He took out the triple peak rake pick and went to work on the cheap lock. He fucked it off quick and easy, and the door to room 9 split wide from the jam. He'd thought about kicking it the fuck in once the lock popped, but he didn't want to catch any kind of heat. If things got too hot in the lot, he'd watch it burn from the rear view. Back behind the wheel, headed for the 110.

He recognized his wife's bare ass underneath her suitor's. Her cheeks jiggled between his wide-spread legs. He had his pickle in her business. Grunted like a chimp, with each thrust. Then the doorknob hit the wall. They separated and shrunk back against the headboard. Both with a look of terror. Unlike in the movies, she didn't bother pulling the bed sheet up over her tits. She just let them hang there. Because why not? Blue and green neon lines wrapped around the lot like a corner in a boxing ring backlit Jason. He'd parted his hair and dressed for a night on the town—slacks, polished loafers, a nice dress shirt with an open butterfly collar. She'd probably noticed he'd left the shirt un-tucked. And that he'd worn the St. Christopher medallion she'd given him. He backhanded the wall switch. "Leanne. What the fuck?"

For Leanne those lethal seconds drawn out and quartered were a first. She'd never expected to get caught. Silence, that hung low and long enough for its legs to stop kicking.

"Who the fuck are *you*?" Jason said, clocking the professor.

"I'm leaving," he said, and Jason watched him slide over Leanne, and into the corner next to the bed, where his clothes were piled up on the floor. Slender in build, but with a well-tanned and toned gym body. Guy drove a Mercedes too.

"Reb. I'm sorry," Leanne said.

"It's okay," Reb said. "I'll let you two work it out."

"You're apologizing to *him*?" Jason said. "What about *me*?!"

Leanne shoved a cigarette between her lips and lit up. "Yeah. What about you?" She took a drag. She blew smoke. Didn't make eye contact.

"How long's this been going on?"

"What difference does it make?"

"Because you're six fuckin' weeks pregnant, Leanne," Jason said. "So what is this guy your pimp or something?"

Leanne still wouldn't look him in the eye. "Jesus."

"More like her paramour," Reb said.

"Shut the fuck up, Reb." Jason didn't know what the fuck Reb just said, but figured it was probably Shakespeare or some shit.

"We all have needs," said Leanne.

"Baby," Jason said. "I've been puttin' the hours in for you. Three more vouchers and I'll be in the union."

"For me?" Leanne said.

"You and the kid," Jason said.

Reb finished getting dressed and shot Leanne a look.

"I'm putting in the hours for *your needs*, and you know it," Jason said. "Every day."

"Those aren't the needs I'm talking about, *and you know it*," she said and took another drag.

"I gotta finish what I started," Jason said.

"You always finish way too fast." Leanne's lips twisted into a sneer. "That's the problem."

Reb let out a chuckle. He'd regret it.

"You...You fuckin' told him about that?" Jason said.

"Not the only thing she told me," Reb said. "She said you like to slap her around."

Slim. A couple inches shorter than Jason. Neat and petit. Jason had him figured for a wuss. "Get the fuck out of here," Jason said. "I don't ever want to see you again. You got me?"

"Sure," said Reb. "No problem. You want to get out of my way?"

Leanne flashed a look like she'd spotted an oncoming car, midway on a crosswalk. "Reb."

Jason made way for Reb. "Put your fuckin' clothes on and let's go."

"No." Leanne was looking at the foot of the bed. "I'm staying."

Jason heard the unmistakable *snikt* of a switchblade. He swiveled. Reb missed his back. Instead, he jammed the blade between Jason's ribs.

Leanne let out a primal shriek, and Reb stabbed Jason again, blood spraying all over Reb's sheer avocado-colored dress shirt.

Jason snatched and palmed Reb's face. In the struggle Reb stabbed Jason again, just below his eye socket. Jason shoved him back into the room, and against the far wall. He pulled a Colt 1911 from the small of his back. It met Reb's eyes soaked in dread before he got two rounds to the face.

Leanne's wail rivaled an air-raid siren.

"Shut up," Jason said. SHUT THE FUCK UP!"

Leanne went numb. She couldn't pull her eyes off the horror frozen on Reb's face.

Jason shoved the barrel under Leanne's chin. "Is it his? IS IT HIS?!"

"I don't know. I don't fucking know! I don't know."

"You fuckin' whore. You better fuckin' hope it's not."

"If it's yours, I'll slit its fucking throat!"

Jason's face slacked. In the mirror above the headboard, he watched it twist into a red hued rage. He backed up and held the .45 with a two-handed grip at arm's length.

All Leanne could do was beg. "No. Please. No…" Then she screamed.

He'd always wondered why people would wrap their arms over their eyes, before someone dropped the hammer on them. Didn't they know there was no stopping a bullet? Jason put a round in her forehead and splattered her brains all over the headboard.

Something kept him there. She had her mother's bone structure. Her mother had been the one who'd introduced them. He felt like he couldn't move. He could hear his own breathing. His heartbeat like the battering of a percussion mallet against the head of a bass drum buried in his chest. He heard a woman's shriek. Someone behind him. He turned and saw her in the doorway. Dressed like a maid. He bolted past her. Hurled himself into the El Camino, turned it over and ignited black carbon against the asphalt like a matchhead on a striker strip. Black smoke trailed all the way out of the lot. He didn't let the gun go until he had gotten back on the 110. Tossed it onto the empty seat next to him. Then let up on the gas and let the needle hover around 70.

WICKED WORLD

"Here come Fat Tony," Pancho said.

He pushed his girth into the motel lobby. Six-four. Could tip the scale at about 400 pounds.

"Tony. How are you?" Sekhar said.

"Hey, hey. I'm good, gents. Just dropped by to give you this," Tony handed over his room key.

"You're leaving us?" Sekhar said

"'Fraid so. One more room for a ah—*honeymoon suite*," Tony chuckled. Before Sekhar could take the key, two loud cracks. Everyone's heads spun towards the parking lot.

"Guys fucking around with firecrackers, again," Sekhar said.

"That sounded like gunshots," Pancho said.

"Those were definitely gun shots," Tony said.

Another thunderous crack. This time louder. A woman screamed. The men clamored by the window. A man bolted out of room 9, and into an El Camino. He peeled out of the lot in a cloud of exhaust. Lucia screamed as she ran for the lobby. Subtly, doors around the lot slid open, just enough for a head to pop out. Then quickly shut again. Faces flashed behind windows, but the curtains were quickly redrawn. People who stayed at The Paradise Motel knew their own business, and how to mind it.

The toilet flush roared. The bathroom door behind the register counter burst open. Gil Dharod, aged 67, stood there clutching the latest issue of *Popular Mechanics*. Unlike his son, Gil had pale skin, and green eyes. His lips, as usual, were in a perpetual snarl. He said, "What the fuck is going on, man?" in a thick Bombay accent.

Lucia barged into the motel Lobby. *"¡Acaba de matar a dos personas!"*

"Yo, two people just got shot. Holy shit, bro," Pancho said. "Call the fucking cops."

Sekhar picked up the phone and dialed. He had the receiver to his ear, when Gil finger fucked the button on the handset, ending the call.

"They'll shut us down," Gil said.

"He's right," Fat Tony said. "Unless you guys have somebody you're paying."

Gil and Sekhar shared a look.

Sekhar followed Pancho, Estaban, and Lucia with his eyes as they bounded over to the room, just as a Pearl White Cadillac Eldorado floated into the lot.

"Here," Fat Tony handed Gil a business card.

Gil read it over. *The Roach King. Best Cleanup in Town After an Extermination.*

"*A cleaner.* Guy comes quick," Fat Tony said. "Since it's two—*when you call,* you tell him he needs to *spray twice.* He's local. Like I said, guy comes quick."

"What's he cost?" Gil said.

"Two k per spray," Fat Tony said. "But it's permanent."

"Thank you, Tony." Gil said, holding up the card. He offered his hand, and Fat Tony shook it. Gil nodded to Sekhar. "I'll page Sally. If she doesn't call, we'll try this guy."

"Don't forget this," Tony said, and handed Sekhar the room key. "Can't say I'm sorry I'm leavin'."

Gil picked up the receiver and dialed up Sally Lieberman's beeper. "Sally, it's Gil at The Paradise. Some trouble here. We need you, please." Gil wasn't sure what the message protocol should be. Did they record these things? Ever since she'd started carrying the thing, he'd been meaning to ask her.

Sekhar watched Fat Tony walk over to his car parked in front of room 7. Pancho and his cousin were chatting it up with Tundra, who was now leaning up against his Pearl White El Dorado, clutching an In and Out drive-thru bag. Tundra, a white pimp who spoke jive, wore his silver blonde hair pulled back into corn rows. Very cocky and loud. And he was clogging up three rooms.

"I don't trust him," Gil said.

Like most families from Gujarat, the Dharods had started with a smaller, inexpensive motel. They upgraded to a larger facility when they had the chance. The Paradise Motel wasn't the Hilton, but it had been a step up from The Crenshaw Inn Motel in South L.A.

"He brings in a lot of money," Sekhar said. The old man knew it, too.

"Because he has the young girls," Gil said. "They always pay more for young."

"How many girls you got?" Pancho asked.

"Just the two," Tundra said. "That's all I need. The one girl, she's a money-making machine."

"Nice ride," Tony said to Tundra on his way into room 7.

"Solid," Tundra said. "Yo, you got style, my man." Tundra also fancied himself a man of style: velour Puma tracksuit, a wide 18k cobra chain around his neck, and a fat gold ring smothered in ice on his finger.

Tony nodded but flashed a look that told Tundra his words didn't match the mouth it came out of. He'd gotten used to it. White people always looked at him like that. Sometimes before he even opened his mouth.

Lucia pulled the door shut to room 13. She nodded to Pancho, and made her way back to the office.

"Had you some drama here tonight," Tundra said. "Damn."

"Some fool shot two people," Pancho said. "Don't worry. Ain't nobody calling five-oh."

"I know that's right," Tundra said. "Ya'll be scandalous."

"Man," Pancho said. "Look at you. Borillo Cabrón. Pot callin' the kettle black."

"Yo," Tundra said. "I just call it like I see it. So who's the little man?"

"Estaban," Pancho said. "Mi primo."

"They call me Little Snoopy," Estaban said.

"Yo," Tundra said. "That's off the hook."

"*Chuco*. Yo, little man's hardcore," Pancho said. "They gonna jump him in any day now."

"For real?" Tundra said.

"Echo Park Locos," Pancho said. "*Órale.*"

The kid threw up a gang sign.

"Yo, you ever seen a naked girl? Ever seen a pussy little man?" Tundra said.

"Hell yeah," Estaban said.

"I mean in the flesh, little g?" Tundra said.

The little man kept silent.

"You ain't never seen a girl's pussy, have you? C'mon. I want you to get a look at home girl. You down?"

"Órale," Pancho said. "You wanna see some panocha, Estaban?"

"Si mon." Estaban said. "Vamanos"

"Right this way, little man." Tundra said. "I'll show you some primo pussy."

CORNUCOPIA

Sally Lieberman's Motorola Dimension IV pager went off. It vibrated at the top of her inner thigh, and she shut it down immediately. Whoever it was, could wait. According to Dan Monahan, a guy she'd come up with from the 77th Street Division—someone she'd gone way back with, all the way back to just-out-of-the-academy, had told her about Wally's Liquor Mart on South San Pedro. Now a dick with the OCID, Dan moonlit and who knew what else. According to him, 'Every neighborhood crum-bum that breathes hangs out there.' He told her there were always guys hanging out there, waiting to strike. Mug some geezer after they cashed their paycheck. Dan said it was 'like a mob scene on the first and the fifteenth.' A grocer, liquor store, and check cashing service (where they probably charged more than the standard 1%). Lot of cash went through there. Definitely worth it.

A couple weeks and she had it down. Lupita opened up sometime between 7:45 and 8, four days a week. Nice girl. Didn't speak very good English but understood it. She also understood the neighborhood. Sally could see she was involved. The 18th Street tattoo told her so.

June first had been a Sunday, so Monday had to be the mother lode. This being Tuesday, Wednesdays were always a bank run. The bank didn't open 'til nine AM, but on Wednesdays, the owner always showed up, bright and early to transfer the money, along with his brother. Both men armed and ready. But Tuesday night? Tuesday nights Consuelo closed up at ten PM sharp. Alone.

When Sally jammed the .38 colt detective special against her temple it wasn't what Consuelo thought it was. Her eyes snapped shut and she froze.

"I'm here for the money," Sally told her.

Her eyes snapped open, and she could see Sally wasn't some vata loca from MS-13. With a black Cleopatra bob, librarian glasses and a surgical mask, Uri Gellar couldn't pick her out of a lineup.

"Back inside," Sally said.

The lights were out, and they were in the doorway in the rear lot.

"Lights," Sally said.

Consuelo flipped the switch.

"Up against the wall."

Consuelo complied. Sally took out a photo. Normally it would be of the person's house. That kind of photo kept people in line. But since Consuelo was involved, she showed her a photo of Consuelo and her brother barbequing in her backyard. Then Sally reminded her what kind of time she could be looking at for harboring a fugitive wanted for a double murder.

No cameras. No alarm. Sally wondered why the place wasn't getting knocked over weekly. "Open the safe bitch."

Consuelo did as instructed. Sally bound Consuelo to a storage locker with knuckle weave fencing using an industrial grade plastic tie for bundling wire.

She opened the duffle bag and filled it with bundles of cash.

"That's not our money," Consuelo said. "You're making a mistake."

There was more than just money in the safe. A couple of guns, probably without legible serial numbers, and passports, legit or expensive. Sally had on gloves but thought she ought to let them be. But curiosity got the best of her. There were three of them. Two were US one for Mexico. Esmeralda Alonzo, born October First, 1927 had a striking resemblance to Sally. Real or fake, it could fool a twenty-year LAPD veteran. She tucked it into her front pocket and finished stuffing cash into the duffle in silence. Then she threw the bag over her shoulder, avoided eye contact with Consuelo, and let herself out.

RAT SALAD

Tony Capra was packed and ready to leave The Paradise for good. He had the door propped open to room 7. His plan was to drop a deuce, collect his bags, and then he was out of this shit hole. No sooner had he gotten through the door when it slammed shut behind him. Tony C spun around to see Dominic "Opti" Russo in the doorway. He had four inches and about 150 pounds on

Opti, but it didn't seem to matter much. He shrank against the far wall. A fresh coat of fear frosted over his fat sweaty face. He stifled himself from wiping it clean.

"Hey Tony. Long way from Suffolk Downs," Opti said.

Not the last face he'd hoped to see. He and Opti went back. But not too far back. Opti was a soldier for the Angiulos. An earner—of sorts. The kind of guy who watched somebody else build something up, then swooped in for his taste. Plain and simple, he was a parasite. The boys back in the North End all respected him for his namesake. Guy took the New England Golden Gloves in '61, when he flattened Jimmy "The Skids" Santiago with a crushing overhand right. Gave the kid a detached retina. From then on, everyone called him "The Optician", or "Opti" for short. But in certain circles, Opti had another nickname. *The Plaster Caster.* Word is his win had been a fix. Tony had gotten the straight dope from Skip Margulies, Opti's trainer. According to Skip, he'd wrapped up the kid's hands in plaster—which hardened with sweat. The result had been bloody, but only Santiago's corner shed a tear. The win made Opti a neighborhood hero. The loss: only Skip's. He ended up homeless in Chucky town, banging H, running his mouth until it caught the wrong ear. Then he disappeared.

The Mystic River would freeze over before he'd have let this guy walk him into a room. And yet, there they were.

"You gonna say something eloquent, or just get it done already?"

"You mean about you being a rat?" Opti said. "Chumming up the waters with my friends to a grand jury? Nah. I leave the monologuing to the movies. Let

Brando be Brando. You know me. I got a short fuse. If I wanted to turn your lights out, they'd be out."

"So what, then?"

"Since you're in the program, I'm assuming you're not mailing Howie Winter his cut of your action down at Hollywood Park," Opti said. "Word is, your take out here makes Suffolk Downs look like a soap box derby."

"Until now."

"This is Hollywood," Opti said. "Consider me like your agent."

"So you want fifteen percent?"

Opti roared with laughter. "What? Fifteen percent of what *you tell me* the take is? I'll take five Gs. Per week."

"When?"

"Tomorrow. Early. But not too early. I'll tell you where to meet me. Give me a number that's good."

Tony grabbed a piece of stationary off the desk and scribbled down a phone number. "Here." He handed it to Opti.

Opti looked it over. "This better be a working number. And it better be you answering. Where the fuck is 424, anyway?"

"Malibu."

"Ho, look at you. Feds set you up nice."

"I set me up nice. I'm not with the feds anymore."

"And they don't need you anymore. Just remember that."

"Anything else?"

"Yeah. You ever thought about joining a gym? Or maybe ordering a salad once in a while? Christ, I thought I was a fat bastard. Your poor fuckin' heart."

"Still driving that '75 Fleetwood?"

"Seventy-three. And it runs like a dream."

Tony realized he'd have to wait on droppin' a deuce. He couldn't shit now, if he tried. But one thing eased his mind. He could see Opti wasn't the earner he used to be. The suit he wore was barely in fashion. "I gotta run." He checked the arms on his Rolex Datejust.

"Little late for post time, isn't it?"

"I take Tuesdays off." He picked up his bags. "Get that for me, would ya?"

Opti pulled the door open.

Before Tony made his way through it, he said. "Tonight's my night to get plastered." He forced the last word out for emphasis. Opti's eyes followed him all the way back to his pearl black '79 Seville. "Call me tomorrow."

He could feel Opti's glare from twenty feet away. He slid behind the wheel. Before he pulled the door shut, he heard Opti say, "*Count on it.*"

BREAK OUT

Sally had parked her '75 Ford Escort a block and a half away from Wally's. When she got to the car, she found the window had been broken, and the radio gone. She dusted the glass off the seat, got in, and prayed it would turn over. When it fired up, she drove two blocks, and pulled into the parking lot of a Jon's supermarket and parked alongside a light pole. She opened up the duffle and counted the cash. There weren't any cars around, and the back of the Jon's swam in shadow. A wide swath of light illuminated the front side of the supermarket. She pulled off her gloves, the paper surgical mask, the glasses, and the black bob cut wig. Looking in the rearview mirror was painful. The dark circles around her eyes. Spider webs around them reaching out for her temples. This is what fifty-seven looked like. But that wasn't the worst of it. The sides of her hair were dark where she'd dyed it, but the gray kept coming in fast around her receding hairline. She had at least an inch more of forehead, than she'd had six months ago. She'd heard about a procedure called a hair transplant. The latest in cosmetic surgery. They used hairs from the back of your head. A hell of a lot better than a wig, paint or wearing a piece. Sometimes they looked like doll hair. But if you got the right doctor in Beverly Hills…She'd heard they cost somewhere around five grand. If she had enough left over in the bag—to cover what she'd taken from Noah's college fund, she'd pay that doctor in Beverly Hills a visit. She counted through the stacks of bills. Mostly 20s and 50s, banded up. In total she'd made off with forty grand. She put the car in drive but couldn't zip up the duffle. She had to count the stacks one more time. It had to be more cash than she'd ever seen at one time. They were thousand-dollar bands, so the second count went quick. So much cash, but there was still room in the duffle.

She heard footsteps before she saw him. His mug flashed a bad toothed grin dipped in venom, and Sally screamed. He held out a chrome .25 automatic, probably a Raven or a Loricon, or some other pop-and-drop Saturday Night Special. "Money, bitch!" he said.

Sally stomped on the gas, flooring it about a hundred feet before she plowed into an elderly man's shopping cart. She locked up the brakes and heard a loud crack—a bullet in her rear fender. The old man shrieked and backed the fuck up. The beating of footsteps on the pavement, as the gunman sprinted after her. She swerved around the man and tore out of the lot, back onto the street.

SWEET LEAF

Tundra opened the door to room 10. Katarina, 19 years old, sat on the bed, watching *Tom & Jerry*. He placed the In and Out drive-thru bag on the nightstand. He unlocked the cuff holding her wrist to the headboard. Esteban hovered next to the open door.

"Close the door, little man," Tundra said.

Esteban pushed the door shut.

"Hey baby. Brought you some dinner," Tundra said. "I want you to meet Esteban. Esteban, this my baby girl Katarina."

Katarina took her eyes off the TV for only a couple seconds to acknowledge Esteban.

"Damn girl. Don't be so friendly," Tundra said. "Shiiit. He's only eleven."

Estaban's eyes fixated on Katarina, who just stared emotionlessly at the TV. A barely audible moaning, and the creak of bedsprings came from next door.

"Esteban ain't never seen a girl's pussy," Tundra said. "I told him I'd show his young ass the hottest motherfuckin' pussy this side of Sunset Boulevard. C'mon baby."

Katarina just stared at the TV. She watched Toodles Galore tease Tom and had a look like she wondered why Tundra would even bother to dick tease a little boy, whose balls weren't even hairy.

Tundra tugged at the sleeve on her oversized tee shirt. She moaned something inaudible and pulled away from him.

Tundra grabbed the remote and killed the picture tube. Katarina turned her head from the tube to the far wall. She pursed her lips into a pout.

Tundra wasn't about to let this bitch disrespect him in front of an eleven-year-old kid. "Take your fuckin' shirt off, bitch." When she ignored him, he grabbed her by the chin.

She said, "Qué demonios te pasa!"

Tundra didn't know what the fuck his bitch just said, but he could see by his expression that the kid knew. "Now bitch!"

"Ay, fuck!" she peeled her oversized tee shirt, leaving nothing but panties.

She had nice full breasts and brown nipples. On her right arm, a tattoo of a flying snake. Her left forearm was branded with block letters burnt into flesh: red letters frosted over in ice, that spelled out TUNDRA. The way it jumped off her skin in three dimensions it just screamed, *can you dig it?*

Tundra tugged on the elastic waistband of her underwear and let it snap against her flesh. "Panties too, bitch!"

Katarina straightened her back against the headboard, hooked her thumbs around the waistband of a pair of shiny pink panties, pulled them down under her ass. Then slid them over her thighs. When they slipped off her ankles, they curled into a ball. Katarina tossed them onto the floor. She opened her thighs towards the awestruck little boy.

"Come over here, little man," Tundra said. "Don't be shy."

Esteban walked up to the edge of the bed, and stared at Katarina's nakedness. The moaning and creaking of bed springs next door got louder. A low guttural grunting, and high-pitched moaning growing even louder still.

"Oh shit," Tundra said. "Little man hip to the groove now," he nearly choked on his own laugh.

Esteban reached out with his right hand and squeezed Katarina's left breast. Tundra knew how warm and soft it felt in the boy's hand. The high-pitched screaming of a woman's voice crying out to God came through the thin walls.

"Okay little man. She's all yours. Imma give you and homegirl some privacy." Tundra walked out of the room and shut the door behind him.

Esteban felt his mouth water, the way it did when his Tia cooked hotdogs with chili sauce. He took in the contours and the thickness of the dense triangle shaped shiny ringlets woven into a dark pubic mound. This wasn't his first time seeing one. Once on a sleepover at his friend Arturo's house, they'd snuck into Arturo's older sister's room when she'd been asleep and pulled back the sheets. They'd laughed and ran out of the room. Just mischief. This time seeing live pussy gave him an electric charge below the belt.

Outside room 10, Tundra and Pancho shared a joint.

"Thanks for hookin' up my lttle cousin, yo."

"Pancho man. You know I got chu."

"I don't think he's ready for no pussy yet."

"He sho' nuff enjoyed getting a handful of that girl's titties."

"For real?"

"Hell yeah," Tundra took a long hit. By the time he passed it back, it was practically a roach. He held the smoke in, till his eyes watered, then blew out a cloud of white smoke, followed by a heavy cough.

"Yo, when he's ready for real, I'll bring him back to you. Meet your price, homes."

They watched Fat Tony pull out of the lot in his black Seville.

"Shit. Big homey got a nice ride too," Tundra watched him go. He turned back to Pancho. "Nah, nah. Look here, when little dude ready, I'll give him Cassandra. She'll be the fuck of his young life. On the house, son. I got you."

"Bet." Pancho killed the rest of the joint.

"Imma check on little dude. See how he doin'."

Tundra pushed the door open to room 10 and burst into laughter. Pancho's little cousin had his pants around his ankles and Katarina's face was covered in jizz. "Oh shit. Yo—"

Pancho walked in and howled with uncontrollable laughter. "Esteban. Oh shit. My little primo. You nasty little fucker."

"Homeboy popped off on that bitch," Tundra said.

"Yo, pull up your chonies, vato!" Pancho said.

Esteban pulled up his drawers.

Tundra re-cuffed Katarina to the headboard, before following Pancho and the kid out the door.

FLUFF

She waited for the door to slam shut behind them, before letting out the air in her chest. She heard the mumble of their voices outside the door. Her nipples were hard, but only because the AC had gotten to her. She didn't feel like getting dressed, or even wiping her face. She didn't feel like flipping on the TV. She didn't feel like moving at all. A takeout bag sat next to her with a burger and fries. Now cold and sloppy. But she wasn't hungry anyway. If she had been high, she might be laughing about how twisted and absurd it all was. Her fucked up life. Some dirty little shit had just tugged on his little prick and taken a cum dump on her face. A malicious little boy, who'd probably grow up to be a rapist, who'd beat his daughters. Her mind took to the skies. On the wings of Kukulcán. If she let herself live in that moment, it would surely kill her bleak future.

SHOCK WAVE

The ladies of the evening shuffled in and out of the lobby as usual. Light flickering over their shiny made-up faces before they walked through the door, only without the drip of diffuse humor from their lips. Street walkers tended to get real quiet in wake of extreme violence. Gil had noticed that to be the case nine months back, when a man had been brutally stabbed to death in front of the motel office. Gil remembered October of '79 like it was two nights ago. The month his wife left him. All eyes were on the hippie girl when she walked into the lobby, but her eyes were on Gil. The full moon lit her up nice in the doorframe. She carried a stench with her.

"Damn," Esteban said. "Somebody been smoking."

"Good evening gentlemen. I'm with the *Women of the Night* street-team. Just wanted to drop off some flyers."

She wore cutoff denim shorts, with Chuck Taylors. Long dreadlocks hung over a rainbow tie dyed Grateful Dead tee with the sleeves cut off. She had a snake print headband that covered her forehead. "I'm Satrina. Are you the owner?" she said to Gil.

"Yes. Gil."

Satrina held out her hand, which had a ring on every finger. Gil shook it.

In her other hand was a stack of flyers. "Pleasure to meet you, Gil. Do you mind if I drop these flyers off? Here at the front desk?"

Gil was a minimalist. He didn't want a pile of Xeroxed papers clogging up the front counter. "Well…"

"Thousands of women are trafficked annually," Satrina said. "Through motels like this…"

Pancho walked up to get an eyeful of Satrina. He'd been checking her out since she walked in. "What's good niña?"

"*Manflor*, ese," Esteban said.

"Yo. *Cállate*, carbon," Pancho said. Then turned back to Satrina. "What do you mean by *trafficked?*"

"Women forced into prostitution," Satrina said. "There have been reports about this motel…"

"What reports?" Pancho said.

The bell went off. A bleached blonde, black woman in a lingerie top, leather mini, thigh highs and fish net hose walked in.

"Excuse me," the bleached blonde said.

Satrina and Pancho made way, as she handed Sekhar the key. She said to Gil, "Got you a New York sized roach in nineteen. In the bathroom."

To Gill it sounded like *Baffroom*. But he took her meaning. "Thank you. We'll take care of it."

"Excuse me ma'am," Satrina said, holding out a flyer. "Hi I'm with the *Women of the Night* foundation. If you need a place to stay. Warm coffee. There are alternatives to a life you didn't choose."

"Bitch, you tryin' to fuck with my money?"

"No," Satrina said. "We're here to help…"

"*Gil*," the bleached blonde said. "What the hell kinda place cha'll runnin' here?"

"It's about your needs," Satrina said, holding out a flyer. "If you need anything…"

"Get that shit out of my face," the bleach blonde said. "You need to shave your motherfuckin' armpits. Gil. You need to get this vagabond bitch the fuck out yo' mo-tel. Goodnight gentlemen." The bell went off as the door swished shut behind her.

"That went well," Sekhar said, and everyone laughed.

"Well," Satrina said. "I'll just leave these here…"

"I'll take *one*," Gil said, rising from the stool he sat on. He peeled the top flyer off the stack and put it onto the desk, below the raised front counter. "We have your number. In case anyone's interested."

"Right," Satrina said. Then exhaled, "Thanks."

She turned for the door, then turned her eyes back to Gil. "Hey, does Roberto still work here?"

"Who?" Gil said.

Sekhar turned to Gil, and said, "Papa. You remember Roberto. He…"

"He's no longer with us," Gil said. "He's moved on."

"He stopped working for us about a year ago," Sekhar said.

"Before my time," Pancho said.

"Do you know where he works now?" Satrina said.

"No idea," Sekhar said. "Sorry."

"Let us know if you need a room," Gil said.

She looked right at Gil, from the doorway. Half her face in shadow. "Truly a god among insects. Goodnight."

The doorbell went off, as Satrina entered the night. Pancho caught it, before it closed.

Esteban cupped his hand around his mouth like a megaphone and barked after him, "Manflor. *Manflor*," as Pancho followed her out.

"Hey, Satrina. Wait up."

She turned with a toss of her filthy dreaded hair. She had a rich tan. Looked sexy on a green-eyed white girl. Rasta voodoo hair sun-bleached reddish down to her ass with dark roots. A tarantula spider around her neck on a chain. No bra. Hairy pits. She looked like she might fuck good after some Mary Jane. A vagabond alright. Someone who hitchhiked. The kind of girl who wouldn't complain about squat pissing in an alley. The kind of girl who didn't wear underwear.

"I'll tell any girls, you know," Pancho said. "If they ask…"

"They won't."

"Satrina. Like *Santeria*."

She had half a smile. "Maybe."

"Where you from?"

"Poughkeepsie."

"That in the valley?"

She laughed. "No, it's in New York."

Her head leaned towards him. Her hand cocked on her hipbone, above the low riding waistband of her dirty cutoffs.

"That's a long way to hitchhike."

She laughed again. "I flew."

No perfume. No deodorant. He could smell her BO, but it only turned him on. He thought he could smell her pussy. But then again, that smell was always on his brain. He guessed that's what happened when you worked at a puta motel. He could smell something else, too. "I'm Pancho."

"Like *Pancho Villa?*"

"Yeah. Exactly."

"But you don't have the big mustache."

He wanted to bury his face in her pussy. "No. I like to keep it smooth. For the ladies."

She laughed. "I see."

He could get used to that laugh. "I see you got a spider around your neck. *Araña.*"

"Spiders are creators. Weavers."

"Of webs to catch prey."

She started to backpedal. "Well, it was nice meeting you, Pancho. I'm gonna go."

"I get off at six. Come back. I got the good stuff. You know? We could smoke. I know you smoke, girl."

"Maybe." She was smiling.

"Go home and change your underwear. We can go to breakfast."

She had to shout from fifteen feet away. "I don't wear underwear."

"Then we can skip breakfast," he shouted back.

"If you're hungry you can eat my ass." She flipped him the bird.

Then she turned around and gave him the rearview. The cutoffs rode up on her ass cheek. One, then the other, as she strode. Until her legs were gone, under the full moon. And all he could see was her rainbow colored back and the snake wrapped around her head. Down where the mouth of the lot met Sunset.

Fuck that bitch, Pancho thought. Probably a dyke anyway. Damn if his pants weren't tight though. His dick didn't know the difference.

JUNIOR'S EYES

The busted-out window roared like a punctured Cessna losing cabin pressure. It kept Sally's mind on edge. The Liebermans lived out in Tarzana. Sally and her husband, Rabbi Levi Lieberman, had been separated for the last six months, which didn't bode well with Noah, her youngest, now a senior in high school.

Levi routinely changed the locks. Sally always found a way in. She'd been LAPD for twenty-two years, what did he expect? She let herself in and climbed the stairs. She saw the door to the master bedroom slightly ajar at the end of the hall. Levi breathed heavy into the phone with his sponsee, a young mentally ill woman of 26. Sally heard him asking her what she had on, and if she'd started to touch herself. Sally must've sighed loudly in disgust, because Levi pulled the door shut, and kept talking into the phone. She thought about leaving the duffle outside the door. Then she caught more of her husband's breathy voice, talking dirty into the phone. She decided to hold onto the money. She crept downstairs, grabbed a beer out of the fridge, and cracked it open. She saw a package addressed to Levi on the kitchen counter. The return address was the mental ward at Cedars Sinai. She tore it open, to find a pair of red lacy underwear—used and unwashed. She recoiled in disgust. She took a healthy swig of the tall boy beer can. But she knew when it went down, the rest of the can and six more like it wouldn't do it. She needed something a lot harder. She stuffed the dirty panties back into the box and hurled it at the backdoor, just as it swung open.

Noah stood in the doorway, scowling at his mother. "What the hell are you doing here?"

"Hi Noah."

She put down the beer can, and walked around the kitchen counter, close enough to reach out and touch her son.

Noah didn't soften. He just glared at his mother.

"I brought back some of your college money I borrowed…"

"You mean, *stole*."

"Yes."

"You know, I was really looking forward to going to Dartmouth," he said. "But I think if you just took the money, and promised to stay out of our lives, it'd be worth what you stole."

Sally's eyes welled up with tears. She didn't want them to. She wanted to fix things. Noah had gotten even more handsome in the last three months. He'd started to look like her brother, Jack. She moved closer and reached out to embrace him.

Noah shoved her away. "You're high."

She wished she was high. "No, I'm not. How's school?"

"It's great. At least whenever the other kids momentarily forget my mother's a drug addict and a dyke."

"Okay." She wouldn't be able to hold back the tears much longer. "See you kiddo." She pushed past him and out the door. She power walked past the front rock garden she used to enjoy tending. Her clammy hand still holding the bag filled with dirty money. Everything dead in the dirt now. Just weeds growing in. The neighborhood and her street looked different too. Cold in June. Sally needed to get high. And she needed to get fucked.

SNOWBLIND

Terrance "T-Bone" Butler was built like a tank, and he terrified Tundra. But Tundra thought he hid it well. "Yo, T-Bone, what's crackin'?"

"What's crackin' indeed, my cracker," T-Bone said, and smiled with a mouth full of gold teeth.

They were inside The Pantry, downtown. Place never closed. T-Bone had a huge plate of scrambled eggs, toast, and hash browns, smothered in hot sauce. He licked his fingers, digging in. "Sit down, T."

Tundra took a seat. There were about five other people in the place.

"Menu's on the wall," T-Bone said.

"I ain't hungry."

"That's because you a junkie, T. Look at you."

Tundra hadn't been hungry since yesterday. "Seems like you always hungry."

"Sixty-five hundred calories a day, my cracker."

His brown skin shone. Giant muscles bulged from leather upholstery.

"Gots to feed the machine. So wazzup?" he said, licking his finger.

"Just confabing, my brother."

"Uh huh. So how much you want?"

"Ounce."

"Shiiit. You movin' up in the world."

"You got it?"

"I got it."

"My secret ingredient. Keeps 'em coming back."

"You still trickin' out them Mesicans?"

"Hell yeah," Tundra looked around, then lowered his voice, and said, "Got me one who's sixteen. Fools pay double for young pussy."

"God damn B," T-Bone said. "But you don't want none of me up in that. I'll ruin that tight pussy."

"But seriously, yo. This F-shit. It's makin' 'em come back."

"Das cuz the shit's highly addictive. Even moreso than snowflake. And your snowflake ain't shit, but that's a whole 'nother thing."

"Tell me the name again."

"So you can aks someone else? *Fentanyl.* You ain't gonna find it. It ain't like findin' blow."

"What if I wanted to buy volume? You got it like that?"

"Maybe. Let me see what I can do."

"Seriously. If I buy volume, I want a discount."

"Sure thing, cool breeze." T-Bone licked his fingers. "I'll give you ten percent off."

Tundra took a hit from his glass pipe. Impure blow. No Fentanyl. He got onto the 10 and got off on Western. The ho stro'. Tundra would often cruise Western in search of new talent, or to size up the competition. Gliding in his pearl white Eldorado, with the chrome Dayton wire wheels, he had the bitches on him like ants on cotton candy.

"Whatchu mean a mo-tel? I tolt you, I got a man," she said.

"What kind of man puts you out here in a wig, with them jagged nails?" Tundra said. "A girl like you needs a curly weave. You a lioness, girl. Need you some polished claws, and a beautiful new coat. Take my number. You a natural. Anyone can see that. You give me a call when you ready." She took his card, and Tundra hit the switch on the power window before she could say anything more. The girl had ass for days, but he didn't wait for her to walk. He'd let her eyes follow him down the Ave, flossing better than any of these guerilla pimps. He popped a cassette into the deck, cranked the stereo and "Chase Me" by Con Funk Shun stomped out of his Bose speakers. He watched her gaze fade from the rearview. The way these hos' eyes would follow him—inside them, a light that reflected back. One they could never catch.

He hooked a right turn onto Third, then another right on South Rampart and cruised into Tommy's burger shack. He got a double chili cheeseburger, fries, and two chili cheeseburgers for the girls. Cassandra been done 19 tricks the whole day long. That ho gonna eat good tonight, he said to himself. "Throw in a chili cheese dog. With the works," he told the cashier with a nametag that said Angelica, and a smile and titties enough for the game.

He kept his pearl handled .38 wedged between the seats, where he could reach for it, whenever he cruised so close to MacArthur Park. "Fire When Ready" by Con Funk Shun rattled his speakers, as Tundra rolled West Temple towards downtown. He took a hard left on North Beaudry, crossed the 101, and rolled back into Paradise. A pest control van with a logo that read The Roach King on the side, took up Tundra's usual spot. He took the one next to it.

He handed Cassandra a burger and the dog from Tommy's. "Ay Papi Chulo," she said.

"A wiener you can eat, instead of suck on, girl." Tundra said. She understood about half of what he said, but she understood intent. Body language. And he could see she had to be really happy to see him. She would always greet him like one of Pavlov's dogs, salivating, one hand on his chest, the other on his package. Especially when he held out that pipe. A fresh spoonful of dirty snow, with that F-shit. He flicked the Bic underneath, and she sucked it like a dick. That bitch loved to smoke. Her eyes orbiting Mars like the Viking probe.

He pressed play. The answering machine jammed pack with messages. Dudes looking to party. During the afternoon (nobody before one PM), the cars would line up for a poke at Cassandra. So much so, Gil's old ass would complain. After 7 in the PM, shit had to be strictly in-call. No exceptions. Baby girl had been told: '*Never mess with the phone.* They were all for her ass but didn't nobody want to talk to her'. Plus, her thick accent made her already bad English even worse. Tundra called back the first three tricks on the machine and gave 'em appointments hour to the half hour. Tricks paid more at night too. Just like at the movie house. And to be honest, he'd always smoke the girls out in the evening, and so they always fucked better.

Cassandra lay on her back, eyes glassed over and still in orbit, when the next knock came. Tundra answered the door with his gat. A pearl handled revolver. Four-inch barrel. Always necessary. Dudes saw he was white, and figured his little dick came with no balls. This dude looked like a schoolteacher: glasses, a cardigan, and a balding comb-over. But dude had evil in his eye. Not like he wanted to test Tundra. But like he might rough up the merch. Cut her or something. Tundra got a bad feeling about him and sent him away. The guy for the next slot, already waiting.

"Yo," Tundra said to the guy in his car, scooping the air in front of him towards his face.

The guy got out of his 10-year-old Buick. He looked like an aging blues guitarist. Leather vest, cowboy boots and hair like Robert Plant. Tundra stopped him in the doorway. "Price is one fitty."

The man held out a single C-note. "Hundred's as steep as I go."

"One fitty, my man," Tundra said. "Baby girl's sixteen."

The man looked in and saw Cassandra buck naked on the bed with her legs spread, hands on her hips, blowing him a kiss.

The man exhaled with punctuation. He reached into his pocket and dug out a fifty. He put the two bills into Tundra's hand, and Tundra slid it into his left front pocket— the one closest to the gun's pearl handle.

"Can I put it in her ass?"

Tundra called over to Cassandra. "Turn over baby girl."

Cassandra smiled wide and rolled over onto her stomach. Below her tiny waist were wide hips with an ass Tundra figured might have been sculpted by one of the ancient Greeks who wasn't a fag. The trick got an eye full. That ass called to him. Tundra stopped him from coming through the door.

"Two hundred extra," Tundra said.

The man's look of protest lasted about half a second. He dug into his wallet, and produced two wrinkled, sweat-laden Ben Franklins.

Tundra palmed the cash and stuffed it into the front pocket of his track pants. "Right on. Got yourself an hour, my man. I'll knock at fitty." Tundra let the man by. Then he let the door close. Easy money. He popped into the next unit over, with the second doggy bag from Tommy's.

Katarina had her usual sour puss face on when Tundra came in. He put the Tommy's bag with the chili burger on the nightstand, next to the bed. She had her eyes on the tube, watching *Charlie's Angels*. Tundra liked to think the girls were like his angels. He leaned in and gave her a peck on the cheek. She kept watching the tube. Didn't even blink. The phone rang. Tundra picked up.

"Hey it's me. Sally."

"Wass up, girl," Tundra said.

"I need…"

"I know what you need baby girl. I got chu. Come on through."

Sally hung up.

Tundra slid the handset back onto the receiver. He ran two fingers across a curly stray lock of hair, that hooked away from Katarina's ear. "It's dark outside, baby girl. Your burger gonna get cold."

Katarina just stared at the tube. A commercial came on for Coors Light. A text popped up on the screen that said, '*The Surprise is how good it tastes.*' Bunch of Cowboys out on the open plain, digging into a cooler. "It's already cold," she said.

Tundra heard voices outside. He got up off the bed, leaned over the circular table, pulled at the very edge of the drawn curtain, and peeked out the window. Gil standing around out there with a guy dressed like an exterminator. He didn't want them spraying his room. That shit complicated business. And nobody, including him had time for that.

PARANOID

"I'm amazed," Gil said. "It's like new. How did you get all the blood out of the carpet?"

"Hydrogen Peroxide," The Roach King said. "But it's all in the application—Peroxide alone won't do it, when it's applied by conventional means."

The chemical smell was fierce. Gil flipped off the lights, and the two men stepped out of the doorway to room nine. Gil pushed the door shut behind them.

By Gil's standards, The Roach King had to be fairly tall. Which meant six feet as opposed to Gil's 5-foot-seven. He wore an auto mechanic's one-piece zip up coveralls with a logo that read *The Roach King* on the back. No nametag over his chest. He wore an unmarked black baseball cap low enough on his forehead that Gil couldn't make out the color of his eyes.

"You're going to want to keep that window open," the Roach King pointed at it. "All night if possible."

During their brief conversation in the lot outside room nine, he'd noticed a prostitute walk out of the motel office, and another one walk in.

"That is, if you can afford to leave the room unoccupied."

"So," Gil chose his words carefully, "Is everything taken care of?"

"*Everything* is in the van," The Roach King said. "And Everything will be gone in two hours."

"Well," Gil clasped his hands together, glanced over at the open window, and exhaled. How quick and efficient this man had been. "Very good."

"There's still the matter of my payment," The Roach King said.

"Oh. I'm sorry. Of course. Right this way."

Gil made a trip to the safe in the back. He walked back out to the lobby with a stack of 100 dollar bills four-inches thick. He handed them to the Roach King. "No need for a receipt."

The Roach King sifted through the stack, quick as a Vegas count machine, then looked up at Gil, and nodded, before walking out.

"That's the guy?" Pancho asked. "*The cleaner?*"

"The very one," Gil said.

Sekhar watched the white van with the words *The Roach King* detailed on the side, back up and pull out of the lot. It disappeared down Sunset, just as a familiar dark blue Ford Escort pulled into the lot. It pulled all the way up to the open spot in front of the motel office. "Sally's here."

Gil gave Sekhar a look.

A see-through can liner and duct tape wrapped up the busted window tight as a prophylactic, diffusing the neon sign. Sally took one last look in the mirror. She'd put on her shoulder length brown wig, that looked a lot more natural with her skin tone. All in all, she looked pretty good, considering she did her makeup in the bathroom at a Shell station. The clean teal colored blouse she had on got tight in the right places. Men had always paid a lot of attention to her D cup chest. She wondered what kind of nasty comments men made with her back turned ('Not much to look at, but she's got great tits') She'd pulled on a pair of tight Jordache jeans that made her butt look good. Truth is, she wouldn't be all that disappointed if she caught any one of them checking out her behind.

"Hey Pancho," Sally said, as she walked into the lobby.

"Sally," Pancho said.

"Hello Sally," Gil said. "How are you tonight?"

"Good, thanks. Got your message," Sally said. "Sorry about the delay. It's a little late for you, isn't it, Gil?" Gil had never been at the front desk past eight.

"Just working late on taxes," Gil said.

"Saw an exterminator pull out of here," Sally said.

"Just someone looking for directions," Sekhar said.

"So what happened?" It must've been from years on the job, but whenever she asked that question it worked on people like truth serum. People always assumed she knew more than she did.

"What do you mean?" Sekhar said.

"A couple of patrons were fighting. Yelling," Gil said. "One of them pulled a knife. That's when I paged you..."

"I got between them," Pancho said. "Told them they had to leave or there was going to be trouble."

"And then what happened?" Sally said.

"I eighty-sixed both those fools," Pancho said.

Out of the three of them, Pancho was the best liar. He also had a criminal record.

"So everything's been quiet," Sally said. "Since the incident?"

"Everything's chill," Pancho said.

A raven-haired prostitute wearing Stilettos, and one of the worst wigs Sally had ever seen walked into the lobby. She handed Sekhar a key, then walked out.

"Very quiet," Sekhar said.

"Cool," Sally said. "Well, the first was a couple days ago, so..."

"Ah," Gil said. Two k a month for protection wasn't as impossible as it sounded, but after what happened earlier, he just couldn't make it. "We're a bit light this week."

"That's fine," Sally said. "I'll take whatever you've got right now."

"Right," Gil said. "I'll be right back."

Sally knelt in front of where Esteban sat on the couch.

Despite his preadolescent macho demeanor, she figured most adults saw a cute kid.

"What's your name?" Sally asked.

"Are you a cop?" Esteban said.

"Yes I am," Sally said.

"Then I ain't tellin' you nothin'," Esteban said.

Sally burst into laughter, stood up and said to Pancho, "He yours?"

"My cousin," Pancho said.

"Adorable," Sally said.

Gil walked out with an envelope and handed it to Sally. Sally sifted through the cash in the envelope.

"That's all there is, right now," Gil said.

"No problem, Gil," Sally said. "We'll worry about the rest when you've got it." She slipped the envelope into the inside pocket of her denim jacket.

"Hey," Pancho said. "Your hair looks good tonight."

Sally couldn't figure out if he'd been genuine, or if he knew she wore a wig. "Thanks. Goodnight, gentlemen."

They watched her walk out of the office. She kept walking past her car, and over to room 11.

"Sally gone lookin' for that good stuff. She looks pretty good for an old lady," Pancho said. "Nice caboose. I'd fuck her."

"And on that note, I'm going to turn in. See you tomorrow." Gil headed for the door.

"Night papa," Sekahr said.

"Night Gil," Pancho said.

SUPERNAUT

Tundra answered on the first knock. He answered the door in a pink silk bathrobe, with velour track pants, and looked her up and down. Then he puckered his lips and gave her a nod. "Sally. Wass goin' on?"

"I'm alone." She said.

"I know that girl. Watched you pull up. C'mon."

She walked in and took a seat at the circular table by the window. She felt her eyes pulled over to the bed. A beautiful young girl lounged with her back against the headboard, watching a rerun of *Charlie's Angels*. One hand cuffed to the bedframe.

"Sally, want you to meet my girl, Katarina," Tundra said. "Say hi, baby."

Katarina looked up from the TV and pursed her lips enough to give Sally a thin smile.

"She kinda shy," Tundra said. "So how much you want?"

"Two grams." She had the cash for more. But if she got more than for her own head, she'd just smoke it up faster.

"Two hundred."

She handed Tundra four fifties from the night's score.

"Solid. Want you to keep baby girl here company, while I go get you the product." He slipped off the robe and slipped on the matching purple velour track top. "Oh, and if I come back here and catch you with yo' face in that coochie pie, it's gonna cost you extra. Just so we're clear. See you in a few."

Sally pulled up one edge of the curtains, and watched Tundra cross the lot to room 22, from the tiny sliver of window. He turned back in her direction, when he reached the door, and Sally reflexively let the edge of the curtain go.

She caught Katarina watching her from the corner of her eye. Katarina's eyes quickly returned to the TV.

Sally walked over to the girl's bedside. Katarina had on sweatpants and a bra. With her hair tied back, Sally could see the beautiful contours of her bone structure. Her features were less central American, and more European. She turned towards Sally and looked up at her with her chin down. Her eyes were so dark, they appeared to be giant pupils. She had a long faint scar on her left cheek.

Sally recognized her tattoo. "Quetzalcoatl?"

Katarina nodded. "la serpiente emplumada."

A powerful flying reptile that according to the Aztecs, helped create mankind. The god of wind. A transgressor between the earth and sky. The patron deity of the urban center, a god of culture and civilization. To Latins truly pagan at heart, he represented the city of L.A. Sally could see her other arm had been branded with the word TUNDRA burnt into the girl's flesh. Red block text with a frosting of snow. Like the letters on an ice machine outside of a 7-11. "Es hora de que dejes este lugar," Sally said.

Katarina's eyes stretched for more illumination— clearly impressed that Sally spoke Spanish.

"How long have you been here?" Sally asked in Spanish.

Katarina laid it all out. How they—she and her sister were taken from their village outside Rosarito. And how she'd been taken as collateral—to ensure her baby sister Cassandra never questioned her role as a 24-7 fuck machine. Her sister was only sixteen. Sally had heard about phony hospitality companies promising young women in Mexico positions stateside as live-in maids. However Tundra had brought them here, they weren't walking away easy. The scar on her cheek wasn't new, but there were likely others hidden from sight.

Sally reached into her purse and pulled out a hand cuff key. Katarina's eyes told Sally it looked exactly like the one Tundra used, when he un-cuffed her to use the toilet. She handed Katarina the key. Katarina closed her tiny hand around it. Sally pointed at Quetzalcoatl. "Like the wind."

The door burst open, and Tundra shut it behind him. "You know, I even charge dudes just to talk to my bitches. I could take it outta yo fix. If I felt like it."

Sally nodded at Katarina and turned back towards Tundra. "Who the fuck are you kidding? I called over first. You should have had my shit ready."

"Wa-ho, Sally baby. Goddamn. Regulating a motherfucker and shit." He cracked a goofy grin. "I can dig it." Tundra pulled a Ziploc bag from his track top, Sally's eyes followed the bag, as Tundra tossed it onto the tabletop. Then he pulled out a glass pipe, as Sally stood up from the bed. He teased it in front of her eyes. "How bout we smoke this. One for the road. Yo stash is still yo stash. *This* is a bonus."

Sally felt herself salivating. "Fire it up."

Smoking coke with Tundra was mostly good. Mostly fine, because when freebasing coke, she could easily ignore his rambling. He seemed to enjoy hers.

"Shit." He passed her the pipe. "You get deep girl, when you smokin'."

Too high to guess what thing she'd said had been *so deep*. She must've been quoting Carl Sagan again.

"Damn baby. Girl you look good tonight." His wandering hand slipped down her pants into her panties and found her hairy crack moist. She froze up but didn't stop him. Staring at her chest, he said, "You got some titties." He slid his hand out from inside her pants, brought it up to his nose and sniffed. Then he reached out and squeezed her double-d's with both hands. Stretching and reeling in his fingers, as though kneading dough.

"C'mon, Sally. *C'mon.*"

It didn't feel good, or turn her on, but they were high as shit. "You like my tits?" She almost cracked a smile.

"These are some perfect titties, baby. These are fine. Too bad you ain't got the face to match. Got tities for days, but you ain't no stunner."

Sally's face iced over. She slapped both his hands away. "Piece of shit," she said, and slapped him across the face.

Tundra reached back and swung his open hand, belting Sally in the eye. Then he grabbed her hair, and her wig slipped off her head. "Holy shit. You bald, bitch. Hahahaha. Oh, shit!"

"You motherfucker." Sally growled. She snatched back the wig, then she plucked the baggie up off the table. "Fucking piece of shit!"

"Take it easy, you wrinkled ass cunt," Tundra said. "I've fucked better looking dudes in prison."

Sad thing is, that wasn't the first time she heard that. "Fuck you," Sally spat. "Fucking motherfucking scumbag." She turned towards Katarina, whose eyes met hers with unspoken compassion. "Como el viento." Then she bolted for the door.

A NATIONAL ACROBAT

"Los Angeles is now the murder capital of the United States," Sekhar said. "I read that today."

"That surprise you?" Pancho said. "After tonight?"

"Hell of a night, man," Sekhar snickered.

"You ain't lying, bro. Holy fucking shit."

Sekhar was reclining behind the front desk, with his head between the folded pages of the L.A. Times. An article on the back page read: *Police Give Up Search: Lady Tomahawk Still at Large.* Pancho had his back against the wall by the front door, as he flipped through the June issue of *Lowrider.* Esteban was fast asleep on the couch.

"Have you seen The Empire Strikes Back?" Sekhar said.

"Oh hell yeah, bro. Took sleeping beauty here to see it. Hey yo, that opening scene. With the ice and the snow. It reminded me of like that flick, *Quintet.* With Paul Newman. You seen that?"

"No, I heard about it, though. I saw a reviewer talk about it on Sneak Previews."

"Never heard of it. What'd they say?"

"They said it was horrible."

"That's 'cause Robert Altman ain't nobody's little perrita. You dig? It was heavy. We're talking nuclear holocaust. It's probably going to happen too."

"Wasn't it all about some game? *Quintet.* It was a game, right?"

"Yeah. A five-sided board. Five players. There's one winner. The losers all die in real life."

"Sounds ridiculous."

"The house always has an unfair advantage."

"I guess if the house wants people dead."

"Nah," Pancho said. "They just want to suck the life out of fools, and hope they'll keep coming back till they're dead broke. You ask me, It's like life. And all you can do is play the game."

TOMMOROW'S DREAM

When Sally got home, she had a message on her answering machine. *'Meet me at Du-Pars tomorrow. Nine AM.'*

Du-Pars bakery on Fairfax and Third might've been the best breakfast joint in all of Hollywood. "Nothing beats their hotcakes." That's how Dan Monahan reminded Sally, right before he said, "I'm buying."

The clock radio woke her up at seven with "Still I'm Sad" by Rainbow. She awoke naked in her empty bed, staring at an empty makeshift coke pipe fashioned crudely out of a test tube, she'd pilfered from one of Noah's old chemistry sets. She got dressed and put on her brown wig, and a pearl necklace. She grabbed the pipe and headed for the stove to light up. Then she put it back down. She never needed to be high to see Dan. Seeing Dan was satisfying enough.

They sat behind empty plates, full bellies, which didn't take much for Sally, and topped off mugs of coffee. Bobby Darin crooning on the juke and the warm L.A. sun had just penetrated the marine layer.

"Remember that place I told you about last week?" Monahan sipped his coffee.

Tall and sturdy, Dan Monahan had a head of thick silver and black hair. His cobalt blue eyes nearly matched the sharp looking off-the-rack suit he wore. His top button left undone, and his tie still tied, but loose. He only buttoned all the way up, when he walked into the Organized Crime Investigative Division headquarters, downtown. While he talked, he had a habit of scanning the room before he put eyes back on her.

"What place?" Sally said.

"That place, ah…" Monahan put down the mug, and snapped his fingers three times. "The place in the southland. Over on San Pedro…Wally's. That's it. Wally's Liquor Mart. Remember we were talking about that place?"

"Oh yeah. Check cashing place, right? You said it gets hit a lot."

"Place got robbed last night. Just heard."

"Well if this place gets robbed tonight, we'll know you're officially bad luck."

Monahan laughed. "You ask my wife, that was official a long time ago."

"It's just the law of averages."

"You mean because this is my third wife?"

"No. Dan." Sally laughed. "I mean about Wally's."

"Right. Yeah, I guess it went a whole two months without getting hit."

"Right."

"So how's Levi?"

"Oh Jesus Christ."

"He wouldn't believe this conversation."

Sally snorted with laughter. "Oh my god, Dan. Stop."

"He still having phone sex with that bi-polar girl?"

"She's now mailing him her dirty panties. Yeah."

"Gross."

"Yeah. He's really reached an all-time low."

"So. You're ah… I heard there was somebody new. A girl…"

"What girl?"

"Just something I heard. That you were…"

"That I was *what*, exactly?"

"Just. Nothing. Never mind. I just. You know. I just want you to be happy."

"Oh, I'm happy."

"Yeah?"

"Yeah. Most days. I'm fine with not seeing anyone. So."

"So?"

"So how's things with OCID? You providing security for Ted Turner? Donna Summer's personal bodyguard?" In recent years, it had become more than a rumor the boys over at OCID had a cush gig—private security details, many of the guys moonlighting as PIs.

"No. C'mon."

"I know about you guys."

"I'm actually leaving the OCID."

"You're kidding me?"

"Seriously. I put in a transfer."

"To where?"

"Bank Robbery Squad."

"Really?"

"Yeah. Figured I'd do some real police work my last seven years before retirement."

"Why?"

"L.A. is officially the bank robbery capitol of the world."

"Oh yeah?"

"Think about it. You're talking six million vehicles on the road. A thousand miles of freeway. Los Angeles is the perfect landscape for bank robbers. Practically every bank is near a freeway on-ramp."

"I didn't think about that."

"Switch to a cold car or just swap out stolen plates for legit ones and... bam. You're gone."

"Sounds like you're passionate for police work again."

"Yeah. Well. It's not all me. I told you about Stacy."

"The realtor. Yeah."

"I think it's. Maybe it's her influence. She re-ignited something in me."

"I see."

"But also. Here's the thing—and, you can't say anything."

"Who the fuck would I be talking to?"

"They're gonna be clamping down. There's gonna be some house cleaning with the OCID. Better I leave now."

"So you put in the transfer..."

"I start in two weeks."

"With the Bank Robbery Squad?"

"Yeah."

"Congratulations," Sally said. "We should celebrate. Remember when we'd celebrate back in the old days."

"Well," Monahan let out a nervous laugh, and glanced at his Seiko.

It was the watch his first wife had gotten him. Automatic, with a chocolate-colored calfskin band. Sally had seen the box it came in, the day he'd popped it open, and watched him tighten it below his fist.

"I have to meet Stacy. We're driving to San Diego."

"I see."

"Yeah, I should get going."

"Right. I'll walk you out."

When they exited through the front, Sally watched Dan stiffen to the rapid-fire sound of a camera shutter. A silver haired man in a tan bush jacket stood in a modified weaver at close range, behind a long lens. Before Dan could confront him, they were ushered out of the way by a rotund woman with salon hair, wearing a wine-colored velour tracksuit.

"Excuse me. Comin' through. You're blocking my shot," she said, in what sounded to Sally like a Long Island accent.

"Fucking tourists," Monahan said in a staged whisper. Sally knew his words weren't for her ears only.

Dan had parked on the far side of the lot. He got to the driver's side, folded his arms over the hood, and said, "Glad we got a chance to catch up. Maybe we'll do this again, in a week or two."

"I'd like that," Sally said.

"Okay. Gotta run." He slid behind the wheel.

He twisted the ignition, as she pulled open the passenger side door.

"Wow," she said. "I didn't know you still had this," running her hand along the dashboard. "AMC Matador Enforcer. 401 cubic inch V8. A real hard charger."

"You got a good memory."

"What year?"

"Seventy-two."

"It's really stood up."

"Yeah. It's still got some get up and go."

"Oh my gosh. Dan, look at that," she said, sliding into the passenger seat. "That is a nasty ketchup stain."

"Oh fuck. You're right. New L-T is definitely going to notice."

"Thought you were headed to San Diego."

"Well. After. I have a quick meeting downtown."

"Here." Sally wetted her fingertips with her tongue. She rubbed at the stain blemishing his trousers near the top of his thigh. "You should've said something in the restaurant. Club soda would've gotten this out." Sally's hand moved towards his inner thigh, rather than away. Before he could say a thing, her hand had closed around his package, now rock hard against her palm.

His lips parted, but the words that wanted to come out took their time. Sally pulled the passenger side door shut. The Matador had a fairly dark tint. All except for the front windshield, which faced hard charging L.A. traffic on Fairfax.

"Remember our first year out of the academy?" Sally said.

"Like it was yesterday," he said.

There had been six of them. They'd all been assigned to the 77th, right after graduation. After the very first week of patrols, they'd all met up at Harris's apartment over on the west side. The Dodgers were on the box, and everyone had a Stroh's tall boy in hand. Five guys in their latest teens and early twenties, and Sally, the oldest rookie at a ripe old age of 35. It must've been around the ninth inning, after the third joint had been passed around—this had been back when the weed was good. Carson, the only black patrolman in the group, giggled when Sally fumbled with his belt. He might've been blushing, but who could tell? When she got him loose, he was hard as a steel rod. Sally gently stroked his nine-inch shaft. Everyone stayed silent until Carter, complete with a porn star handle-bar mustache, said, "Damn."

Sally was the older woman with confidence and a huge braless bosom. She stared directly into a young Dan Monahan's eyes when she lowered her head into Carson's lap. Then her voracious lips gave the young patrolman the blowjob of his life. The rest of the evening became a blur. Sooner or later everyone came unzipped. They were all in various states of undressed civvies. Sally was dressed in a tight pair of jeans, Harris's patrol hat and nothing else, with nipples like thimbles. Dan's memories were less imagery, and more about a feeling. A camaraderie. Brothers in blue bonded by sharing the warm skilled mouth of a sister in uniform. The first of many such parties that would follow. The five of them getting more and more intimate, one by one with Sally. Despite her being a Catholic, there were rumors within the group that Sally had visited a free clinic more than once. Astonishingly, they'd all managed to keep it to themselves, long after each and every one of them had found spouses and solidarity. Then came Sally's substance abuse and gambling problems. One by one, they all fell out of touch. Except for Monahan.

She unzipped him, and pulled him all the way loose, so his balls hung over his pants. "I miss those days," Sally said, a tiny smile growing from the corners of her lips, as she gently stroked Monahan's hard cock.

She wasted no time going down. He could smell her perfume, and felt her soft breasts on his thighs, as she descended onto his lap, and wrapped her warm mouth around him.

WARNING

"Why don't you slow down, you greedy pig," Angelo said. "Take it easy."

Tony Capra had his brother-in-law Angelo meet him at The Hong Kong Café, over by Dodger Stadium. They had a three-dollar all-you-can-eat buffet, of which Tony routinely made the most of. And if he was being absolutely honest—they—the Chinamen that ran the place, hated his fucking guts.

"Buffet's only open for two hours," Tony said, with half his mouth full.

"So you're not in a hurry…"

"What'd I just fuckin' say…"

"For your next heart attack." Angelo pushed his paper plate over to Tony's side of the table. "Here. You can have mine."

"You're not gonna eat?"

"This shit goes right through me anyway. When you sent the cab to pick me up, I thought it was taking me to Musso & Franks. Or someplace nice."

For the first time since he'd walked over his heaping plate of food, Tony looked up from his plate, and gave Angelo a wide-eyed *Are you serious?* look. "I'm trying to keep a low profile."

"Sorry to hear about Farenheit."

"That was three months ago," Tony said between bites. "I've had time to get over it."

"Fuckin' prophetic. Still. A stable fire. Jesus. What a way to go. That means it was hotter than 451."

"What?"

"What paper burns at. It was hotter than four hundred and fifty-one degrees. To burn flesh."

Tony just stared.

"You never read a single thing outside of the sports page, have you?"

"I prefer picture books," Tony said. "So'd you bring 'em, or what?"

"Yeah. If you want to stop feeding your face for a minute." Angelo pulled a manila envelope from the inside pocket of his tan safari jacket.

"I can do two things at once."

"Suit yourself," Angelo tossed the envelope onto the table.

Tony opened the envelope, pulled out the photos and did a slow shuffle, while his mouth moved like a washing machine with a glass door. Angelo's index finger stopped him on the fourth pic.

"Giovanni Russo's place. Opti's staying there. His wife threw him out. Plus he used to own it. It's an interesting story…"

Tony made circles with his index finger in profile, like film on a reel.

"Yeah, yeah. Anyway—flip to the next one. Keep going. The next one. *Stop.*"

Someone Tony didn't recognize walking in through the vehicle bay. In the next shot, Opti greeted his guest inside the garage.

"How the fuck did you get this shot?" Tony said between bites.

"It's called movement. See how they're in profile? Okay, remember that face. Now shuffle ahead."

Opti shuffled about ten photos ahead and saw the same face in profile talking to a man in a parking lot. A man Tony immediately recognized.

"Monahan?"

"Yeah. Mister Gangster Squad himself."

Tony finally swallowed, then wiped the chow mein off his face. "So. What, Opti's being set up?"

"That'd be my guess. Probably RICO. Could be an indictment."

"Good. He'll flip. Then I can call *him* a rat. So, that's it? I should be happy he's going down, so when they put him in the program, he can't extort me?"

"You don't see the bigger picture here?"

"What bigger picture?" Tony stuffed more food into his mouth.

"You can use these as leverage."

"What? Sell 'em the photos?"

"No. You don't fuckin' sell 'em. You *give him* the pictures. Tell 'em it's a heads up."

"And that's gonna get me out of him paying tribute?"

"Yes."

"You don't know Opti."

"Bullshit. I met him at your wedding."

"But you never did any business with him."

"The Plaster Caster? Thank god."

"Exactly. That fuckin' finook's gonna do whatever he can to get over."

"Which is why when you hand him these. You meet him somewhere nobody connected's going to be. Like when guys would meet at that place in Reading—Wayside Bazaar, back home. Or like a Chuck E Cheese or somewhere. You meet him out front. Then, when you hand him the photos inside. You tell him, 'The guy who shot these, just shot the two of us together'. Then you threaten to mail them back to Providence. I mean, they're supposed to cap you on sight, right? Guess what that makes him?"

Tony licked his fingers and wiped the corners of his mouth.

They were inside a Toys "R" Us in Huntington Beach. They were walking down one of the boys' aisles, that had a bunch of giant robots with Japanese writing on the sides of the boxes, when Tony handed Opti a fat manila envelope.

"Wrong envelope," Opti said. "This is a bunch of photos."

"You're gonna want to have a look at those," Tony said.

Opti cocked his left brow. "This was already a hell of a fuckin' drive."

Tony's sleepy looking eyes kept a serious pitch.

Opti sifted through them. Quick at first, like shuffling a deck, then he slowed way the fuck down. "Jesus.

They're still damp." He pulled the stack of pictures closer to his face. He took his eyes off the stack to study Tony's mug. Tony rotated his finger as though dialing a phone. Opti put his eyes back onto the stack, and slowly shuffled all the way through. "So?"

"So remember when I told you I didn't want to come out that way," Tony said. "That I wanted you to meet me out here?"

"Yeah."

"Who the fuck calls at seven AM? By the way. Anyway, I got curious. I wanted to see how you were living, seeing as I'm supposed to be floating you 5 Gs a week. I took a ride over to your place. Nice neighborhood. Plenty of parking."

"My place?"

"Yeah," Tony said. "In Beverlywood."

"I don't live in Beverlywood."

"I thought I heard you did."

"My cousin bought up the mortgage."

"Giovanni?"

"Yeah."

"Was it the property taxes? You stayin' there now because of that thing with your wife?"

"Yeah—you want to get to the point?"

"So anyway, I swung by the place. I saw your ah, friend—the one in the pictures with Monahan." He pointed to Opti's right hand. "Figured it was a mark. Probably asking for an extension. Rather than use the phone."

"Yeah, *and?*"

"And what?"

"So what do you want from me?"

"Just thought you might want a heads up. It was a coincidence really. I was keeping tabs on Monahan for obvious reasons. I put two and two together and…"

"You got what I came for?"

"Sure." Tony reached into an inside pocket of his guinea gray barracuda jacket, and handed Opti the envelope.

A mother and two kids turned the corner, pushing a shopping cart down the aisle. Opti twisted profile, but Tony had started to walk away. There was no way he could share the width of a toy aisle with anyone or anything.

He stopped inside an aisle of Huffy and BMX bikes. Opti followed behind, quickly sifting through the bills, only pulling them an inch out of the envelope. He had the photo envelope stacked underneath it.

"Looks like it's all here," Opti said. But he knew Tony wasn't finished. "So that's it. You think these photos are gonna get you out of paying tribute."

Tony turned back around to face Opti. "That was the idea."

"No dice, rat. Word came down from the old man himself. *Il Patrone*. Anybody sees you, they're supposed to put you on ice. Nice try." Opti held out the photo envelope.

"Guy who shot those was out front when you pulled up. Why do you think I asked you to meet me out front?"

"Bullshit."

"Maybe I'll just mail 'em to Federal Hill, and you can explain to the front office how the guy in those pictures with you, is just some guy who looks a lot like me."

"Okay, fat man. You want to be off the books? Free and clear?"

"Just like that?" Tony smirked. "I knew you'd come around."

"Whoa. Slow your roll. About that mark you saw—still got your FBI contact?"

"Hey, hey."

"Hey hey, nothin'. You make my problem go away, and I'll forget I ever saw you."

"How the fuck am I supposed to do that?"

"You're the handicapper. You figure it out. Just hang by your phone in Malibu, and I'll call you with instructions."

"Hey. That's all bonus, from where I'm standing. What's it worth to you?"

Opti swore if he had vision like Superman, there'd be a giant smoking hole in Fat Tony's forehead. He peeled a C-Note from the cash envelope, "For gas money." He pocketed it, then tossed the remaining $4900 into Tony's waiting grip.

The corners of Tony's mouth lifted a sliver.

He had to know smugness wouldn't let him get away with anything. "And just remember—they come around for me, whether it's in a car, or they walk me into a room. I'll still have enough breath in me before the piano wire sinks in, to tell them where to find you."

Tony's grin now bordering on smug.

"5944 Cavalleri Rd."

Tony's grin faded, then migrated onto Opti's face.

"I'll call you tonight," Opti said. "With instructions."

WHEELS OF CONFUSION

Opti threw the parking attendant for Langer's Deli a little something extra, as always. Fucking neighborhood was atrocious. Sally Lieberman was waiting for him in a booth overlooking a stretch of Alvarado just down the block from MacArthur Park. Opti walked up to the table, unbuttoned his double-breasted blazer, and glided into the booth. He pulled the Porsche Carrera sunglasses off his face and slid them onto the tabletop. Sally looked out across 7th Street, as if in a trance. Like there was something poignant over in needle park.

"Beautiful isn't it." Opti snickered.

Sally turned her eyes from the street over to Opti. "It used to be." Her eyes a little sad.

"How are you?" Opti said.

"I'm good, Dom," Sally said. "How are you?"

Opti pursed his lips and nodded. "Good."

The clock on the wall said three, and they had the place mostly to themselves. The waitress came over, dropped a couple menus and poured them both glasses of water.

"Hey sweetheart," Opti said. "I'll let you know in a bit."

"Take your time," the waitress said, and walked off.

"Remember when that meant something?" Sally looked over the menu.

"When what meant something?"

"*Take your time*. Then one day you wake up and realize most of it's been taken away. You know what they say. Life's like a roll of toilet paper."

"You mean because you're either on a roll or taking shit from some asshole?"

"No. The closer it gets to the end, the faster it goes."

Opti nodded, but she couldn't see. Her eyes were looking down. He didn't need to look at the menu. He knew what he wanted, and that they'd do it right. The AC chilled the air enough to make the vinyl seat cool.

Glancing out past Sally, he could see the sun still high and bright in the sky.

"So many choices," Sally said.

"Figured a nice Jewish girl like you would know her way around a delicatessen."

"I'm a nice Irish girl, Dom. I married a Jew."

"That's right. I should've remembered. And you're a lush, to boot."

"You forgot drug addict," Sally said.

"No I didn't. I was just being polite."

The waitress had a quizzical look when she popped into the conversation. "All set?"

"I think I'll go with Corned Beef Sauerkraut and Swiss Cheese," Sally said.

"And for you, sir?"

"The Same." Opti had a *great minds think alike*-inspired grin.

"Excellent." The waitress scratched at fresh Monarch butterfly tattoo on her neck as she headed back to the kitchen.

"Care to explain this?" Opti held out a scrawled note—*Call me later tonight. It'll be worth your while.* She'd handed it to him at his house, said nothing, and then left. They had an understanding that Opti's house might've been bugged. And that no mark had any business coming to Opti's house, but with Sally he made an exception. Typically Sally dropped her vig by The Cockatoo Club, and it was always in order. Meticulous as a heroin addict about the fix, that's how Sally was about paying her vig on time. Truth be told, Opti really admired that about her. "Not that I'm complaining. I love this joint."

"I want to break even."

"You going somewhere?"

"No. Just. I just want to be free and clear."

"Works for me. I always figured you'd kick, and I'd have to just take it as a loss."

"Very sweet of you to say."

Opti laughed. "These vices we're bound to. We have some in common, you know? Looking at you, sometimes it's a mirror."

"My heart, Dom. My heart. It's takin' its toll."

"Worst thing is…When I'm doing well. I want it even more. When I'm riding high—and that's a good way to put it. The more I earn. The more it goes up my fuckin' nose."

"Yeah," she said. Nodding like everything he'd said had been her conscience. "If I can't go straight, at least I can break even."

"You still fuckin' the Hadjis over there at the Paradise?"

"I provide a service, okay?"

"Do they know you quit being a cop six months ago?"

"What do you think?"

"I think you've got a nice vig comin' in."

"I perform a service. Hey, what they're doing…"

"Hey…You don't have to tell me. They got underage trim tricking out a' that place that rivals TJ."

"See. Now that shit pisses me off. If a girl wants to sell it at eighteen. Hey. But selling underage pussy is fucked up. I mean, you got kids…"

"Absolutely. I get it. It's sick. I'm fuckin' thirty-nine. If I want to play step daddy when I buy pussy, I'm good with nineteen."

"Thirty-nine. Jesus. I remember thirty-nine," Sally said. "You're a fuckin' kid."

"Sometimes. Sometimes I'm a responsible adult."

"Nice touch, by the way. Not ordering a drink."

"Yeah, well. I still might just powder my knuckle, and sniff."

"So. How are your other endeavors going?"

"What do you mean by that?"

"I'm not asking for specifics. Just you know, in general."

He paused, and he knew she knew she'd gotten him. "I mean, there are some things. I deal with a lot of people. There's always something. Could be better. Think I might have something new I can bank on. How's your marriage?"

Sally chuckled. "Oh my god. You had to go there. Dumpster fire."

"That bad?"

"Worse. You just emptied a can of Sterno on it."

Opti laughed.

"But I might have something new I can bank on."

"Escort?"

Sally took a long blink, and exhaled. "That's such a dirty word."

"So you've got an expensive love life, a drug habit, and a weakness for gambling?"

"Nope. You're only two thirds right. I haven't placed a bet in six months."

"No shit?"

"You ever think about retirement?"

"Got a Roth IRA. A place in Florida. No. Not really. You must have a nice nest egg."

"I did. But then I gambled and lost it. Stole from my kid—who hates me, then gave his college fund back. Or tried. He still hates me. So no, I'm broke and I'm old. Can't sell my eggs. And I couldn't sell my ass to a death row inmate."

"Wow. Sure you don't want a quick bump?"

"Don't tempt me. Yeah, mortality's a real party, Dom. You're gonna love it."

"I'm sorry."

"Sorry enough to squash my debt?"

Opti laughed.

"How about giving me an extra week…"

Opti exhaled with punctuation. He hated seeing someone beg.

"One week off, and my next payment will be my last. The principle plus the interest. One shot."

"You got that kind of bread?"

"I will. Promise."

Opti took a deep breath, the way his pediatrician told him to, with a stethoscope to his chest. Then he let it out. "Sure. That's including the extra week…"

"No problem."

"So…After you break even. What are you gonna retire on?"

"I'll figure something out."

"What? The motel racket?"

Sally put on the airbrakes with her lips. "Fat chance. That fuckin' place is going to implode any day now. They had a double murder there. They covered it up without me. They think I didn't hear about it."

"You could rob a bank."

Sally snickered. She broke eye contact.

"I got a thing," Opti said. "It's on you. But. Something that could help you out."

"That new something you can bank on?"

"Yeah. As a matter of fact." Opti laid it all out—Hollywood Park, Fat Tony. The fix. Only he left out the part about the fat bastard being a rat, and the RICO case back in Boston. Also, he neglected to mention what he'd started squeezing Tony for.

"And what's your percentage?"

"Nothing."

Sally cocked an eyebrow.

"Call it a favor. It's a one-time thing. A sure thing. But you don't ask questions, and follow all my instructions."

"I can do that."

The food came. When both their plates were down, Opti said "I'm starving."

"This looks delicious," Sally said. "For once I've got an appetite."

DIRTY WOMEN

The door slammed, and Sally slid her ass down the length of the bed. From the end of the bed, she could see Lena and Francis inside the front door of apartment 12B at Franklin Towers. Lena took off Francis's leash, and the six-year-old Pomeranian bounded through the living room, its tiny collar jingling into the bedroom onto Sally's lap. The dog jumped up and started slobbered all over Sally's face.

"Awww. You're so cute," Sally said in a high-pitched nurturing voice. "You're a cute little baby boy. Yes, you are. Mmmmuah." She kissed the wriggling, high strung pooch. Lena sauntered in, with that long legged seductive gait she had. The way tall sexy women walked when they weren't even trying. All legs at only five-foot-five. Lena glistened with sweat. She even had a moist shadow of sweat triangulated between her thighs. "Oooh girl. Look at that sweat on the sweet spot."

"Stop it," Lena said.

"That's the Burmuda Traingle, baby."

"No, stop. You making fun of my sweating vagina. This is not funny. You are embarrassing me in front of Francis."

"Until today I always thought you had a cat," Sally said.

Lena cracked a smile. She had a mole above the right side of her upper lip. Her smile always just the tiniest bit crooked. She had the most alluring lagoon blue eyes.

"Well," Lena said. "It's tough out there for a working girl. One hungry pussy is all I can afford."

Sally's heart sped up. She must've been drooling, when she said nothing. Lena moved closer to the bed. Lena pulled down her leotard—not off, just down about six inches below the top of her thighs. Her neatly trimmed auburn bush glistened in the light coming in from the bedroom window. She stood at the edge of the bed, with her hands on her hips. Sally grabbed her buttocks with both hands and buried her face in Lena's pussy. She felt Lena's hands cradle Sally's head, gently— not the way a man would, but affectionately, guiding her nursing mouth, to that sweet spot that made her moan.

Pancho spent his afternoons as an intern at Video Drama on La Brea near Hawthorne.

"So what do you do there?" Tundra asked, pulling away from the curb, as they headed towards Hollywood Boulevard.

"Mostly I make coffee, stack and label film stock," Pancho said. "Also, I pick up the lunch orders."

"For free?"

"That's right."

"Shiiit. No wonder you wanna learn the game."

"I'm not trying to be a pimp, bro. Just, you know. I want to learn *about it*."

"Yo, whatever you say," Tundra said. They cruised Hollywood Boulevard. When they passed The Roosevelt he said, "Never know. You might fall in love with the game."

Pancho stayed silent for at least a block.

"So why bother?" Tundra said. "Working for free."

"Hey bro. Cause that's what I want to do. You know? I want to be a film maker."

"And hanging around, getting lunch is gonna help you do that?"

"It's learning a trade. You know? I'm there to learn."

"Right on. So, you learned anything?"

"Yeah man," Pancho said. "All kinds of stuff. Like today, right. These two Japanese guys came in. They wore these like black FBI suits you know? They were asking my boss about filming death. Like watching it happen. Putting it on film."

"Damn. That's some heavy shit."

"You know, like death has a look. When it passes over you. Before it takes you. You know what I'm saying, bro?"

"Word to your mother. Like you can see death…"

"On a fool's face. Yeah. They want to capture that. On film."

"Wow. Fuck. That's some crazy shit."

"I know, right? But that's what they lookin' for."

Tundra gestured towards the Masonic temple. "Yo. You know about that place, right?"

"For sure I heard some things, bro. So how 'bout you?"

"How 'bout me, what? You askin' if I know what death looks like?"

"Nah, man. I mean, watchu want to do? In the future."

Tundra banged a right onto Highland. "Expand my empire, yo."

"Your empire?"

"My empire. Check it—When the time is right, Imma buy The Paradise Motel."

"Man, you crazy. Gil ain't never gonna sell."

"That's what you think, my dude. Trust me, he lookin' to move up and out. And for the right price…"

"I hear you."

"I'll give you a fat raise, yo. Make you my personal bodyguard."

"Bet."

When they turned onto Sunset, there was plenty of eye candy. Tundra couldn't help but clock every ho who chased after the Caddy with their wandering eyes. He watched Pancho check them out. "Hos just can't say no to a man inside a pearl white Eldorado. But on a serious tip. I'm looking to expand. Move beyond the game. You dig? There's something maybe you could help me with."

"How? Lay it on me, bro."

"Talkin' about slangin'. My snowflake game is strong, too. Got me some primo product."

"So you talkin' distribution."

Tundra took a right on Vine. "Bingo."

"My tio an O.G. Down with the Echo Park Locos."

"Of course I'd hook you up with a referral fee."

"Solid. Imma rap with tio this weekend. Let you know. I got you."

Tundra pulled up to the curb at the 1400 block of Vine, just before where it met DeLongpre Ave.

"This is the spot?"

"This is it bro," Tundra said. "Best place in L.A. to find you some talent."

They watched a bus pull into the Greyhound Station across the street.

"Every day. All day. These young bitches arrive, starry-eyed. No place to stay. No money, no nothing. They get off that bus, and they all end up right there," Tundra pointed out a small café lounge.

"The Grapevine Room?"

"That's exactly what it is, my man." Tundra said. "You tell 'em you a talent manager, and they all loosey-juicy, ripe on the vine to be taken. That's the easy part. All you gots to have for that is a hard dick and a sweet tooth. But what come next, you got to have a cast iron stomach for. That's the difference between a pimp and a simp. A player ain't nothin' nice."

"Oh man. Girl I can't remember the last time somebody munched my pussy carpet like that," Lena said, taking a drag, then handing the cigarette to Sally.

"I had a lot of pent-up angst," Sally said. "Figured I should channel it constructively. Last three days have been an all-time low for me."

"You and me both," Lena said.

Sally took a long drag. The cherry glowed bright red. She blew smoke. "Are you serious?"

"Yeah. I just lost two regulars. The fucking shit landlord is raising the rent. Plus, I owe him for last month. And I can't get a job, remember?"

"I remember, sweetie," Sally handed back what was left of the cigarette. "They denied your entertainment visa. Again?"

"Yes. My auditions for Kool Aid and the Bosom Buddies doesn't count. Plus, I can't tell them I dance at The Seventh Veil, because it's under the table."

Sally snubbed out the cigarette in a blue glass ashtray by the bed. "Oh, sweetie."

"I don't want to go back to Ukraine," Lena said, folding her arms over her beckoning breasts with medium sized ariolas: cinnamon-colored and perfectly centered. Vivacious nipples pointed upwards at a 20° angle. "So far I have failed very badly at the American dream."

"No sweetie. Your American dream is only beginning."

"You are very sweet to me."

"I love you." Sally felt a tinge of regret. Too much too fast. Lena wouldn't reciprocate, and Sally would slowly implode...

"You do?" She looked at her with those wonderful blue eyes.

"Yes."

"Then I promise to love you back. With my mouth." Then her lips cracked a playful smile, and she burst into laughter.

Sally's eyes kept a serious pitch. "How would you like to go away with me?"

Lena turned to her, still pouting. "Where would we go?"

"Wherever you want."

"I want to go to Fort Lauderdale."

"Florida?"

"Yes. It is near Walt Disney World I am told."

"But there's a Disney..."

"This one is much better I am told," Lena said. "For vacation, no?"

"To live."

"You want to take me to Florida to live?"

"If you want..."

"I want."

"We'll live like queens."

"Are you rich, Sally?"

"I will be. Soon."

Francis jumped up onto the bed and nestled in between Lena and Sally.

"You have to make me your only client," Sally said.

"I don't understand."

"If you agree to go away with me," Sally said. "There can't be anyone else."

"*No one else*? For sexy time you mean?"

"Yes." Sally thought about the passport she'd found at Wally's. The one with the photo that looked like her. A new start.

"I understand. We will be together. I would like very much to be a rich queen in Florida."

SPIRAL ARCHITECT

"So what are we talking about here, bro?" Tundra said. "You want to get me on camera talkin' it up with these girls?"

"I want to see how you lay it down, bro." Pancho said.

"And this is going to be like a movie?"

"Documentary."

"You want to watch me talk to bitches?"

"Exactly. Among other things."

"What other things? You want to watch me fuck 'em?"

"Nah man. I ain't doin' a porno."

"So what other things, then?"

"I want you to tell the audience. How it is. Stories of how shit went down."

"Such as?"

"Man I don't know. They're your stories. I mean didn't you go to war with some spade over one of your girls?"

"Yeah. Another pimp. He go by the name Ocelot. He cold."

"So what happened?"

"What do you mean?"

"With Ocelot?"

"Oh. Yeah. Shit, homeboy ran me off the block. Put me out of business," Tundra said. Truth be un-told he was terrified of Ocelot. "And then I found The Paradise. I stole two of his hos. Sisters. One's a money-making machine. The other one's got some kind of power over her." Katarina had called Ocelot, Tezcatlipoca. Whatever the fuck that meant. "Sure you don't want to film them fucking?"

"Yeah man. I'm looking for something deeper."

"So you want to get inside a motherfucker's soul?"

"Yeah. Maybe."

"Maybe I should just kill a bitch. You know, like those two Japs wanted to see. The life fading from someone's eyes."

LADY EVIL

Katarina got up with the sun. She had just woken from a nightmare she had interpreted as a vision. In the scope of a dream, this vision revealed events past and present. Kukulcán had rescued her from Tezcatlipoca. But the feathered serpent then traveled to the underworld, where he joined IxChel, lunar goddess of war. Hunab-Ku, the supreme was also there. And he commanded Kukulcán to swallow the moon.

When she awoke, she knew she had to leave this place. Without moving, she rolled her eyes to the left and saw Tundra lying on his side, facing her, snoring. She reached down into the crevice between the mattress and the box spring. She grasped the key. The one Sally had given her. Without making a sound, and with very little movement, she reached up, and unlocked the cuff that bound her to the headboard. She slipped on her clothes and inched towards the door.

Satrina was standing by the payphone on Sunset next to the giant neon motel sign. She watched a black 60s Ford Falcon with a lowrider suspension rumble into the lot, then idle in front of the motel office. The driver blasted something that sounded like Rainbow, with "Lady Evil" in the chorus. She watched Pancho exit the motel office. He and a little boy got into the Falcon, then it barreled through the lot, and exited through the Bellevue Ave side. She waited until the engine rumble got weak, and she could no longer hear the voice of Dio.

She walked into the lot and started pushing the flyers for *Women of the Night* under the motel room doors. She slid them onto the windshields of the cars in front of the rooms. Tucking them under a windshield wiper. Nobody stirred inside the rooms. The sun had just gotten there, and it had that eerie orange glow, the kind that made her hair look like a brush fire. She watched a couple ladies in thigh highs walking in opposite directions. One to the motel office, the other clickety clacking out of the lot towards the street. The end of another shift.

SYMPTOM OF THE UNIVERSE

Katarina felt like she had the wind at her back. She gripped the knob and pulled the door open. The sky looked like Xibalba—the inferno. She froze in the doorway. Her eyes were locked with whom she knew to be IxChel, goddess of war. Her eyes green as the snake wrapped around her head, her hair doused in flames. IxChel said, "I can help you. You know I can."

Satrina felt a firm hand clamp down on her shoulder. She spun around to see Gil flashing a hateful glare, his arms crossed.

"What do you think you're doing?" Gil said.

"I'm offering these women a way out," Satrina said. "This entire motel is a brothel. And you know it."

"People are free to do as they like. It's no consequence to me. But I respect their privacy. And their business."

"Their *business*." She glared at Gil with a malice, that made him take a step back. "I'm sure you do. There are under aged girls being trafficked through this motel. Did you know that?"

"I'm going to have to ask you to leave."

"You did know that."

"You must leave now."

"When I'm done distributing these flyers."

"Then you'll leave?"

"Maybe. Maybe I'll stick around and ask some of these closet-rapists if their wives know they like sodomizing runaway teenagers."

"You're going to make this difficult, aren't you?"

"I know for a fact this was the last place Roberto was ever seen. And so do you."

Gil's face froze, with his jaw slack in what Satrina surmised could only be guilt. His eyes burned.

"I have a feeling there's a lot more than prostitution going on at this motel," she said. "You fucking slave master."

"You bitch! GET THE FUCK OUT."

"Papa," Sekhar said.

Gil turned in the direction of Sekhar's voice, as he walked up.

"Papa? Is everything okay? It's Ramon," Sekahr said. "He's asking about the Mercedes. He needs your card number to authorize a tow."

Satrina turned back into the direction of room ten. The girl in the doorway was gone. She pushed a flyer under the door.

When IxChel broke away from her gaze, Katarina realized her freedom in that moment. Free as a quetzal bird. Someday soon she would return to liberate her baby sister Cassandra. She felt her heart ready to take flight. Then she felt the coil of the serpent around her throat. Why Kukulcán? Why? The red skies vanished, and everything faded to black, as the doorway to freedom shut.

THE THRILL OF IT ALL

Sally had never been to Hollywood Park. A thoroughbred racetrack worthy of old Hollywood, located in the middle of the ghetto. It had an intriguing architecture. A long smooth chute that looked like a giant slide, extended down from the circular sign that read *Club*

House. With a classic 1940s look to it, like Union Station downtown. She'd had to fight traffic to get there ahead of post time, then found out she was early. She always thought waking up past noon to be way too late. It had been all Lena's fault. For 110 pounds, man could that fun-size Ukrainian drink.

She met her contact outside the entrance, at the foot of the stairs. The man standing in front them was hard to miss.

"Cary Grant's in the winner circle doing a photo op. If you hurry you can get close to him," the big man said.

He towered over her and had hands the size of catcher's mitts. He must've been about the width of her car. He wasn't exactly a modern fashion plate, dressed in a gray silk bowling shirt and scally cap.

"No thanks," Sally said. "I was never a big movie buff. And I was never cute enough to be a star fucker."

"That makes two of us," he said.

He had big sleepy-looking eyes, like Billy Joel.

"Tony C?"

He nodded. "You know this is a one-time thing, right?"

"Yes, I know," Sally said. "And I plan on making it count."

By noon, Gil had finally chased Satrina out of the lot. There had been a leaking toilet in unit 24, and he'd been dealing with the plumber most of the afternoon. It wasn't until two thirty that he finally sat down to eat the plate of cold tandoori chicken he ordered two hours ago. No sooner had he pulled it out of the microwave, when Jessica—one of the regulars, burst into the lobby.

"Gil. Who is this fucking puta with the camera?" Jessica said. "She just run off my date. What the fuck?"

"What do you mean?"

"She just run off my fucking date. I'm not paying for the room."

"Who?"

"That bitch. *Mira*. Out there!"

Gil stood up and went to the window. Satrina returned. This time she'd started photographing the johns and their cars. "Fucking hippie bitch." He reached into the register and pulled out a twenty. He handed it to Jessica and said, "Come back tomorrow. This will all be taken care of."

Nine months ago his wife had left him. Khushi was a strong woman, but she never quite assimilated into the culture. She never really accepted how American capitalism worked. When she left, he brought on Roberto. Roberto had been ignorant the same way— despite being born and raised here. No understanding of how complicated business was. The people who ruled the country understood that. But too many of the people they ruled did not. It wasn't long before Roberto had become involved with Sekhar. Gil had walked into the boy's unit and found them together. Like a beast with two backs— shrieking like two Bellbirds below a wall poster of Freddy Mercury. 'They don't tolerate this sort of thing here', he'd told his son, but the boy didn't listen. So when Roberto swiped financial records, and decided to go to the authorities with serious allegations, there was only one thing to be done. Sally, then dead broke owed a hefty sum of money to a leg breaker. It had been the reason they'd first gotten acquainted. She helped with the Roberto situation. What had become their sordid legacy.

"**O**pti says you're quite a handicapper," Sally said.

"He ought to know," Tony said.

She noticed he'd slipped on a pair of aviators, as they'd entered the betting area.

There were several people in the middle—almost all of them men, gathered around a bank of TV sets with tickets in hand. Most of the wagering windows were open and had lines. Tony walked Sally down to a line of three closed wagering windows and pulled a daily racing form from his back pocket. She watched him take a quick peek at his gold Rolex wristwatch, and purse his lips.

"Okay," Tony said. "We got a little time. I picked you up a DRF. I'm going to make some suggestions," he said. "But what you tell the teller is your business."

Sally's head was spinning—still. She reached into her purse to grab an aspirin, when some hapless son of a bitch practically shoulder checked her trying to stack up at the betting window.

"Asshole!" Sally said.

"People get real serious about placing bets this close to post time." Tony took out a retractable ball point pen, then thumbed through the racing form. First he circled a horse named Malta Majesty. "This is your win."

Sally cocked an eyebrow. "But it says right here, the odds are fifty-seven to one on that horse."

"Imagine that."

"It says here, Easy Rider, Pharaoh, and Quintessa are the odds-on favorites…"

"Which is exactly where the big payout isn't. Maybe you'd rather do this yourself…"

"No. No, no—I'm sorry. Please continue."

"For your parimutuel, you're gonna want these horses," Tony circled Outrageous Fortune, and Rebel Incarnate. Then he drew a two and a three next to the latter then the former. "Twelve horses in this race. You get all three of these. In that order, and you win the trifecta. I don't know how much you're wagering, so I can't speculate on the win."

"So you guarantee these horses?"

He made a sound like a breathy cough. "Guarantee? There's no guarantees sister. But now you know what I know. Good luck." he turned to walk off.

"Wait," she said. "Aren't you going to bet?"

"Here? I never bet in person. Too many of the attendants know me. Good luck."

"Wait—I've never placed a bet before. Not like this. Couldn't you..."

"Jesus Christ, lady. Look I can't hold your hand."

"Just tell me what to do." she said.

Tony sighed. He walked back to her, just as he saw her take notice of a guy staring in their direction. Guy must've thought he was slick—with his head pointed away from them behind mirrored sunglasses. Sizing them up from the corner of his eye. "How you doin'?" Tony said, and the man nodded casually. Tony waited, watched him pass by. Then he turned to Sally and said, "Okay, look. All you gotta do, is tell the teller the racetrack and race number, the amount of your bet. The type of bet you're placing, and the horse's program number—that number," he said pointing to the one next to Malta Majesty. "Now you're gonna want to spread your bets around to different tellers. I don't recommend dropping 10 g's at one window. This is a crash course I know, but that's just how it is. Opti mention anything about me? Besides I'm a handicapper?"

"No," Sally said.

"It's better that way. Especially since you're an ex-cop. You're gonna be grandstanding this one alone, sister," Tony said. "I gotta run. Tell Opti we're even."

"Thanks, Tony."

"Sure thing."

She hoped it was.

SWINGING THE CHAIN

Tundra got a call at about three.

"Wass up my cracker," T-Bone said. "You still lookin' for that twenty percent dis-count?"

"Sho'nuff am, T," Tundra said. "When and where?"

"Hollywood and Western. Ten," T-Bone said. "We straight?"

"I'm hip."

"Sharp," T-Bone said.

"On the square."

"Solid."

T-Bone hung up, and Tundra considered leaving the game behind in a cloud of white dust. Superfly dreams with that f-shit. Full time.

It would be another two hours before Pancho showed up. Sekhar, still sound asleep—and for what Gil needed, that boy was useless. Gil had spent time in Goa and had befriended a few Dacoits there. They'd taught him a thing or two about kidnaping—skills he never thought he would use, let alone in America. The Dacoits had been using Scopolamine for years—the real life equivalent of Chloroform, what they always used on American TV. Scopolamine wasn't available over the counter, but Belladonna was. And it did the exact same thing.

A concrete room in the basement had been outfitted with a post war era bomb shelter. Gil had since sealed it off with a wall of knuckle weave fencing. Truth be told, it made a perfect cell.

He could smell her dirty ass before he saw her. He waited for her to set up her next shot. She had backed herself into one corner of the lot, so she could get the license plate of a big gray Lincoln, one of the johns drove. She bent down into a crouch and aligned the camera with her eye. Gil rushed in quick, with a cleaning rag soaked in Belladonna. Just like a Dacoit with Scopolamine, he wrapped it around her face, with his other arm he held her tight. Until her knees buckled, and she went out.

So many questions ran through Sally's mind, as she walked between the grandstand, and the teller at the betting window. She didn't have any idea how much she'd won. She knew her horse had come in first followed by Rebel Incarnate and Outrageous fortune. Every line at the club house cashier had to be ten deep. She caught a glimpse of a newsfeed. She saw the KNBC logo in the corner, and the young Hispanic news anchor standing in front of a check cashing joint. She recognized the sign from the street view before they threw up the bright yellow text that read: Wally's Liquor Mart. Then they flashed up the faces of Consuelo and her brother, with the text that read: Victims of a Gang-Related Slaying. It shouldn't have, but it eased her mind. She was pretty sure Consuelo wouldn't have reported the robbery to the police. But now it was official. She wouldn't be reporting anything. Sally had a smile even before he reached the clubhouse cashier. In all, she collected $80,440. Not a bad start for a new life.

When Gil had knocked on Tundra's room, Tundra insisted he'd given his rent money to Sekhar a couple of days ago. Gil held his hand up and told him he wasn't there about the rent.

They were standing on the roof of the motel office. The neon had just come on, and in an hour the sun would bleed out. Tundra could see the downtown skyline over his right shoulder. Gil was taking a long pull of his mini cigar as they both watched Pancho retrieve flyers from the front windshields of cars, and from where they had been shoved under the doors of the rooms.

"Yo, it's nice up here, Gil," Tundra said. "Straight up."

"I've been thinking about making some changes," Gil said.

"Oh yeah? Like what? You puttin' in a pool?"

"No. Regarding our agreement."

"You want more money."

"In a manner of speaking, yes."

"How much more?"

"How much do you have?"

"Yo—just what kind of conversation we havin' here boss man?"

"You said you want to buy the motel," Gil said, turning to him. "Pancho told me." He dropped what was left of his smoke and ground it into the shingles. "How much have you got?"

"Shit. 'Bout thirty-five. How much…"

"Not enough."

"What's your price?"

"Property is valued at eighty. But I could go as low as sixty-five."

"I could have that fo' you in six months, big G. On the square."

Gil took out another mini cigar and lit up.

"Why you askin' me about this now?"

"I have a problem, and I need your help."

"With what? One of these bitches? You know I got you big G. I can regulate a bitch. Whoever it is, you know me. I'll put her in line. Set her straight. This the Ho-tell Paradise, here."

"Good." Flames consumed the L.A. skyline. Gil took a long drag and blew out a plume of scented smoke. "I want you to kill her. Tonight."

SHE'S GONE

Sally couldn't wait to celebrate. She found a payphone in the betting area and dialed up Lena. She wanted to give Lena enough time to get ready. Tonight, would be a celebration. In her wildest dreams, she'd dazzle Lena with a night out at Ma Maison. But that was a little out of her reach. Pacific Dining Car would have to do. It rang five times, and she got the machine. Lena had probably gone to the gym. On the beep, Sally hung up. Why bother telling her on the phone? She'd surprise her with the news, in person. They could be gone in a week, or a month. It really all depended.

She made her way through the cacophony of sparring voices. Angry men cussing and tossing betting receipts. She trampled discarded wager paper, navigating the crowd as lines at the widows swelled. On one of the TV sets in the middle of the area she saw the hair transplant ad flash up on the screen. A Doctor Ayers the third, an Osteopathic Surgeon in Beverly Hills. No quote given. Didn't matter. She could afford it now. The ad cut short by breaking news. Again, Wally's flashed up on the screen. Consuelo's picture. The brother's picture. If it happened inside Wally's that meant there would be crime lab technicians. An eyebrow hair, a fingernail shaving. That's all it took.

"You want me to kill a bitch?" Tundra said. "Watchu gon' pay me?"

"You're going to pay me," Gil said.

"Yo—*what*. Yo, you sure that's tobacco you smokin'?"

"You give me the thirty thousand, and you'll be a full partner. Your name will be added to the deed."

"I'll give you twenty. I got operating expenses."

"Done."

"And I can buy you out, when I raise the other forty."

"Done."

"Okay, big G. Give me the lowdown. Who dis bitch you want rubbed out?"

There was still the matter of her promise to Opti. The principle and the interest squashed, and she'd be free and clear. Just a short drive from Hollywood Park over to The Cockatoo Inn in Hawthorne, where Opti held court. She could finally be debt free. But the steering wheel had a mind of its own. The car wouldn't let her deviate the course. Like a homing pigeon, she was headed back to Franklin Towers.

Sally waved and shouted to Philip at the front desk, who offered nothing more than a dismissive wave. He seemed to be engrossed in the evening news. She hit the call button.

When the elevator doors swish-parted she could hear the rhythmic throb of a familiar bassline at its haunting faintest. When she got to 12B she recognized Donna Summer's "Hot Stuff." The song that had played at the gay bar where they'd first met. With music so loud, it shook her joints, she pounded on the door like the LAPD responding to a domestic. Finally, she just tried the knob. As she walked in, she was immediately greeted by Francis. She could smell pasta—damn, Lena must've already eaten. Drinks would have to do.

"*Lena*. LENA." Goddamn that deafening music. It was so loud she couldn't figure out where it came from. She cracked open the bedroom door. A sharp pain in her chest hit her, a railroad spike pounded through her solar plexus.

Underneath the large muscular tanned body of a man who resembled Arnold Schwarzenegger, were eyes on a face—two eyes the palest shade of lagoon blue, that expanded in shock. The rest of Lena's beautiful face obscured by the hulking man's shoulder. Her eyes told one story. Lena's soundless mouth moaned in ecstasy, which looked very similar to cries of pain. But her hands told another story, as they gripped his buttocks, flexing with every grunting jostle, to the rhythmic pulse of Donna Summer. Sally moved closer. On the back of the man's neck, he had a tattoo of a rooster's head. The bed shook under pounding thrusts. Frozen in a moment of pure hatred, she considered shooting them both dead. In that half a second drawn out like it was ten years, she lived inside that malediction. Lena's lagoon blue irises now seemed cold as ice. The gaze said their goodbyes. The song forever ruined.

Tundra had learned a great deal before and after his time at the NSP lockup in Lincoln, Nebraska. Back when California was just a glimmer in his eye. "So who else knows about this Roberto dude disappearing?" He'd made Gil tell him everything.

"Just Sally," Gil said.

"You better page her."

"You mean?"

"You know exactly what I mean, big G."

When they got down to the basement, his mind took a trip—like on a time travel tip. Childhood memories of the Cuban Missile crisis flooded through Tundra's head.

Tundra lowered his voice. "No one can hear us down here?"

"It's sound proofed," Gil said, shutting the basement door behind them.

They descended a set of concrete steps.

"Damn, big G. You got a bomb shelter down here?"

Right before the entrance to the pod, a padlocked section of knuckle-weave fencing closed it off. Inside the cage—the dirty hippie ho Gil had described, down to her Bob Marley hair. Her fingers were wrapped tight around the weave of the fence. She had a hateful look in her eyes.

Gil handed Tundra her purse, and said, "Okay. Tell me when it's done."

The pimp put his hand on the old man's shoulder and said, "Not how this works. We partners now, big G. You gonna watch. Then you'll know. Dig?"

"Oh look. It's the slave master and his boyfriend the pimp," Satrina said.

"Did you sleep well?" Gil said.

Tundra fished through her purse.

"Fuck you, old man," Satrina said.

Tundra pulled out a prescription bottle. "What's cy-clo-spor-in?"

"I had a liver transplant..." she said.

"Bitch is crazy," Tundra said. "These be her crazy pills."

"Doesn't matter," Gil said.

"Fuck you in your ass," Satrina spat. "You motherfucking pieces of shit!"

Tundra tossed the pill bottle at her through the weave in the fence. "She 'gon need a little crazy for what happens next," he said, drawing the chrome Smith & Wesson .38 from the small of his back. He leveled the four-inch barrel on Satrina.

"No. *No*—wait. Please. I'll suck your cocks. PLEASE. You can both fuck me. I won't say anything…"

"Bitch, I wouldn't fuck your dirty ass with his dick," Tundra said.

"If you let me go," she said. "I'll disappear. You'll never see me again…"

"Do it." Gil said.

Tundra pulled back the hammer. "I know that's right…"

"WAIT. I can tell you your future. I do fortunes."

Tundra chuckled and his laugh made a sound like a wheezing cough. "What?"

"I do fortunes," Satrina said. "I can see the future."

"She's crazy," Gil said. "Just. Do it."

Tundra de-cocked the Smith and said, "Okay." He lowered the weapon, letting the pistol hang by his two hands, over his crotch.

Gil shot him a look that said: just get it done already.

Tundra said, "Tell me my future, bitch."

"Twenty years from now. This place will still be here. Gil will be dead, but…"

Tundra brought the pistol back up to arm's length, holding it on her and said, "MY future, bitch."

"Okay," Satrina said, shutting her eyes. "I just need to focus…"

"NOW BITCH!"

"*Okay*. The deal you're making with him…"

"What about it?" Tundra said.

"She's fishing. She doesn't know anything..." Gil said, in a low tone.

"He's going to back out," Satrina said. "He's...."

Tundra turned to Gil and stared at him menacingly.

"She's trying to say anything she can to survive," Gil said. His dome wobbled like a bobble-head. "It's not..."

"Fuck that," Tundra said. "Give me the key."

"What?"

"The key to the cage," Tundra said.

"I don't have..."

"Now!" Tundra growled, putting the barrel on Gil. "Sound proofed. Remember."

Gil turned his eyes away from the barrel, blinking reflexively. He fished the key out of his pocket and handed it over to Tundra.

"Now go get that motherfucking deed. Imma wait five fuckin' minutes, and then I'm letting this bitch out."

ALL MOVING PARTS (STAND STILL)

The elevator dinged, and Sally rushed out into the lobby. She hurried past the front desk.

"Hey," Philip said.

Sally looked up—her eyes must've been glazed over in rage, because he now looked at her with new intensity. They also reflected concern. Did he know? Jesus Christ, can't he mind his own business—then she recognized her face on the TV screen in front of him. It looked like her. But it wasn't.

"Everything alright, Sally?"

"Everything's fine, Philip. Goodnight."

When she closed the rickety door to her shitty little Ford Escort, it was like she'd closed a vacuum. The plastic she'd wrapped around the smashed driver's side window was still air tight as a condom. Outside the car the world looked normal. She saw a woman in a leotard and headband walking a dog that looked like Francis. One block up, an elegantly dressed woman climbed out of a Taxi, and watched it drive away. Everyday people on the street biding their time, chasing a dream that wasn't real. The railroad spike had sunk even deeper. Now it had migrated to the middle of her chest. *That photo*—she immediately scrambled, searching through her pockets, the glovebox. Under the seats. On the TV—the photo from the fake passport she'd stolen from the safe at Wally's. This couldn't be good. A handful of scenarios flooded her mind. She thought about putting the money in a safety deposit box for Noah. She thought about turning herself in. She reached into the glovebox and wrapped her hand around her .38 service revolver. She thought about shoving it between her lips. Felating the barrel and finger-fucking the trigger til it popped off in her mouth. What was left?

Her pager went off. She recognized the number. Gil. His message in green computer text floated left to right across the tiny screen: *Sally I need your help*. Come quickly. She twisted the ignition and put it in drive.

"Hey," Satrina said. "Hey man, I get why you do what you do. You're not a bad guy."

"I'm good to these bitches. They work hard, but I take care of 'em." Tundra had lowered his weapon. He still had both hands on it, and the cylinder resting up against his Johnson.

"You're their protector."

"That's right."

"But not everyone has someone like you," she said. "I can see you've got a magnetic presence. Women trust you. But the other prostitutes. Gil treats them like cattle. He's a slavemaster."

"Imma buy this place," he said. "That's my plan."

"I was a working girl," she said. "In New York. For a while. I never had a pimp, though. No one to take care of me. I could work for you."

"I don't think so. You ain't..."

"I could clean up. Shave. I could—you could get me some nice clothes. I could be pretty. I can fuck good. I can take it in the ass. Whatever you need..."

They heard Gil's footsteps on the stairs.

"Here," he said, with a shifty look. And a pronounced layer of brow sweat.

Tundra took one hand off the gun and took the deed. He looked it over. It looked legit. He folded it and shoved it into the front of his track pants. "My name goin' on this bitch come Monday. Then Imma hold onto it until I cop that thirty Gs. You dig?"

"Done," Gil said. "We have a deal."

"Guess my future's bright after all," Tundra said.

"She's a manipulator," Gil said. "Trying to play you against me."

"You think I'm stupid, big G?" Tundra said.

"No."

"Then why a motherfucker got to state the obvious?" Tundra brought the .38 back up to arm's length and leveled it on the girl.

Urine tumbled onto the concrete. The crotch around the hippie girl's cutoffs were soiled. She collapsed onto her knees, clenching the knuckle weave of her cage, and started pleading. Her face clenched into a balling fist. "Oh fuck. Oh god. I fucked up. Please."

Tundra poked the barrel of the gun through the fence and probed her forehead. "Get up bitch. I want the rest of my fortune."

Satrina balled, and her hysterical wailing started to shift into uncontrollable maniacal laughter. She parted the nasty dreadlocks that were clinging to the tears and the drool on her face to reveal eyes of pure malice. Her face dirty and flushed.

She stifled the laughter. "You're going to a meeting tonight. It's a drug deal," she said. "T-Bone is there. So's *Ocelot*."

That name sent a chill down Tundra's spine.

Satrina stood up. "There's a hooker named Lace, who lures you into his house. Then T-Bone takes your stash and your cash…"

Tundra backed away from the cage. He swallowed hard.

Satrina pressed her face against the fencing. "And they tie you to the bed at gunpoint. Then Ocelot rams his big black dick inside you. And you scream, but nobody hears. Your eyes snap shut, and you take it like a man. *A broken man*. Sobbing and pleading, just like you did in the showers of the Nebras…"

Five gunshots rang out. Every one of them a head shot, and Satrina collapsed. Her brains blown all over the doorway to the bomb shelter. Blood snaked along the concrete like the bottom of a metal sink in a slaughterhouse. Her face now unrecognizable.

Gil froze in shock. His ears must've been ringing. Tundra breathed heavy. He'd never killed anyone with a gun before. It was a lot easier than using a shank.

THE WRIT

The Paradise Motel was two minutes away from the Bill Keene Memorial Interchange. The oldest four level freeway stack in the country. Made for a quick getaway in any direction. Sally pulled off Sunset and drove straight up to the motel office. She picked up her .38 service revolver from the passenger seat, and slid it down her waistband from behind, until the two-inch barrel tickled the top of her ass crack. The cold metal felt awkward, but it wasn't going to stay there for long.

When Sally entered the lobby, the two young guys and the old man were looking at her like she had three heads. Then she saw her face on TV. There were two images thrown up on the local news. One of Esmeralda Alonzo (the passport she'd stolen—how they got that, she still couldn't figure out) as an alias, and next to it, one from her last four years at vice. Her name across the screen in bold text.

"Holy shit," Pancho said. "You're on the news."

"Yeah," Sally said.

Gil had one of his typical expressions. One Sally called *the angry watchful old man gaze.*

"Can I talk to you outside?"

"Sure."

To his credit, Gil never smoked in the lobby. And when he did, he smoked those awful smelling mini cigars called Black & Mild.

Sally watched Gil light up. Then he offered her one. She said, "Sure." Fuck it. Why not? Her heart pounded inside her chest. Her hands sweat. The gun barrel worked its way into her ass crack.

He lit her up. "According to the news, it said you're no longer a police officer. So you've fraudulently been extorting me?"

As though there could be any other kind. Sally took a drag, and exhaled. "Yep."

"Tundra knows about Roberto," Gil said.

Sally felt her pulse rise higher—if that were even possible.

Gil cleared his throat. "I don't know how he knows…"

About that, she could see he was lying.

"But it's a problem," he said. "You should kill him."

Sally cocked an eyebrow and took another drag. Comical how candid the old man could be.

"Always wondered who the bigger pimp was," she said. "Now I know."

He reached into his pocket and pulled out the keys to his '76 Buick Sentry. "Take my car. I'll report it stolen in two days. You won't get very far in yours."

She took the keys and nodded. But he also knew she'd gotten rid of Roberto's body. The old man had a vested interest in her good fortune as a fugitive. "Thanks."

Gil pursed his lips and gave a slight nod. "Take care of yourself."

"You too," she said. If her pulse wasn't through the roof and she didn't feel like the jaws of life were closing around her, it might have been funny. Neither of them were doing a very good job. She saw Tundra in the doorway of his room, reaching for a bill fold from a john. The john faced the lobby, and Tundra had his back towards them. He took the money and disappeared behind the door. Sally dropped what was left of her Black & Mild and stamped it out. It tasted like shit. She knew now what had to be done. She'd liberate Katarina and her sister. She wouldn't stop driving 'til she reached Rosarito.

She grabbed the duffle bag full of cash out of the trunk of the Escort and walked towards room ten.

LORD OF THIS WORLD

Gil dialed from the phone in his back office.

"Hello."

"It's Gil. From The Paradise. I need a fumigation. You'll need to spray twice. Two different rooms."

"That complicates things. The cost is *three sprays.*"

"I have it."

"Forty minutes." The line went dead.

YOU WON'T CHANGE ME

Sally knocked on the door.

"Who is it?" he said.

Like he didn't know her by her cop knock, and like he wasn't looking right at her through the peep hole. "It's Sally."

"Fuck off. You too hot, girl."

"I've never been accused of that before," Sally said. "I brought money." She held up the duffle and cracked open the zipper. Just enough to show it was bursting with bootie.

The door swung open. "Look at you. Shiiit. I look like a Colombian dictator? I ain't got powder enough for *that.*" He didn't have the pearl handled chrome revolver, normally poking out of the waistband of his track pants.

"I'm here for your entire inventory," she said. "Girls too."

"Well goddamn baby," Tundra said. "Guess this my lucky day." Tundra pulled the door open wide, and let Sally in. Katarina stayed silent, sitting on the bed, as her eyes followed Sally into the room. They told a sad story, along with the long fresh gash under her right eye. Now she had a matching set. Her focus flipped back to the TV.

"You a TV star Sally. Straight up. They talkin' all kinds o' shit about you. Robbed a liquor store. Fixed a horse race..."

So that's where they got the passport. They must've swiped it at Hollywood Park. Sally's heart sank. On the TV she saw the press chasing after Levi outside the Synagogue. And Noah, outside the house. Her life was over. She held the tears back. This baby-fucking cash whore wasn't going to see any waterworks. "I need to get high, Tundra. Right now." Sally pulled her eyes away from the TV and stared at Katarina, who wouldn't return her stare. Her arm still cuffed to the frame, the way it always had been. The girl's baby soft kissable lips quivered.

"Baby girl tried to escape," Tundra said. "I had to regulate; you know."

"You don't mind damaging your own merchandise," Sally said.

Tundra snickered, and it pushed its way into Sally's brain like fingernails on a chalkboard. He turned and pulled open a drawer on the nightstand. "She just collateral really. Bitch ain't nothin' special. Her sister be doing all the fuckin'. Her sister's pussy is gold." He slid the drawer to the nightstand shut.

"I hope you got a fix for me, baby."

"I got you," He put both his hands on her ass, and squeezed. It drove a shockwave through her system. Then she felt his hardon through his sweats against the bottom of her back, ashamed that it felt so validating. His obnoxious flamboyant cologne brought her outrage back. As he moved past her, she thought about reaching for the .38. She said, "So how are you, baby?"

"Been thinking about expanding," he said. "You know…"

She wrapped her right hand around the cold metal handle. Felt the kinetic energy begging to be employed.

Tundra turned around sharply. Sally let go of the weapon. Let her hand hang by her side.

"Imma buy this whole motel," he said. "Every one of these bitches gonna be mine. You'll see."

He turned back around and worked his hand into the nightstand on the other side of the bed. "Now that I can finally afford to buy it."

She knew as soon as he wrapped his hands around it, that it wasn't a dime bag. She knew he had his hand on his gun. With the speed of a coke fiend, the pimp spun around and leveled the chrome barrel. But Sally already had her service pistol at arm's length, with the hammer cocked back at the ready.

HOLE IN THE SKY

The giant neon motel sign at his back pointed down to the bowels of the devil. A black and starless horizon crackled, threatening acid rain. He looked out on the Boulevard, with the payphone to his ear. His man picked up on the third ring. "Hey. It's Pancho. Yo, bring your camera and meet me at the Paradise Motel. On Sunset. Yeah. I got one. What the Japanese guys talked about— how death has a look. I got one. Fading fast. Get here as soon as you can, so we can capture the face of death."

HAND OF DOOM

"So what happened with Sally?" Opti said.

"You want the whole story?" Tony said.

"No, I want the corporation-friendly L.A. Times version."

Tony just stared at him blankly. No understanding at all of nuance.

"Yeah. I want the whole fuckin' story."

"Okay, so you know it was Malta Majesty for the win, right?"

"Sure."

"What you didn't know—what nobody on earth was wise to. Up until three weeks ago. Is that Malta Majesty is really Fahrenheit."

Now Opti had the blank stare. "What?"

"*Fahrenheit.* C'mon, you must've heard. He took The Belmont Stakes in '79. He was all hands and heels…"

"Okay. Okay. Enough with the Horse Track stats," Opti said. "Stick to the Cliff's Notes on that. I want details on the long con."

"Okay. The gist of it is, they had similar coloring. You couldn't really tell 'em apart. Fahrenheit supposedly died in a stable fire in Rockingham."

"But it was really Malta Majesty."

"Now you're catching on," Tony said. "The Identifier was paid off. The reality is it would have passed anyway. Both horses had the same number except Malta Majesty had a final digit of eight. Fahrenheit's was Three. Easiest fix."

"So Malta Majesty wasn't favored to win…"

"Right."

"And you'd pulled this same scam a few times."

"With that horse? Once. But then a jockey who was wise, flipped. I had no choice but to sell Malta Majesty off. Now it's on him—the buyer. And Sally. Did the feds bag her?"

"They had enough on her—including that passport your guy lifted. But she just sort of vanished, you know?"

"Hey, you mind if I smoke?" said a voice from the back.

Opti turned around and looked over his left shoulder. He glared at Angelo—Tony C's brother-in-law. "I just quit."

"Then it won't be a shock to your system," Angelo said. "An early meeting like this on a Saturday with no breakfast. It's fuckin' with my stomach."

Opti turned around and glanced at his cousin, Giovanni, who sat behind him. He cocked an eyebrow and gave him a *can you fuckin' believe this guy?* look. "Sure Ange. Crack the window."

"We ought to be smokin' Cubans," Angelo slid a cigarette into his mouth, and lit up. Out of one side of his mouth, he said, "Did you hear what this fat fuck just pulled off? Malta Majesty is fuckin' Fahrenheit. You slick sonovabitch."

Tony hit the power windows and gave Angelo six inches of open air.

They were inside Tony's Seville on the edge of a deserted parking lot about the size of the one outside Dodger Stadium.

"Where are we, anyway?" Angelo said.

"Torrance. It's a chemical plant." Opti said.

"Saw a sign that said Montrose," taking a drag.

"Yeah," Opti said.

"They've been dumping DDT in the bay for over a decade," Angelo said.

"Yeah. Your cigarette smoke ain't gonna make this air any more toxic," Opti said.

"Jesus Christ, Tony," Angelo said. "This guy brought us to Cancer Row, for fuck's sake."

"Relax, Ange." Opti said. "If the smog don't kill ya, something else will. Trust me. I'm an authority."

Tony tossed an envelope onto Opti's lap.

"What's this?" Opti said.

"Five Gs," Tony said.

"For what?" Opti said.

"For listening to my proposal," Tony said. "Remember?"

"The book thing?"

"Yeah," Tony said, pulling an immaculate manila file folder from a leather document holder wedged between the two front seats. "Here. Have a look. It's the synopsis. And the logline. There are some photos of me in there, too."

"I shot those," Angelo said.

"Fixer: The Tony Capra Story. The life and times of the greatest horse racing handicapper in history," Opti quoted. "Very modest."

"I understand you know Neil Olsen," Tony said.

"You want Mario fuckin' Puzo to write your biography?"

"Hey," Tony said. "I had Sports Illustrated contact me. Listen, I'm gonna get some big writer to do the book and then I'm gonna be a star. Then they're gonna make it into a movie."

Opti turned around and gave Giovanni a look. "Listen to this guy."

"Hey," Tony said. "You know movie producers, don't you?"

"Yeah," Opti said. "I got a meeting with one this evening."

"No shit," Tony said. "Who?"

"Jackson Steel," Opti said.

Giovanni belted out a hearty laugh.

"The porno guy?" Tony said.

"Hey—beggars can't be choosers."

"Hey, do they make Sulphuric acid here?" Angelo tossed his cigarette butt to the pavement. "Tony, you can kill this window now."

Opti gave Tony a look that went over his head. Then he turned to Angelo. "I believe they do," Opti said. "Acetone too. That's what you use to develop pictures, right?

"That's right," Angelo said.

"You know, you're quite the photographer," Opti said.

"I've got years of training," Angelo said. "*Hey, stugots! I'm breathing in the fumes.*"

Tony flipped the switch and powered up the window.

"Sorry I couldn't give you a discount," Angelo said. "But you know. A guy's gotta earn."

"Right," Opti said. "Money's like the sea to me—it ebbs and it flows. I get it back one way or another."

"As requested," Angelo said, handing Opti an envelope. "The negatives."

"These all of them?" Opti said.

"God as my witness," Angelo said.

There were two sharp cracks, and Angelo's brains looked like a side of meat loaf shot out of a leaf blower. All over the rear driver's side door. The window demolished. Crystalized shards of glass on the leather.

"Jesus Christ," Tony said. "I just had the interior cleaned."

Opti gave his cousin a look. Giovanni's 9mm had twice the barrel length with the silencer. Smoke wafted from the ejection port.

"I tried to get your attention. But you had to roll the window back up. Maybe you'd rather you didn't have to worry about it," Opti said.

"That it?" Tony said. "You gonna whack me too?"

Opti reached into his blazer.

"Oh Jesus," Tony said.

Opti's hand came out with a business card. He handed it to Tony. "Neil Olsen's number and address. Write to him. Drop my name. He knows better than to tear it up. Maybe we'll make a million bucks with this thing. Me as your agent."

"Hey thanks, Opti."

"Hey look," Opti said. "The old man is old. And you know, Howie Winter is probably going to die in the can. And the guy out front for Winter Hill's a bigger rat than you are. And we both know it."

Opti nodded towards Tony, then turned around and nodded at Giovanni. Then he said to Tony, "I suggest using acetone. As an astringent. On that." Then he pushed open the door.

"So...Fifteen percent?" Tony said.

"More like fifty," Opti said. "A guy's gotta earn."

"Looks like you're doing okay," Tony said, chinning towards the pearl white Cadillac Eldorado parked next to them.

"I needed a new set of wheels. Recently acquired. Guy wrote me into his will at the last minute."

THE END

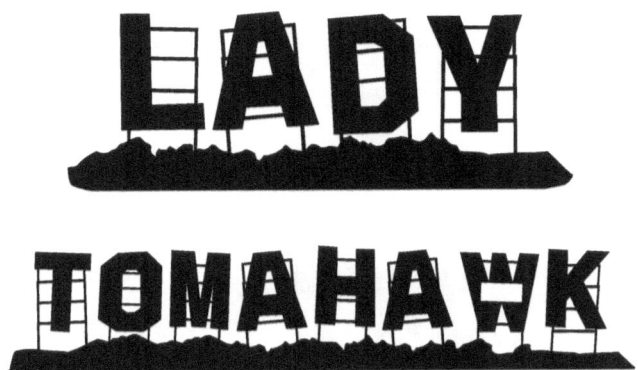

by
Andrew Miller

One

Licensed masseuse Dustin Skye drove his blue '79 Ferrari 308-GTB along Bayshore Drive in Newport Beach, passing all the homes situated along the water's edge. The sky was clear and a steady wind coming in from the ocean tamed the rich heat from the sun. Dustin pulled into a driveway and parked by the side entrance, as his manager Frank instructed. Then he took off his Porsche Carrera sunglasses and combed his blond moustache.

A note was taped on the side door: *Wait for me at the bar—M.*

The bar was in the corner of a modern living room with a glass wall overlooking the ocean. Dustin sat on a stool. The house was quiet. Sailboats were out and Balboa Island was in the distance. On the wall above the bar he noticed a framed picture of Hank and Mavis Shepherd, the residents of this house, with John Wayne.

Dustin knew the Reverend Hank from his billboards. They were all over L.A. He was a well-known conservative political commentator and the host of the nationally syndicated program *The Hank Shepherd Show.* This opulent house might not be what most of his fanbase would expect from a man who branded himself as "the voice of the people," but Dustin had long accepted hypocrisy from the rich.

Mavis Shepherd walked in wearing a sheer black kimono that hung open over a tight green bikini. She smoked a cigarette.

"Were the directions I gave Mr. Carson sufficient?" she said.

He could smell her tanning oil from across the room. "Totally easy."

Mavis walked toward him and stubbed out the cigarette in the ashtray on the bar next to where Dustin sat. When their heads were close, he registered the want in her eyes and kissed her on the lips. Mavis lit a fresh Pall Mall from the pack on the bar.

She had a decent body for her age. Her skin was tan and leathery. She was too old to be hot by Dustin's standards but he was turned on by her confidence.

He pointed at the picture. "Is that really John Wayne?"

"Yes, it is. When the Big C finally killed the Duke last year, it was as if a great and powerful force had been sucked out of the world. We didn't know if it would return."

"A great and powerful force?"

"The Duke was our neighbor for years." She pointed at the house next door. "His wife Pilar and I played tennis together."

"My Dad would get jazzed when his movies came on TV."

Mavis took Dustin's hand and led him over to the Italian leather sofa. They sat. She picked up a small black box from the coffee table and handed it to him.

"Tell me what you think," Mavis said.

He opened the box and looked at a brand-new gold Rolex.

"You don't have one already, do you? I asked Sherry if you already had one. She said she didn't think so, but she wasn't sure."

Sherry Michigan was the wife of a studio executive who Dustin had been on a date with at Ma Maison last month when they ran into Mavis. Curious about the pretty new stud Sherry was showing off around town, Mavis made inquiries and found out Dustin was available. Sherry gave Mavis Frank Carson's number, and arrangements were made.

"You needed something special for our first date. It's the newest model."

An erection formed in Dustin's pants. Fancy things often got him hard. "I already have a gold Rolex but not the newest model."

Mavis placed her Pall Mall in the ashtray, still burning. "Do you think this will do?"

Dustin closed the box. "I think this situation is calling for us to forgo the introductory massage." He reached, and with his thumb and forefinger, took hold of a string that tied her bikini bottom together. He undid the knot, pulled her bottoms off and threw them onto the carpet. Dustin then put a pillow down and had Mavis lay back and spread her legs. She closed her eyes. Dustin went to work with his tongue, trying not to tickle her with his moustache.

Mavis moaned and said, "Merciful Jesus" and "Holy Father Above." Dustin knew Mavis was a famous Christian so these phrases didn't surprise him. As he continued licking and kissing, Dustin rapidly felt the vibrations of her body reaching a crescendo.

"Hosanna in the Highest!" Mavis shouted.

Then she came.

Mavis took a moment to gather her senses. She pointed at the glass walls. "We shouldn't be here. That wasn't the plan. There's a room upstairs."

Dustin picked up his Rolex box and held it at his side. "Lead the way."

Bottomless, Mavis took Dustin's hand and led him to a second-floor guest bedroom. The curtains were drawn and a mirror was above the bed. Mavis closed the door, turned to face Dustin, and unzipped his pants. Her mouth gaped open.

"I thought Sherry was exaggerating."

"Twelve inches exactly, when it's at attention like this." Mavis stared. "You can use a tape measure if you don't believe me."

Mavis got into bed. She positioned herself on all fours with her face right in front of the mirror. Dustin got behind her and went in.

"Judas Priest, that's a huge cock!"

Dustin watched himself in the mirror. He was perfectly tanned and perfectly toned.

He often found it difficult to remember what his life was like at all before it had turned so pleasurable and luxurious. His origins, and much of the long road he traveled to get here, felt foggy and remote.

After a long while of admiring his own reflection, Dustin got a strong sense that someone was watching on the other side of the mirror.

Allison Mae Dummar got off the freeway in Echo Park. She cruised past the lake, which was plagued with the homeless. Her white '73 Ford pickup with Arizona plates was low on fuel so she stopped at a gas station on Sunset Boulevard. As she refilled the tank, a bald Mexican shouted at her from the next pump over.

From her angle, Allison saw he was covered in tattoos. One of them said *Echo Park Locos*. He was refilling the tank of a car built with a frame bizarrely close to the ground. Other Mexicans were in his car behind him, laughing at their friend's routine. Allison didn't understand. She didn't speak Spanish.

From the Mexican's angle, all he could see was Allison's face—her deep blue eyes, her high-set cheekbones, her clear white skin, and her long golden hair. She stepped out from behind the gas pump so the man could see all of her body—her thick neck, her muscular legs, and her beefy, bulging biceps.

The Mexican went quiet. He waited until his tank was full and took off east on Sunset in his low riding car.

Allison drove the other way. Graffiti was everywhere in L.A. So were the homeless. At least two out of three

Angelenos she saw appeared to be Mexicans. At the peak of a hill in Silver Lake she saw the Hollywood sign.

In a McDonald's on Vermont she ordered a Big Mac combo. At a booth she watched through the window as a homeless black man dug through a trash bin for food. He found the remains of an old hash brown and ate it.

Allison sighed and dipped the edge of her sandwich in barbeque sauce. L.A. was big and bizarre. Finding her brother wouldn't be easy.

At the bottom of the stairs, on Dustin's way back out to his Ferrari, the Reverend Hank Shepherd appeared and stood in his way.

He wore an unbuttoned tropical print Pierre Cardin shirt covered in hula-dancing girls and held a glass of cold white wine.

He didn't seem upset. Dustin got the impression that the Shepherds had an understanding and the Reverend probably just watched through the mirror.

"Let's talk in my study," he said.

Carrying his Rolex, Dustin followed Hank back to the far end of the ground floor. His study also offered a view of the water. Hank left the door open and took a seat in a black leather, high-backed swivel chair. A record of a church choir singing "Our God is an Awesome God" played softly on Hank's stereo. The waves rolled in outside the window.

"Pouilly Fumé?" Hank pointed at a chilled open bottle sitting on a small wine fridge.

Dustin shrugged. "Cool."

"Pour it yourself."

Dustin poured himself a glass and stood quietly. Hank's study was full of Christian books and pictures of him with people Dustin assumed were famous in the Christian world. The Stetson Hank wore in all his famous billboards hung on the wall.

"I know your manager. He's ambitious for a colored fella."

Dustin smiled.

"You're partial to just women?"

"All the cool kids go both ways these days. It's 1980, Rev."

"I've seen some of the boys who work for Clark Debussy." Clark Debussy was Frank's biggest competitor. Clark's parents came from incredible wealth. Frank always seemed to be playing catch-up to his rival's superior connections. "Mavis and I have always had our routines to stay exciting. I've always dabbled with boys. But ever since I saw *Caligula* last year, I've felt encouraged to expand my horizons and intensify my dalliances." Hank looked at Dustin's bulge. "Clark Debussy's boys are hot, but they aren't hot like you."

Dustin looked down the hall. Mavis was still up in the guest bedroom. The smoke from the Pall Mall she left burning wafted their way.

"Not here," Hank said, massaging his crotch. "My wife doesn't like it when I poach her boys. It's one of our rules and if I break her rules, she's promised to inform the liberal media about my true orientation. We'll have to meet somewhere. Tell me how I get in touch with you."

He handed Hank his card. It had the number for his answering service.

"One thing," Hank said.

"What's that?"

"Fire and brimstone would reign down upon you if you talked about my private life."

"Ask anyone about me, Rev." Dustin finished his wine. "I'm a trustworthy guy."

Allison unpacked her things in her room at the Galaxy Inn and looked out at Hollywood through her barred window. Semis filled the lot. In the distance she saw a circular tower that said Capitol Records at the top.

The carpet below her was torn and stained. It smelled like urine. A recurring meow told her a cat was trapped somewhere in the walls.

Down on Sunset, she noticed all sorts of strange people. She focused on the prostitutes, or people who seemed to be prostitutes. The further she walked, the more she noticed men and women who appeared to be selling their bodies in public.

She began to engage them. Starting a conversation wasn't easy. Allison was blunt and lumbering, an evident outsider. All the boys she tried to chat up changed the subject or walked away. Maybe they thought she was a cop. One lip-glossed boy wearing just a jean jacket and speedo bottoms laughed in her face.

Allison decided to change her approach. She would focus only on women. For a while that didn't go much better. Allison didn't know what to say and she scared the women off, or maybe they weren't really hookers at all. She couldn't be sure.

The streets got stranger. She watched a colorfully dressed black man take a thick wad of cash from a white woman in front of the Crossroads of the World.

Dustin walked into Chasen's and took off his shades. The staff here knew him. The famous chili scent was on the air. He told the pompadoured maître d' that he would wait for Frank, who was already here with some big shot, at the bar.

A beautiful blonde stared at him as her cocktail was being mixed. She seemed familiar to him. She eyeballed his bulge. Over in the corner he noticed Alpha and Amani, Frank's top guys. Both drank pink Greyhounds which matched their suits.

He ordered an Absolut Martini. "Busy night?" he said to the bartender.

"The cast of *Three's Company*'s having a season finale wrap party."

Dustin realized the blonde was Suzanne Sommers. She took her drink and returned to the party. Dustin's Martini came and Frank sat down beside him.

"You're never home lately, man," Dustin said, taking a sip.

Frank wore a pewter green double breasted Armani suit. Other than Alpha and Amani, he was probably the only black man in the restaurant. He certainly wasn't the only Republican. Frank ordered an Absolut Martini for himself.

"Plus you said to tell you directly about this afternoon." Dustin handed Frank a stuffed envelope. Frank put it in his jacket pocket.

Frank's Martini came. "So?" Frank said.

"The Reverend asked for my card. He wants his own date."

"Righteous development."

"He'll call the answering service when he's ready."

Frank nodded. "This is good for us. It could mean a higher elevation."

"Yeah?"

"We could get a very important contract."

"You've been talking about this contract. What is it, exactly?"

"Some very powerful people are looking for the services of a business like mine." Frank chose his words carefully. "But they're secretive."

"Everyone's secretive."

Frank sipped his Martini. "These men are on a different level of private. You started on the streets and you've come a long way. But you're still on the grind and so am I. If we can guarantee the efficiency and secrecy these men need, if nothing gets in our way, you won't have to worry about hustling ever again."

"What's the hold up? What could get in our way?"

"These men are delicate. They take their time before making a deal. Plus, we aren't the only ones they're considering. A little birdie told me that silver spoon Clark Debussy's also in the running. These men are putting Clark and myself through a series of interviews. I've got nine girls and six boys. There are other popular faces on the roster. But you're my star, Dustin. All the old rich ladies and old rich men in this town are thrilled by your huge cock and your empty soul. If we win, it will be because of you."

"I totally treat them good, man," Dustin said.

"You sure do. The reality is that Hank Shepherd's a good friend of Governor Reagan, who's going to be nominated by this summer as the GOP candidate for President. That's the kind of elevation I'm talking about." Frank finished his drink. "The game's changing. In the '80s, people will want everything and they won't be afraid to admit it."

"What's next then?" Dustin said.

Frank patted his chest where the envelope was. "When the Reverend calls, be sure to rock his world."

At Sunset and La Brea, Allison studied faces and bodies.

A white woman stood on the sidewalk by the gas station. She wore high heels, cutoff jeans and a flower print wife beater. A peace sign was tattooed on her arm. She seemed like a friendly face.

"All these women," Allison said, "appear to be prostitutes."

The woman turned. She scoped Allison's imposing body and got confused. "How does that make you feel?" she said.

"You too?" Allison said. "Really?"

"My name's Karen." Karen smiled. "And I like to fuck."

"I didn't think you were one of them."

"Lady, you a cop?"

"No."

Karen said, "I have to ask. Nothing personal."

Under her wife beater, Karen wore no bra. Stretch marks crossed on her exposed stomach. "How many kids do you have?"

"Three."

"What are their names?"

"Miles, Coltrane, and Bird."

Allison waited. "What happened to them?"

"What do you mean?"

"Did you lose them?"

"They're at home with my husband, asleep. It's a school night."

"You're out here, but you still have a family?"

"Yes. I'm a substitute teacher. Mainly in North Hollywood, where I live, but I teach all over the Valley. I don't have class tomorrow, which is why I'm out late tonight."

"Your husband knows you do this?"

"My husband knows I believe in female liberation. Just because I married him years ago, that doesn't mean my philosophy about sex stayed frozen since our wedding day. I'm out here without a pimp, you know. I'm special. The money I make's my own."

"Don't you care if your husband is hurt by your actions?"

Karen laughed. "Usually, Donald doesn't mind listening when I tell him dirty stories about all my female fucks. But even if he didn't, I've given him enough thought and consideration. I have needs and urges. This is the only life and body I'll get. If I can have the town, why don't I take it?"

Allison became worried Los Angeles might destroy her. Then she became full of rage and more determined than ever to not let anything destroy her. She took out the picture. "I'm searching for my brother." She held up Randy's face. "Have you ever seen him?"

Dustin walked into the pool house. Tania was already home, painting her toenails on the couch and watching a black and white Jane Fonda movie on TV.

"What's this one?"

"It's called *Walk on the Wild Side*."

His roommate Tania worshipped Jane Fonda, who not only had won the Best Actress Academy Award the year before for *Coming Home*, but was also a brave and outspoken left-wing political activist. Earlier in the day, Tania had been at a protest march against a nuclear power plant on Hollywood Boulevard.

"Jane show today?" Dustin said. This morning Tania's heart was fluttering about the possibility of getting a glimpse of her hero.

"Maybe. I didn't see her. I don't know," she said. "But it was still a good day. Why? Did Frank complain about me going?"

"He didn't bring you up at all," Dustin said.

Frank lived in the main house here in Studio City, though he was hardly ever home these days due to all his hustling. Dustin and Tania lived here in the back, as a reward for being his two top earners.

"What'd you and him talk about then?" Tania asked.

Dustin sat and told her about the Shepherds and the possible upcoming contract.

"Sounds like some cashew-dick Republicans selling Frank a bill of goods," she said.

"You think?"

Tania's girlfriend Laverne walked down the stairs. Moving sluggishly, she got herself a Tab from the fridge.

Laverne went back upstairs without acknowledging either of them. Dustin could tell that she was once again in a Librium haze.

"Laverne go with you to the protest?"

Tania didn't answer.

Laverne, a black woman from Oakland twice Tania's age, was a former Black Panther. Tania wanted to reignite her lover's passion for politics, but since moving in with them two months ago, Laverne's life with a woman who fucked others for a living began to take its toll. Laverne mostly stayed up in the bedroom, getting heavier and more spaced out.

"So you like, really don't think this deal of Frank's is real? He said important people are interested in his popular roster. That means you too."

Tania shrugged.

"You think he's getting scammed?"

"Whatever it is, it's obvious to everyone by now that you're the star of the show," Tania said. "And besides, I really will be like Jane Fonda. No BS. I know seeing success as an actress is hard, and I know most people don't think I've got what it takes, but screw them. I'm determined. I'm making real moves, moves Frank doesn't know about. This world won't be mine much longer."

Dustin searched for words. Their relationship was important to him. He cared deeply for Tania, but it was hard to relate to her anymore. His world was flesh and material. This used to be her world as well, but somewhere along the way she developed dreams, began focusing on ideals. They were now on different paths.

"Your optimism's cool," he said. "I'm going to go use the steam shower now."

Allison walked down to Santa Monica Boulevard, now unable to stop sweating. Unlike Sunset, male prostitutes were dominant down here. Harsh neon lights outlined their bodies. Each boy looked like a homosexual. Just changing boulevards flung you into a different realm.

At a hot dog stand called Oki Dog she saw crowds of punks attired in bizarre leather jackets and torn pants. They looked back at her like she was the weird one. Due to Allison's imposing figure, they seemed reluctant to engage her. She wasn't just some tourist to antagonize.

Allison got in line for a hot dog. While she waited, a young boy in tight cutoff jean shorts got out of a green Camaro and stepped out onto the sidewalk, where all the punks could see.

"Little fruiters after some sweet sausage!" a punk shouted.

"Shouldn't have gotten out here, faggot!" shouted another, who threw an empty can of Schlitz at the boy's head.

A pack of berserk punks charged the boy. They punched and kicked and beat him senseless. The boy shrieked for help but didn't fight back.

One punk drew a switchblade. Allison heard him shout, "Buena Park Punks!" before he stabbed the boy repeatedly in the gut.

The Buena Park Punks sped off. She watched all the others casually leave the scene as the boy cried for help and held his bleeding gut. No one seemed to hear him. Eventually, his cries stopped and he turned lifeless. Allison thought of the Old Testament and the Leviticus admonition of homosexuality. As far as she could tell, no one called the cops.

Allison walked back to the Galaxy Inn and fell asleep to the rhythm of the trapped cat still meowing for help inside her wall.

Two

Tania stood at the corner of Hollywood and Western wearing a ripped jean skirt and a tight pink halter top. On the job she almost always dressed lavishly, but not today. She dressed down for one special client. It was morning, already eighty-five degrees, and she wiped sweat away from her forehead.

A Rolls Royce pulled up. Tania walked to the back window. It rolled down partway.

"Need a ride, toots?" an old woman asked from the darkness. The voice was hoarse and haggard from a long life of smoking.

"Wow. You've got a nice car," Tania said.

"Plenty of room in here."

Tania smiled. "Is everyone in L.A. so nice?"

"Not everyone. But I'll be nice to you if you're nice to me."

Tania smiled. This was all part of their routine, a fiction they acted out. Lucille Ball, currently sixty-nine years old, opened the door of her air-conditioned Rolls and Tania got in.

Lucy wore a mink coat and shades. Her hair was redder than the last time Tania saw her. Fresh dye job.

"Where are we going?"

"Roxbury in Beverly Hills. One of my houses."

"You must be a powerful woman."

Allison came to a pawn shop on Vine. It was under a huge billboard for *The Hank Shepherd Show*. Her father loved that program. Father saw the Reverend Shepherd as the embodiment of Christian decency and a culture warrior for true American values.

Inside, a salesman with a ducktail sat in the corner listening to Sinatra. He calmly watched Allison as she looked over the guns displayed in the glass case.

"What's your situation, sweetie?"

"I'm hunting my brother."

He scratched his chin. "You worried he might be dangerous when you catch him?"

"We've been separated a long time. The people he's with might be dangerous. I honestly don't know about him. I just know I need something that shows I won't be intimidated. Something primal."

The salesman pointed at a small automatic handgun. "This Saturday Night Special could fit easily in your purse."

"I don't carry a purse."

The salesman nodded, intrigued by the challenge. "Primal," he said. He waited and then directed Allison's attention to the wall behind him.

"I suggest taking time to practice throwing it, but something like this shouldn't be too difficult to wield for a lady with your build."

Hanging on the wall was a tomahawk.

"I got that from a retired Green Beret," the salesman said. "He used it to kill gooks in Vietnam. It even comes with the original manual on how to throw it right."

Tania removed the red wig that Lucy always made her wear and placed it back on top of the dresser on the far side of the bedroom. Naked, she picked up her clothes and walked to the bathroom to clean up. When she came back out, they laid down together in the pushed together beds. Lucy's husband Gary was in Palm Springs, at another home of theirs.

"I had a big moment this week in my acting class," Tania said. She was allowed to stay for a short while and permitted to forget about their role playing. "My partner Herbie and I did a dramatic scene from *Klute* and I cried. I was supposed to cry and I really did. I became the part and the sadness just happened naturally."

Lucy lit another cigarette. "Good for you. But stop placing all your hopes on the acting classes." After the first drag, a fit of congestion hit Lucy hard and she hacked into her hand. "I think you're the bee's knees but it's hard to get ahead, kid. You'll need to get over your idealism and start spreading your legs for the casting directors."

Tania laughed. "When I make it as a star, I'll have earned it straight."

"I've got plenty of money, but I don't have a say in who gets cast in anything anymore. Take my advice. You're a beauty and you might actually have a chance that way. After you've got your foot in the door, that's when the acting classes pay off."

"I know why I have to wear the red wig," Tania said gently.

They never spoke about the wig. "Enlighten me."

"For so long in your career, you never had power. All those studio heads and executives did. Those men. Now that you've got it all, it gets you off to be reminded that you're the one in charge now. The wig reminds you that everything you had to do was worth it."

Lucy whistled. "You don't make it in Hollywood, you might do as a good shrink."

"The point is that I will make it. The road I need to take isn't as harsh because women like you cleared the way for me."

Lucy smiled. "Oh, before I forget." She reached into the nightstand drawer and pulled out an envelope. Tania looked in at the cash. "Remember, you earned that, not the smoke."

Dustin sat poolside at the Beverly Hills Hotel, slowly drinking a salt-rimmed Paloma and reading *The Shining* by Stephen King. Malcom McDowell said hi as he walked by

Dustin's chair. So did Jamie Lee Curtis, wearing a red bikini.

When Dustin had time off, he always worked on his tan. He could have used the pool at Frank's to lay out. It was only a few feet from his front door. But Dustin understood it was important to be seen whenever possible, so he came here.

"I saw you drive in up front," a girl's voice said. "Cool Ferrari."

Dustin turned. A beautiful young brunette looked down at him. She was backlit by the sun. She looked about sixteen. "Thanks."

"Are you Dustin Skye?"

"Who might you be, pretty lady?"

She clearly found it endearing Dustin didn't recognize her on sight. "My Dad greenlit *American Gigolo* at Paramount."

Dustin sat up.

"Is it true Richard Gere based his character on you?"

"The script for *Gigolo* wasn't based on me at all," he said. "But when Richie was preparing for the role, a friend in common hooked us up and we hung out together. He said I inspired his performance."

Long ago, during his first year in Los Angeles, Dustin had a job as a pool boy at this hotel. He shared this detail with Richard Gere when the actor was shadowing him as research for his role. When Dustin saw the final film, released in February, this detail ended up on the screen as part of the fictional history of Julian Kaye, Gere's character in the movie.

"I throw good parties." The girl took some hotel stationary and wrote her room number down. "Come by sometime."

She handed him the paper and walked off. Dustin slid it in his shirt pocket, laid back down, and returned to his paperback.

Allison sat alone at a corner table in Café Tropical, sipping a coffee. She watched the people around her and imagined what the woman she was waiting on might look like. Her large green camouflage backpack was under the table at her feet.

"Allison?" a woman said.

Allison looked up. The woman before her had to be Tania.

They made their greetings. Tania apologized for being late, then stood in line to get a coffee. Allison watched her. She expected someone sleazier, like how prostitutes looked on television. Tania got herself a mocha and they sat down together back at the corner table.

"Thanks for meeting me," Allison said.

"Karen spoke highly of you," Tania said.

Allison waited. "I was standing beside her when she called you. She told you I have money."

Tania smiled.

The lie Allison had forced Karen to say about her last night, about Allison being rich, had worked far better than she expected.

"You could say it was sort of entirely random how Karen and I happened to meet," Allison said. "I wanted someone who... does what you do..."

"You wanted a date with me. But you wanted to talk first."

"Is that all right?"

"Of course." Tania was touched by Allison's innocence. "My relationships with people vary. Usually, I start by just getting to know a new client. First, I learn about them as a person, then I go from there."

"Works for me."

Tania took a sip of her mocha. "You seem new to L.A."

"I arrived yesterday."

"From the Midwest?"

"You're a good guesser. Yes."

"I see that you work out a lot." She nodded slightly at Allison's shoulders.

"Back home, I've got a routine."

"Seriously, your physique is impressive."

"Karen has a husband and children, but she spends all that time on the street, selling her body to strangers. She doesn't seem to think anything could go wrong, behaving this way. Do you have romantic relationships outside of work?"

"Yes. I'm with a woman named Laverne."

"You're gay?"

"At work, I sleep with men and women. But my only love is Laverne."

"She... understands what you do?"

"She's not closed-minded. As long as my work stays work, she supports me. Laverne knows I bring people happiness."

"You don't like men at all? You aren't just saying this to make me feel better?"

"Men don't actually attract me. Trust me, my roommate does the same work I do. He's about as hot as guys get and we've never fooled around. I sleep with men, but that's all just a performance. To do this work for as long as I have, you've got to have some talent as an actress."

"Karen told me about your roommate."

Tania watched Allison's face closely. "Would you like to meet him?"

"Maybe."

"I could arrange that too. I've thrown my roommate dates before." Allison finished her coffee. "Maybe we can continue this conversation someplace private?"

Detective Sergeant Howser walked across the lot of Hollywood station and got into the passenger seat of an unmarked department-issued Black Matador. His partner of four years, Detective Lieutenant La Rocca, was already waiting with the engine running.

"I'm telling you Tony," Howser said, continuing with a rant he'd begun earlier at their side-by-side desks. "This *Heaven's Gate* picture's going to be a disaster for UA."

La Rocca pulled out onto Wilcox toward a fresh murder scene.

"It might even bankrupt the studio," Howser said. "Retakes, insane cost overruns, all because some megalomaniacal director with a bleak vision was given too much power."

"Uh-huh," La Rocca said.

Howser was a homicide detective, but his real passion was for screenwriting. He'd been through an MFA at USC and cranked out a new script every two months, regardless of how demanding being a detective was. A sci-fi title of his called *Cyber Samurai* had been optioned three years ago but was stuck in development hell at Paramount. He'd been frustrated and depressed about the holdup, but a series of highly publicized and still ongoing complications with director Michael Cimino's follow-up to *The Deer Hunter* was giving him hope about the future of his baby, which was big-budget escapist fare in the style of *Star Wars*.

La Rocca, older and the senior detective, always enjoyed his partner's Industry rants, even if he didn't always follow them. La Rocca didn't have a side hustle or an outside passion. For him there was just his wife and four kids, his devotion to the Catholic church, and the job.

"The American public doesn't want *Heaven's Gate*," Howser said. "This country's done with depressing movies. It's a new era in Hollywood."

They pulled up to the scene in an alley off Hollywood and Cherokee, behind Musso & Frank. Howser and La Rocca got out of their Matador and walked under the yellow tape. The lab guys were at work. The patrolman who took the call saw them and approached.

"We found the victim's I.D. stuffed in the dumpster beside the body," he said. "Her name is Karen O'Hara. She's from North Hollywood."

They looked in at the body. She wore cutoff jeans and a flower print wife beater. A peace sign was tattooed on her arm. She had bruises all over her body and a large skull fracture in her forehead above her right eye. "I'm estimating the time of death as being between twelve and eighteen hours ago," an ME told them.

Howser pointed at the legs. "She's only got one stocking."

"Maybe the object down her throat is the other," the patrolman said.

Howser and La Rocca looked closer.

On the other side of the tape, down by the alley, a commotion broke out. There was shouting. The uniformed officer guarding the tape restrained a man.

"Let me see her!" he shouted.

Howser and La Rocca walked over. He was white and in his thirties. He obviously knew the victim, or thought he did. They had the officer let him go.

"Why are you here?" La Rocca said.

"Because one of my wife's whore friends called me and told me she was dead."

"Who is your wife?" Howser said.

"Karen O'Hara. Her day job is as a substitute teacher but at night she sells herself on the street." He pointed at the dumpster. "Is she in there?"

Howser and La Rocca waited.

From their faces, the husband knew. "I told her some maniac was going to cut her up. Did she listen? No, she came out here and sold her pussy on the street because she wanted to be sexually liberated. Look what it got her."

From his answering service, Dustin got a message that "Rev" wanted to get in touch with him, along with a fresh number to call after 1 p.m. The clock on the hotel wall read 1:15. Dustin dialed the number.

"Is this Mr. Skye?" Hank said before Dustin spoke.

"Are you a mind reader too, Rev?"

"Just anticipating that sexy voice."

"Where are you? What are you doing?"

"I just finished my three-hour broadcast that airs across the nation. I'm at my studio. We've got a country to save."

"It must be stressful, talking so much every day. How do you relax?"

"Politics is always downstream to culture, so for my job I have to see and review a lot of the products Hollywood manufactures in order to educate the public about the danger they represent to the average American. That's a mission from God and I take it seriously. However, between me and you, on a personal level, I enjoy many of these movies far more than I would ever let on to my listeners. Sometimes I relax at the cinema."

Through the window, Dustin saw Jamie Lee Curtis again, out by the pool. "I remember you liked *Caligula*. Malcom McDowell is a friend of mine." He watched Jamie Lee rub suntan lotion over her long legs. "That was you, right, who liked *Caligula*?"

Hank laughed. "My, you are just a big ball of perfection, aren't you?" He took a long sip of something. "You're right, Dustin. My job is stressful. I'm a very public face in a coming war. It may be a spiritual war, but it's a war nonetheless. I have powerful friends and benefactors above me that I have to make happy. Masses of Americans look to me for moral guidance. I can't let them down so I have to stay even-keeled."

"I'm a licensed masseuse, Reverend. I could give you a massage."

Hank gave Dustin an address in Encino. He told him to be there at 9 p.m.

Allison got out of her truck and followed Tania inside the Harvey Apartments on Santa Monica Boulevard. In the lobby, a thin black man sat on a stool smoking a peach flavored blunt and reading the *Wall Street Journal*. A decaying cigar box overflowing with rumpled bills was on the table beside him. Tania stepped over congealed dogshit on the carpet.

"What up, Tan?" he said

"Monroe, this place is disgusting."

Monroe shrugged. "Cleaning lady took the week off. Bitch's whole family got smoked in El Salvador."

Monroe gave Tania a key and Tania led Allison up the stairs and to the door of a second-floor apartment. Inside the place was dingy but not as bad as the lobby. Allison laid her backpack down on the couch.

Tania removed her jacket. "You like me, Allison. I can tell."

They were just a few feet apart. Allison struggled to find the proper response. She began to breathe heavily. "I still just want to talk."

"Of course." Tania took a chair from the dining room table and turned it to face Allison, who sat on the couch, beside her bag. Tania sat. "What else would you like to talk about?"

Allison stared at Tania's chest.

Tania said, "Maybe you'd like to watch me undress?"

Allison tried to respond. Gibberish came out.

Tania smiled. She unbuttoned her shirt and let it fall to the floor, exposing her pink bra. "Take all the time you need sweetie," Tania said. "You can have me. Later, you can have my roommate too, if you want."

Allison stood.

"Just pay me up front."

Allison reached into her bag and removed a bundle wrapped in a blue Galaxy Inn towel. She unwrapped it to reveal the tomahawk.

"What is that…?" Tania said.

Allison stepped closer and made a rail splitting swing down into Tania's right arm. Tania screamed. The blade carved smoothly through to where it stopped at the bone. A silent sputtering geyser of black blood spewed out.

Allison threw her off the chair and down onto her back, on the floor. She covered Tania's mouth with her hand and ripped the bloody tomahawk loose. A second, wider-spraying geyser of blood coated the carpet.

"Don't scream," Allison said.

Tania agreed with a nod.

"Your roommate. What does he call himself?" Allison took her hand away.

"Call himself?"

"What is his name?"

"Dustin Skye."

"Where can I find… Dustin Skye? What's your address?"

Tania looked at her bloody arm and was suddenly overcome by a rush of adrenaline. She jumped to her feet and pushed Allison's chest. Allison lost her balance and fell.

Tania looked at her arm and shrieked. A dog in a nearby apartment howled. Tania ran for the door and down the hall. Allison got up and followed.

Tania made it to the top of the staircase but twisted her ankle on the first step down and fell forward. She took a blood-spattered plunge and landed in the lobby below with a crunch. Her neck was twisted in a deeply unnatural angle.

Allison went back to the apartment, got her bag, and rushed to the window at the end of the hall. She heard violent screams and the sound of Monroe below calling Tania's name. Allison opened the window and took the fire escape down to the ground floor. She went around the building and made her way up the block to her pickup, which was parked in front of a meter on Santa Monica. Just when she unlocked the door, a strong hand grasped her shoulder.

"Eh, bitch!" The hand turned her around.

It was Monroe with a switchblade.

Allison swung the tomahawk into his neck. Monroe's eyes widened with surprise. He fell back and onto his side. He let go of the switchblade to cover his bleeding wound with his hands. Allison stepped over him and with two hands brought the tomahawk down again hard into his skull. People screamed and ran. Allison swung again with great force, and again. The white sun illuminated flecks of misting brain.

Allison's skin was now the color of beets. She looked around. Many had witnessed her kill. Someone clapped violently. It was a virginal looking man at the corner wearing a cardboard sign that said REPENT OR BURN. "Hosanna!" he shouted, raising his hands to the sky. "Don't stop there! Bring the flood!"

Back at the pool house, as he walked to his room, Dustin passed Tania's bedroom and saw that Laverne was in bed again with the TV on.

He called the answering service and learned that Frank needed to meet him in Hollywood at eight. He changed into a charcoal gray Armani suit with white pinstripes and drove to the lot of a Masonic temple on Hollywood between Highland and Orange.

The moon was full. Alpha and Amani stood beside Frank's Maroon Continental. Alpha opened the back door of the Lincoln so Dustin could enter.

Inside, Frank sat in the driver's seat smoking a Newport. Dustin had never seen Frank smoke inside his own car, out of fear of damaging the upholstery. In the back seat, next to Dustin, there was a middle-aged black man wearing cream-colored Persols and a conservative black trench coat of a brand Dustin couldn't place.

"My brother Milton here is a busy man so we won't take up much of his time," Frank said and tossed his Newport out the window. "You heard about Tania?"

Dustin got the feeling he was on display for Milton, whoever he was. "Last time I saw her was last night."

"That'll be the last time ever."

"What do you mean?"

"Tania's dead. Killed in a way that she won't have an open casket."

Dustin laughed nervously. "That's not funny."

"See me smiling?" Frank said.

Milton watched Dustin closely.

"She's really dead?" Dustin asked.

"She brought a trick into the Harvey. Trick tried to cut her arm off with a baby axe and pushed her down a flight of stairs. Broke her neck. Monroe tried to chase down who did it and got himself hacked to death in front of about a dozen witnesses."

"Baby axe?"

"A tomahawk," Milton said, speaking for the first time. His voice was slightly fey.

"Tania had her weekly date with the old redhead this morning," Frank said. "But she was already done with that by the time she walked into the Harvey. A woman was with her. You know who the woman was?"

"She didn't tell me anything."

"You've got no idea who this lady trick could have been?"

"No."

In the Gold's Gym in Hollywood Allison asked to sign up for a membership. She was directed to the desk of an employee named Ivan.

During the past few years she transformed her body. The key, she knew, was to keep up with her routine. Lately, on her journey, she hadn't been able to. A price had been paid for her laziness. She needed to get back to basics.

"I'm telling you, baby," Ivan said. He had a Swedish accent and was obviously on steroids. "There's an added level of attention brought to all the pretty ladies here. This is Hollywood. What I need to know is, do you need me to be your personal trainer?"

"Let me sign the paper." She leaned in. "Now."

Frank looked at Dustin. "Tania was one of my girls, which means she was a part of that deal I told you about. The one with the group of men who Milton represents. All the cash she brought in is gone. I'll just have to take that loss. I've been paying off the LAPD to keep me out of any investigations, so I'm not worried about that. But we need to show Milton's clients that our operation is under control. Your date with Hank Shepherd will have to be postponed."

"The Rev won't like that."

"Hank already knows and he understands it's just temporary," Milton said. "Hank likes you, Dustin. He told me so. The men above him are excited to meet you. They just don't like surprises."

Dustin said, "I'm willing to do what's needed."

Milton looked to Frank and nodded, satisfied.

"Go back home now, Dustin," Frank said. "Wait up for me."

Allison worked the leg press. Working out felt good. She moved on to leg extensions. While she did reps, she heard Tania's voice, that line from earlier:

"He's about as hot as guys get and we've never fooled around."

That sentence played in a loop:

The Dummars were from Willard, Ohio. Talking-in-tongues Pentecostals. Father was the principal of a Christian grade school. Mother was a homemaker. Kathleen was the first born. Next came Allison and Randy, two years and four years later. Allison and Randy had the same birthday. Sometimes Father dressed them up like twins for their joint celebration. Allison was always made up to look like Randy. Randy was never dressed like Allison.

Father favored Randy. When Allison was eight, she found a letter he'd written to his unborn son, the boy he hoped Allison would turn out to be. Father kept the letter, long after Allison was born a girl. She dreamed that she was a boy, so Father would love her. Randy, the male, was supposed to be a star athlete. Randy was no good at sports.

Randy would hide in Allison's room. Sometimes he watched when she changed. When they were alone in the woods, they swam naked in the river down at the end of the family property. Allison never spoke about these moments. She never told anyone that she liked watching her brother swim naked—

Allison moved on to the bench press. She was the only woman in this part of the gym. All the men watched her. Every man here seemed to be doing a cheap impression of Arnold Schwarzenegger. She did reps until she maxed out.

One summer night, Allison was called upon by her youth pastor to bring a book or record that was ungodly and throw it into a church bonfire. It was humid and rife with mosquitoes. Bites decimated her thin arms and legs. She'd brought a David Bowie album she knew Father would not approve of. When her turn came, she tossed it into the fire. She fought off tears. She loved that record, even if it was un-Christian. As she watched it burn, she prayed the Lord would deliver her from the endless feeling of being a prisoner inside her own body.

That night, Randy woke her up and said they should take a walk out to the river in the woods. She followed him and they sat down on their favorite log and looked out at the water. Randy leaned in and kissed her. After a moment, Allison pulled away.

"Don't worry," he said. "I'll show you."

He was gentle. Allison felt ecstasy. The next day, she felt shame. She told no one. Late one night the following week, Randy entered her room and they made silent love in her four-poster bed. Their parents were just down the hall—

Allison moved on to the free weights. Her biceps were still strong, something people noticed. There was an open space in front of a full wall mirror. She watched herself do curls.

Changes came to her body. When she was sure, she told Randy about the situation. Randy said he would take care of it. Allison wondered why God had seen it fit to put a brother like this in her life.

They created a fiction for their parents about a Christian youth retreat at Malabar Farm but instead they drove to a strip mall in Sandusky. Randy gave her instructions and an envelope.

She had no idea how Randy was able to manage this arrangement. She waited. A strange doctor arrived. He led her to the back room of a dentist's office with a floor covered in old editions of the Sandusky Register. He put her to sleep.

After the procedure, their lovemaking never resumed. Allison murdered a baby for him, and now Randy refused to touch her. He never even offered an explanation—

She decided to wrap up with cardio. On the way to the treadmill she passed a muscle-bound man who looked familiar and gave her an approving nod. Allison nodded back. She later realized he was Lou Ferrigno.

Allison became suspicious. Randy knew too much about the world. He coasted on his smile and charm. Her demented little brother was a disgrace to their family and to the Lord. He had turned her into a disgrace as well. She had killed her baby.

Allison began to secretly follow him. At night he got picked up by mysterious trucks that returned him at four in the morning. Another afternoon she found him under the middle school bleachers with Mr. Brusco, one of his teachers. Mr. Brusco's penis was in Randy's mouth.

She confronted him by the river that night.

"You're evil," she said. "Father and Mother need to know. I'm going to tell them."

"They won't believe you," he said. "I'm their special baby boy."

Allison walked back home, leaving Randy there on the log. When she got home, she lost her courage. She couldn't tell Mother and Father yet. She would wait until morning. When morning came, Randy was gone without a word.

She hadn't seen him since the river—

Sweat soaked her and the treadmill. Allison had come a long way. Out in the world, she had power. She was becoming less afraid of using it.

The pool house was empty. Dustin poured himself an Absolut on the rocks and drank it in the kitchen. He focused hard and tried to summon his old survival instincts, the way he naturally behaved long ago, when his life wasn't so casually touched by fortune every day.

Laverne returned home. She looked worried and exhausted. She knew Tania was dead. Dustin could tell.

"You've talked to the cops?" he said.

"Yeah. They called and ordered me come to the police station. Pigs treated me like I had something to do with it. I didn't tell 'em shit."

"They want to talk to me?"

"Your name didn't come up."

Dustin exhaled a deep breath. "I'm really sorry."

Laverne started crying. "I used to have faith, but I lost it." She wiped away tears.

Dustin knew about Laverne's life as a Panther. "Belief gets you nowhere," he said.

Laverne walked to the bathroom and opened the medicine cabinet. Dustin followed with his vodka. Laverne took two Libriums from a bottle and dry swallowed them.

"My faith came back when I met Tania." She cried some more. "She was so goddamn smart and foxy and full of life."

"I was always impressed by the relationship you two had. It was brave."

"But I just sat and agreed to let her fuck whoever she wanted. I wasn't okay with it, but I pretended like I was. What kind of a way is that to behave with someone you love? Tania sold herself every day and I pretended like after that, we could still have something special." Laverne fell to her knees and sobbed.

Dustin put his drink down. "I've got to tell you something."

Laverne looked up, teary-eyed.

"We don't know who did this. You should leave. There's a chance more bad things could happen."

Moving slow, Laverne got up. "I'll get packed now." She got some toilet paper and wiped her tears away. Now she looked determined to leave the pool house. "I'm sad, but you know I'm not really surprised. Deep down I always knew some guy would kill her."

"It wasn't a guy."

"What?"

"The killer was a woman."

Back down on Santa Monica, far west of the Harvey, Allison asked random street boys if they knew a hustler by the name of Dustin Skye. She got a lot of brush-offs and nos. One boy said he'd heard of Dustin but didn't know him or how to find him.

Everyone was jumpy. A tomahawk killer was on the loose. It was in the papers and on TV. Regardless, Allison felt measured and in control of her strength.

Two LAPD patrolmen stopped her in front of a neon-lit pornography shop on Santa Monica and Poinsettia. Her tomahawk was wrapped up inside the bag on her back.

"Everything good, miss?"

"Yes, everything's good."

"Can we help you?"

"I'm looking for my brother. I don't know if you can help me with that."

"Where'd you see him last?"

"In Ohio, years ago."

The officers looked at each other.

"I heard that he was living here in Hollywood, on the streets, selling himself. I thought that some of these people might know him." She showed them the old picture of Randy.

"It's not safe to be out here among these degenerates, especially not at night," the first officer said. "Your best chance at finding him will be to file a report at the station tomorrow morning. You'll want to speak with someone in missing persons."

"Thank you," Allison said.

They parted ways.

Howser parked their Matador on the Strip in front of a meter, then he and La Rocca walked to the Whisky a Go Go. Unwashed punks were everywhere, headed to the Whisky for a show. The marquee said a band called The Germs played tonight.

Howser spotted the woman they were after. She was a curvy white woman with a red mohawk, torn leggings, and a Black Flag shirt. She smoked a Kool.

"You Nancy?" Howser said.

"Blowjob Nancy," she said. Nancy was a hooker CI who had been referred to them by Vice. "You know, after Nancy Reagan. Back in the day she used to be called Blowjob Nancy. Mrs. Reagan used to suck the best dick in all of Hollywood. Now I do."

Howser went silent. Like his partner, Howser was a Republican. Generally, he avoided talking politics, especially while doing business as a screenwriter. But the trajectory of Ronald Reagan's golden life was an inspiration to him. The man was living proof that America was the greatest country in the world. Reagan would want Howser to make money, so Howser wrote scripts that would sell. He didn't like hearing rogue fragments in the official narrative of the Gipper's biography, but something about Nancy's tone told him this tidbit was true.

"Want to talk in the car?" La Rocca said to Nancy. "It can't be good for you, being seen with us."

"No. Irish Karen was a friend. We worked parties together. She was out here on her own. No one deserves to get their head kicked in and dumped in a trash can. If anyone out here's got a problem with me helping you guys, they can kiss my big, beautiful ass. Just give me the money."

"First, we get the information, then you'll get your money," La Rocca said. "When was the last time you saw Karen?"

"The night she died."

Howser got his head back in the game. "You see what happened to her?"

She stubbed out her Kool on the sidewalk. "I saw her at Sunset and La Brea, talking to this weird looking woman. They walked off together."

"Where'd they go?" La Rocca said.

"Toward Hollywood."

"How was this woman weird-looking?" Howser said.

She thought about it. "Hard to say. I was across the street, half a block away. At first, I thought this lady might be some square missionary, trying to save Karen's soul. But the more I watched her I could tell she had a seriously weird vibe. Much more so than the average Jesus freaks. I've never seen her around before, but I'd recognize her if I saw her again. She was muscular, like a bodybuilder."

Dustin had settled into the hot tub by the time Frank unhooked the gate and went back to Dustin's part of the property. Frank brought a chaise lounge over toward the edge of the water and sat. His tie was loose around his neck.

"I pay for this pool house, but I barely ever come back here," Frank said.

The water in the hot tub bubbled. "I still can't believe she's gone, man."

"Tania was unfocused, living out a fantasy about getting ahead in show business or whatever. I can't figure out why this happened. I've been reaching out to the streets for answers, but so far, I haven't heard a thing. The regulars at the Harvey don't know shit. None of the people in the neighborhood gave me anything useful. We're still looking, but it seems like it was just... some random woman." Frank was mystified. "Tania's the second girl to get killed on the streets in twenty-four hours."

"Who's the other girl?"

"Some bitch that worked Sunset and La Brea independent is what I heard."

"You think the two are connected?" Dustin was struck by a feeling that they were. He wasn't sure why.

"I don't know. What I *do* know is that the leaders we need to impress right now are turned off by these bodies. We've got to control their perception of our business, steer it away from the negative. If these men see us dole out justice swiftly, then they'll understand that they can trust us. To make ourselves look good, we've got to show them a body."

"Show who a body?"

"*Focus*, Dustin. The men Milton represents. The top dogs. These men I speak of will still hire us if we can prove that we handled this. I've made a plan."

Dustin's eyes widened. "Involving what body?"

"Involving the body of whoever killed Tania and Monroe."

"You just said we don't know who that was."

"I said we're still looking. We could be patient and let the investigation run its course, but according to Milton, our potential employers aren't the patient type. Maybe we'll figure out who the woman with the tomahawk was. But for now you're right—we don't know. We have to give them someone anyway."

Dustin didn't like the sound of this. "Who?"

Frank waited. "Like I've told you, that Skull and Bones motherfucker Clark Debussy is also competing against us. He's who."

"You're going to kill Clark Debussy?"

"He's got that woman who works for him. His cousin, Helen." Dustin knew Helen Debussy. He'd seen her around sometimes at Ma Maison and the Polo Lounge. "After we smoke Clark, we'll make it look like she's the bitch with a tomahawk. We'll blame the Harvey on her and eliminate our only real competition at the same time. As far as I can tell, that's the best offense in this situation."

"I don't know, man," Dustin said.

Frank stood and took off his tie completely. "I didn't work my ass off getting this close to real money only to just sit back and let some random shit pull the whole deal out of our hands. We've got to make an offensive move."

Dustin finally felt the fogginess of his brain beginning to clear. His old and familiar survival instincts finally rose to the surface. "We?"

"Clark would never trust me. I've got to send you."

"Why would Clark trust me?"

"You're the golden boy, the man of the moment. If Clark sees you want to meet him, Clark will take that meeting." Frank opened his suit to show his holstered .38. Frank didn't usually carry a piece. "For this gig, you'll need a different kind of gun."

Dustin wondered if Frank was playing some kind of game. "This might really help us get this mysterious contract?"

"Of course. There's no might. Trust me."

Dustin had never felt less trusting of Frank. Taking Clark Debussy out of the picture would solve some problems, but not the actual threat. "But the real killer is still out there," he said.

"We won't forget about her."

Dustin looked up at the stars. You could see a few from where he sat in this hot tub.

"Everything was going so good," he said.

It was Hollywood station, late at night. Howser and La Rocca were called into the captain's office. Their shift was almost up.

Howser wanted to go home and work on a script. He worked best late at night, when the world was quiet. Writing blew off steam.

When they walked in, Captain Hudson sat behind his desk in his swivel chair unwrapping a pack of Tums. He had them take seats in the two chairs opposite him. "This is about the double at the Harvey," he said.

"RHD caught it, right?" Howser said.

"They read the description of your perp on the dumpster job," Hudson said. "A bodybuilding missionary?"

"Who fed them that?" La Rocca said.

Hudson shrugged. "The description of your assailant matches the witness descriptions of theirs. They made an attempt to dump their case. Claimed a whore and some pimp as victims weren't high profile enough for their roster this month. They succeeded. Since both bodies fall under our jurisdiction, I was asked to provide my two best detectives, which is obviously you two. So, you're being assigned to the Harvey as well."

Howser said, "That's bullshit." He knew this was RHD using all their political juice to cut loose from a case they had no chance of clearing.

"The Higher Ups have already ruled. All three bodies are now yours. Close them promptly. A contact at the *Times* told me they've already given your perp a name. Don't give the media a chance to sink their vampire fangs into this thing."

"What name?" La Rocca said.

"Lady Tomahawk." Hudson chewed Tums. "That's gonna sell some papers."

Allison paced back and forth, clenching the handle of the tomahawk. She pictured herself using it in combat in the jungles of Vietnam. She threw it up in the air and caught it. She vowed to get better at handling it.

Further trawling on the streets felt dangerous. She'd gotten many suspicious looks. Still, she couldn't leave. Not after all she'd already done.

First things first. The most pressing problem was money. After the gym membership fees, tomorrow would be the last night she could afford her room. She needed a lifeline.

She decided to call home.

"What is it?" Father sounded groggy. It was 3 a.m. in Ohio.

Allison laid the tomahawk on the corner of the bed. "Daddy? It's me."

"Allison? Are you okay?"

"Sorry to call so late."

"Where are you?"

"Los Angeles."

Father waited. "You really went all the way to California?"

"Randy's here."

"Have you seen him?"

"I've met people that know him." She realized she needed to sound like her old self. "He needs someone to bring him back under the banner of heaven. It should be me."

"I almost can't believe it." His voice sounded full of joy. "My son."

"Father, it's just…"

"Just what?"

"This trip hasn't been easy. California is expensive and I'm running out of money."

"I told you that might happen."

"Could you loan me some?" she asked.

"I don't have any money to give you."

"None?"

"None," he said.

"Didn't you just go visit Kathleen and Evan in Delaware?"

"We just got back Saturday."

"You have the money for that, but none for your son?"

The trapped cat in the wall began meowing again. It had been quiet since this morning. Its cries were slower and more labored.

"I'm not going to do this with you in the middle of the night," Father said. "If you need money, ask the Lord to provide. If you see my son, tell him I love him."

Father hung up.

Allison grabbed the tomahawk from the bed, twirled it again and caught it. The more she practiced handling it, the more comfortable she felt.

She walked to where the noise of the cat was coming from and, with the tomahawk, made a square incision into the wall. Plaster bits spilled on the floor. When the square chunk was loose, she ripped it out. In the dark she saw a small and emaciated tortoiseshell cat, a baby, looking up at her. Upon seeing her, the cat chirped. Allison reached all the way in but couldn't get her, so she cut out a larger chunk of the wall. Then she scooped up the small animal into her arms. She cradled it and paced with it until it stopped crying. Then Allison took some sheets from the bed, put them in the bathtub and made the cat a nice bed.

It got loud again. The cat was hungry. Allison promised herself that she would take care of this cat forever, no matter the cost. There was an all-night grocery store on Hollywood that had pet supplies, so she decided to go out and get some food and a litter box.

She would worry about money tomorrow.

In the parking lot of the Galaxy, she saw the passenger side door of a truck open. A hooker wearing a silver haired wig and a faded sequin dress stepped out. Allison watched her walk across the lot and give her money to a black pimp standing by a Cadillac parked on the corner. She'd witnessed scenes like this a few different times since she'd been in L.A. The pimp counted bills. It was a lot of cash.

Three

It was early in the evening and Clark Debussy was sleeping between two naked teenage boys in the second-floor bedroom of his beachfront Malibu mansion when his cousin and manager Helen knocked on his door.

"Fuck off," Clark said, his face buried in a satin pillow.

Both of the boys were aspiring actors hungry for work in Clark's dad's movie studio. Helen had arranged their visit under the pretense of having a meeting about being in a new mega-budget sci-fi drama the studio was producing. Clark, despite having no authority in any casting decisions at his father's studio, had greeted them wearing nothing but his black Versace robe with barocco sleeves, given them ludes and Dom Perignon, and taken them both to bed.

Helen cracked the door open, and stuck her head in. "I know, but hear me out."

"Saturdays are my off day."

"Even for Dustin Skye?"

Clark raised his head. Drool streamed down his chin.

"Yes," Helen said. "Dustin called."

"About what?"

"About meeting with you. In private, tonight."

"What was his tone?"

Helen thought about it. "A little worried. Like he thought you could help him."

"He's holding on the line now?"

"Yes. What should I say?"

Clark smacked one of the boys on the ass. "Time to go!" He looked at Helen. "You should say one hour."

Walking down Western Avenue, Allison passed a newsstand and saw the front page of the morning's edition of the *Los Angeles Times*:

Lady Tomahawk Kills Two on Santa Monica: More Suspected.

She was not the type of person who appeared in newspaper headlines. She thought about the name as she marched deep into the neon-lit streets once again and decided that she liked it.

On Santa Monica, a black and white LAPD patrol car cruised slowly. Allison stayed calm and kept walking. They passed her by.

Back at the Harvey Apartments, she watched strangers in the area. She began engaging with them again, playing the part of the virtuous missionary character she'd spent so much time rehearsing in her room. She was getting good at meeting new people in L.A. She introduced herself to people and asked them how they were doing.

Most blew her off. She was used to that by now. Eventually, across the street from the Harvey, she encountered a thin white woman with ratty brown hair.

"Looks like you're having a hard time," Allison said.

"I heard you talking to those other girls," she said. "You're some kind of missionary."

"What's your name?"

"Ginny."

Allison pointed at the Harvey. "Hear about what happened yesterday?"

"It put heat on my game. I haven't been able to get back in."

"You use the rooms?"

She nodded. Allison saw needle marks and bruises on her arms.

"Was the man who got killed your pimp?"

"I paid Monroe thirty percent of every fuck to be able to use the room. He said I wasn't foxy enough to be a part of his stable. Still, here's better than the Paradise Motel, where I used to work out of. Over there they took fifty."

Ginny's worried eyes reminded Allison of the cat. "You need protection. Someone strong to look out for you."

Clark looked over his reflection one last time in the mirror. There were spots on the lenses of his tortoiseshell Christian Dior glasses. He cleaned them off with the end of his robe.

The doorbell rang.

Dustin wore a long-sleeved black and white striped Commes des Garçons shirt, white Brioni pants, and a black Armani bomber jacket. He walked in and took some time to close the door behind him. "I didn't know Dolph worked for you," Dustin said.

Dolph, the man outside, was one of Clark's security guards. It was his job to frisk anyone that came close to the house. He was sitting out front in a Mercedes 450 SL, the same car Richard Gere drove in *American Gigolo*. Everywhere Dustin went these days, people seemed to be trying to emulate the style of Julian Kaye.

"You and Dolph know each other?" Clark said.

"We were at the same escort service years ago. I was just getting started." He took off his Porsche Carreras and put them in his front pocket.

"We've been rivalling a long time," Clark said.

Dustin shook his head. "You and Frank have. Not me."

Clark led Dustin into the nearby living room. There was a bar. "Dom?"

"Sure."

"Let's be honest, though," Clark said as he popped a fresh bottle and filled two crystal flutes. "You've talked shit about me."

"All I said was that I didn't want to turn tricks for you," Dustin said.

Clark took a shaker full of a powdered yellow substance and shook a bit of it into the top of his drink, watching it dissolve. He held the shaker up over the other flute. "Quaalude chips?"

Dustin shook his head no. "Frank's been good to me. He treats me straight. I give him his cut and he lets me be. When one of my clients gave me my Ferrari, he let me keep it."

Clark handed Dustin his flute and held up his own. "To protectors," he said. They clinked. "Still, when the biggest cock in L.A. trashes me, I lose credibility."

"I was doing right by my manager." Dustin took a drink.

"It was hard to stomach, that someone with my connections was playing catch-up to some coon independent. My family alone should have sent me to the top of the food chain at whatever line of work I chose. These days I'm ahead, though. My stables become far bigger than Frank's has ever been."

It was true Clark now had a longer roster of workers than Frank, but the quality of Clark's first-string line-up couldn't beat Frank's third. Clark ran a bunch of pool boys and strippers from the Valley.

"Frank's losing his grip," Dustin said.

"Do tell," Clark said.

"Two of our people got killed by some lady with a tomahawk. Right when this deal with these rich men who value privacy is about to go through."

"That's what he told you? That the deal was about to go through?" Clark laughed.

"Yes, and I believed him."

"But you don't anymore?"

"He's losing his grip. He doesn't know what he's doing."

Clark put his drink down on the bar. "Is this an audition?"

Dustin put his drink down on the bar. "I want the part."

Clark smiled. "Kneel."

Dustin got on his knees.

"Apologize for everything bad you ever said about me."

"I'm sorry, Daddy. I take it all back."

Allison and Ginny went to a Chinese food and donut shop on St. Andrews. Ginny was a regular. Allison bought her a coffee and two glazed donuts.

"I came here from Ohio to find my brother," Allison said.

"He ran away?"

Allison nodded. "He was in trouble so he took off."

"In trouble for what?"

"For hurting me."

"How?"

"That doesn't matter. You see, our parents saw him as the special one. The only boy. I wanted them to treat me the way they treated him. I was always by his side because I was jealous. He sniffed out the weakness of my mind and made his move."

Ginny nodded, listening closely. "Yeah?"

"Even though I was older, somehow, he was strong enough to hurt me. When I got the courage, I looked him in the eye and told him I was going to expose his evil."

"Did you?"

"He ran away first. After he was gone, I let myself be scared and confused. Terrified of the world. Then I decided to not let anyone hurt me again. I became physically strong. I lifted weights every day." Allison flexed her right bicep. "Over time, I accepted that I had to actually confront him. He's somewhere here in L.A."

"I bet you'll find him," Ginny said.

"I got strong because no one was there to look out for me. Now I clear my own path. No one gets in my way." Allison reached across the table and touched Ginny's hand. "I'll look out for you now."

"Look at me, thinking you were a missionary," Ginny said.

Clark looked down at Dustin, there on his knees. "You want to jump ship?"

"Be my new Captain," Dustin said.

"I have to test the merchandise."

"Usually, I start with a massage. I'm licensed, you know."

"We'll forgo that." Clark opened his robe.

Dustin crawled forward and took Clark in his mouth.

The first man Ginny picked up for Allison was a Canadian auto mechanic from Monrovia named Beau. He sat on the edge of Allison's bed while Ginny kneeled in front of him and sucked his cock. Allison sat in the corner, watching.

The tortoiseshell cat was in the bathroom, sleeping in the tub.

Ginny had been street walking at Hollywood and Highland when Beau flagged her down from his car. Ginny got in and directed him back to the Galaxy. While they waited in the parking lot, Allison made an arrangement with the manager, which was easy, and they came up here to the room. At first, Beau expected Allison to leave. But Allison decided to stay and watch. Beau didn't argue. Allison had never watched other people have sex before. It was exciting to her.

Beau spoke between moans: "My fiancé Angel and I are pillars of our church community. God's been good to us, or at least that's what I tell people. I run my own shop and I'm only twenty-three. Angel thinks I'm a virgin. She thinks I'm saving it for my wedding night." Beau pulled Ginny's head away and looked her in the eyes. "Get into the bed." Ginny complied.

Allison had long known that Randy led a secret life of wild and secret sexual assignations. He'd somehow found a way to achieve that in middle-of-nowhere Ohio. Since coming to L.A., it now seemed to Allison like everyone in the world had a secret compartmentalized portion of their life where they didn't bottle up their desires but just let them roam free. Allison saw freedom and money in this new world.

Beau was gone now and, Ginny, still naked, walked into the bathroom to clean up. The cat began to chirp from inside the tub. Allison came in and picked it up.

"Have you decided what you'll name her?" Ginny asked.

"Not yet," Allison said. "While I think about it, go get me some more money."

Three fast gunshots popped off out front. Clark pushed Dustin away. He ran for cover behind the bar. His robe was still open, his erection exposed.

Dustin crawled to the corner and pulled up the right leg of his pants. A small .25, given to him by Frank, was holstered to his ankle. He drew it. Dolph could have frisked him earlier but didn't bother. They were old friends. The gun was so small it was hard to notice if you weren't looking closely.

"Clark?" Helen called from upstairs. "Clark? What the fuck is going on? Did you hear that?" She rushed down. "Clark?"

Clark rose from behind the bar.

When Dustin got a visual on his target, he raised the .25 and aimed it at Clark's face. But he remembered Frank's warning: to do dependable damage this gun needed to be much closer when firing it.

The front door swung open hard.

It was unlocked, as Dustin left it.

Alpha and Amani, wearing track suits and plastic gloves, entered. Alpha, a few feet from Helen there at the bottom of the staircase, aimed his .45 at her and pulled the trigger twice. Helen was hit in her throat and fell back, clutching her wound and gargling.

Amani stepped forward. He saw Clark standing behind the bar. He let go with three shots into the chest. Clark fell to his knees and toppled over.

Helen convulsed on the ground. Alpha stepped closer and fired again into the center of her forehead. Her body went still.

Seeing that it was all over, Dustin lowered his .25.

"You good?" Amani said.

"I'll be fine. Yeah." Dustin returned the .25 to his ankle holster.

Amani took off the backpack he was wearing and removed a tomahawk from it. He held it up for Dustin to see. He wrapped Helen's fingers around the handle. Then he left the weapon beside Helen's hand.

Dustin followed Alpha and Amani out the door. In the driveway Dolph was still in his parked Mercedes but now had three bullet holes in his head.

The cat sat in Allison's lap purring while she counted cash. It was four in the morning and Ginny had been with two more men since Beau. When Allison was finished, she looked up. "You did good." She put the cash in the front pouch of her bag.

Ginny looked around. "This room is nicer than the Harvey."

Allison put the cat down onto the bed, and then reached into her bag and took out the tomahawk. Earlier she had polished the blade. It gleamed.

Ginny looked at it. She didn't seem surprised. "I had a feeling you were her."

Her meant *Lady Tomahawk.*

Allison threw the tomahawk up in the air and caught it smoothly, demonstrating her accelerating proficiency. "Tania, the girl from the Harvey, knew my brother. They were roommates. I wanted to know where they lived but she died before she could help me."

Ginny gulped.

"Anyone who tries to stop me, I'll hack away." Allison put the tomahawk down on the bed. "He's calling himself Dustin Skye. What else do you know that might help me?"

"Dustin Skye? He's the hustler *American Gigolo* was based on. He's hot shit."

Allison took a deep breath—the wild life her brother was living.

"It's a movie with Richard Gere that came out earlier this year. It's just what I heard."

"What else did you hear?"

Ginny thought. "There's this punk chick I know who mainly works the Strip. She gives alleyway blowjobs and lets the punk gangs pay to run trains on her, shit like that. She's been busted a handful of times but gets out of it by snitching to the Vice. Apparently, she saw you talking to Karen. She told a few other girls about it and it got around."

"I used Karen to get to Tania," Allison said. "If this punk girl was a friend of Karen's, who knew Tania, then maybe she also knows my brother."

Ginny thought. "It's possible."

"What's her name?"

"Blowjob Nancy."

"What?"

"Like I said, she's a punk. I think if you asked her why she goes by that name she would say that she was being transgressive or something like that." The cat, warming up to Ginny, crawled into her lap and purred.

"I've decided to name her Jane," Allison said. Jane was her grandmother's name. It was also the name she would have given the baby who was scraped out of her years ago.

That night, Ginny and Jane slept beside her. It was the first time in her life that Allison hadn't spent a night sleeping alone. Randy had always returned to his own bed whenever he was through with her. Besides him, there was no one else.

It was a luxury beachfront house in Malibu, the scene of a fresh triple homicide. Howser and La Rocca were at Clark Debussy's. The L.A. County Sheriffs, who had jurisdiction over the city of Malibu, had been first on the scene.

"What a cluster fuck," Howser said, looking at the fresh bodies.

County techs milled about. Captain Barrera, the lead Homicide investigator at Malibu Station for the L.A. County Sheriffs, had called them because of the tomahawk found beside Helen Debussy's body. The partners had driven straight over from Hollywood and made their way past the gauntlet of media personalities and their crews that were gathered in the street.

Howser knew the names of all the big studio heads. He read the trades daily. Clark Debussy's dad, Henry Debussy, was a big deal at Warner Brothers and his son was a known scumbag pimp with high profile clients and expensive lawyers on his payroll. He bet that an army of publicists and high-powered fixers employed by

Debussy's wealthy parents would soon be descending to make sure that this story was killed in the press.

La Rocca walked over Helen's body and kneeled down to look closely at the tomahawk by her right hand. "So," he said. "It appears that Helen Debussy, the cousin of Clark Debussy, was our mysterious Lady Tomahawk. She went out and killed some people…"

"Then someone came here and killed for payback," Captain Barrera said.

Howser looked back at Clark Debussy's body, behind the bar, and then back at Helen. "She doesn't look strong enough to throw a tomahawk."

"I'll bet the victims were competitors of her cousin and that's why she targeted them," La Rocca said. "But why with a tomahawk? When you're this rich, why not send someone to do the killing for you, like the dead muscle out front?"

Captain Barrera said, "We've got at least three unsolved 187s going back four years that I think Debussy ordered. His past MO was never anything like a tomahawk."

Howser thought. "Helen Debussy works for her asshole cousin, and here's her body with a tomahawk, which she was carrying at the time someone busted in shooting."

"It sounds like one of your movie plots, like someone's making up a story," La Rocca said. "And you're right. She doesn't look strong enough to throw a tomahawk."

Howser said, "Let's track down Nancy again and show her a six pack with a picture of Helen here mixed in. See who she picks."

Dustin drove under a full moon. He arrived at Damon's restaurant in Glendale, parked and went in. It was late.

The lighting was dark red. Closing time was near. He found Frank's booth and took a seat.

"What are we doing in Glendale, man?" Dustin said. "Are you ever coming home?"

"I like this place." Frank was on his third Mai Tai. He ate a rare steak with a side of coconut fried shrimp. "I grew up around here. Went to Glendale High, just like John Wayne. My mother forced me to go to church just up the street from here."

The waitress approached. Dustin looked at the cocktail menu and ordered a Singapore Sling. She smiled at him flirtatiously and cleared away empty glasses.

"I spoke to that closet case Milton," Frank said. "I blamed the whole mess at the Harvey on Clark Debussy. He bought it. Hopefully his Jesus freak clients do too."

"What do you think they would say if they heard you talk like that?"

"Doesn't matter because they never will. I really am a Republican, but as far as they're concerned, I'm on board with all that Christian shit too, and so are you."

Dustin said, "I chickened out."

"What do you mean?"

He leaned in, whispering, "I left the door open, but I couldn't shoot. I told myself I couldn't get close enough. The truth is I was scared."

"Don't worry about it." Frank sawed into his bloody steak. "I had Alpha and Amani there in case that happened. They took care of it. That's all that matters now."

Frank pushed his plate of shrimp Dustin's way.

Dustin didn't take any. "Now all we need to know is who Lady Tomahawk really is."

Frank pulled his shrimp back. "I still haven't heard a thing."

Dustin's Singapore Sling arrived. He waited until the waitress was gone. "I think whoever really killed Tania and Monroe could be ready to give us more trouble and you just want to move on, pretend like our real problem is handled because you just killed some dude you wanted to kill anyway."

"I'll protect you, Dustin. But I can't eliminate all of the threat. If you wake up in the morning, there's no guarantee you make it all the way through the day." Frank downed his third Mai Tai.

Dustin waited for more. "That's it?"

"I'm going to be out of town for a while so I can let the heat from this Clark Debussy hit cool down. We stirred up some shit."

"Where are you going?"

"Palm Springs. I'll be finalizing the deal over the phone."

"So I'm just supposed to go back to the pool house and stay there all alone? You're leaving me and everyone else who works for you to fend for ourselves?"

"No one will know you were involved with what we did today. Tania's dead, but you didn't need her."

Frank paid the bill and they walked outside.

"You're the star, Dustin." In the parking lot the ivory light from the full moon covered Dustin's face. His blank eyes could have been the eyes of a doll. "All of L.A. wants you. Just focus on being your same old self."

Four

Allison waited alone in her parked pickup on Leland Way in Hollywood, across the street from a run-down Victorian house rented out by a popular punk band that let everyone come and go. Ginny said it was called Skinhead Manor.

Ginny returned to the car. "Nancy'll meet us out back."

Allison got her backpack and followed Ginny down an alley to the backyard where a ragged orange couch and a few other ramshackle pieces of furniture were arranged. Empty beer cans and liquor bottles littered the ground.

The back screen door kicked open and Nancy walked out holding a torn-open box of Schlitz. Her clothes were ripped and filthy. She sat in a lawn chair, reached into the box and opened a fresh can. "You wanted to talk to me?" Nancy was still waking up.

"You remember me?" Allison said.

Nancy looked Allison over. It came to her.

"Do you, Nancy? Do you know my name?"

Nancy burped nervously. "You're Lady Tomahawk," she said.

Allison waited.

"Want a drink?" Nancy said. She raised a can. She wanted to cut the tension.

Allison looked at the can, there in Nancy's hand. She had never before in her life drank alcohol. All the people she had ever known in Ohio were sober Christians. This moment seemed to her as good a time as any to try it out. She took the can, cracked it open, and tasted it. Nancy handed Ginny a Schlitz as well.

"You knew Karen?"

"Karen was a friend." Nancy looked worried. People on the street knew she snitched for Vice. "I wasn't trying to start trouble. I just felt bad about what happened to her."

Allison downed a big slug and felt the beer flow through her system. "It's none of your business what happened to her." She waited, giving Nancy a chance to challenge her. No challenge came. "What's good for you is to answer all my questions."

"What else do you want to know?"

"Did you know any other people in Karen's life? Did you know friends of hers?"

"You mean, like Tania?"

"Yes, like Tania."

"I knew who Tania was."

"What about Dustin Skye?"

Nancy paused. "Tania was his roommate."

"So, you know him too."

"We've never met but I know about him. They say his cock is a foot long."

Allison gulped. "Where does he live?"

"In a pool house. Somewhere in Studio City. Their manager lives in the main house."

She was so close now. "What's the address?"

"I don't know. Karen and I worked a party in that neighborhood a few months ago and I remember her pointing out where Tania and Dustin lived when we drove by." Nancy saw the displeasure in Allison's face. "It was a while ago, but if you took me up there, I think I could point it out to you. At least I could get you in the right area."

Allison chugged more Schlitz. She realized she was starting to get drunk. "How often do you talk to the cops?"

"When they pay me. Sometimes I need money to survive."

"You won't be talking to them anymore. Understand?"

"Yes."

Allison realized that Nancy would become her second girl on the street. If Randy could thrive in this world, so could she. She crushed the empty can and tossed it over her shoulder.

Dustin woke up late in the empty pool house and spent a few hours drifting on a raft in Frank's pool, working on his tan. Then he spent time reorganizing his clothes, his shoes, his watches, his jewelry. After, he washed his Ferrari.

Late in the afternoon he called Hank Shepherd. Hank was at his radio show and had once again just signed off for the day.

"Glad to hear from you," Hank said.

They confirmed that their new date would be tomorrow night, at the same Encino address.

"I can't wait," Hank said. "Milton mentioned that there was some trouble."

"No trouble," Dustin said. "Everything's fine now."

"I don't think Clark Debussy will be missed too badly."

"Clark wasn't trustworthy. Not like us." Dustin waited. "Can I ask you a question?"

"Depends on the question."

"Are you and your friends like the Freemasons? Is that it?"

"The Freemasons don't have power anymore. That's not what we are."

"What are you then?"

"I'll explain what I can." Hank cleared his throat. "As I've told you, there's a war on for the future of America, Dustin. A spiritual war. Some people think that they can ignore it or stay neutral, but each and every one of God's creatures will have to pick a side. My brothers and I are all men in positions of power with a common goal, a mission from God we are on the cusp of achieving. But just because God put us where we are, that doesn't mean he created us perfect. We're all sinners. It's imperative that the world not learn about our contradictions, because the forces of Satan would use them against us. My associates and I need to maintain our warrior status, but also live with the urges inside us."

"So, you're in good standing as a Christian?" Dustin said. "I was born in the church and that's not what I was taught. I was taught that everything was black and white."

"I am a good Christian. You can still be one too."

Dustin thought about the church and all the times he had wondered if he could ever really outrun the God his parents taught him to fear since he was an infant. He had never sought anything but material goods from the women and men he went on dates with.

"Maybe sometime you could help me with that," Dustin said.

"Help you with what, son?"

"On how to be a good Christian, after backsliding." Dustin was surprised at his own words.

"Yes, yes," Hank said, sounding aroused. "That's an approach I like."

Howser got a location on Nancy from another Vice CI, a girl who worked as a cashier at a punk clothing shop on Melrose called Poseur. The CI knew Nancy, who shopped there regularly. She confirmed Nancy was there now, browsing the aisles. He and La Rocca sped over with their bubble siren blaring. They arrived just as Nancy was coming out of the twin red Poseur doors, below a sign that said, "Fuck Parents." She carried a full bag.

"What do you guys want?" she said.

Groups of punks stood in front of the store, passing out handbills to pedestrians. Nancy looked nervous about being seen talking to the cops. La Rocca raised a picture of Helen Debussy and held it close to her face.

"Who's that?" Nancy said

"You don't recognize her?"

"Should I?"

"She's not the woman you saw walk off with Karen the night she got her head smashed in and left in a dumpster?" La Rocca said.

"No, that's not her."

Howser looked inside her bag at a spiked belt, bondage pants, and a studded bracelet. "What's with all the new gear, Nancy?'

Nancy looked down at the sidewalk. "I was told to upgrade."

"Upgrade? Why? By who?"

She hesitated. "When we spoke before, I meant it when I said I wanted to find out whoever killed Karen. But my situation is different now." Some punks watched her suspiciously. "Can we go to the car this time? It'll be my ass if it gets back to her that I'm talking to you again."

They walked her up the block to the Matador. Nancy sat in back.

"You need to talk to us, Nancy," Howser said. "Did Lady Tomahawk contact you? Is she why you're suddenly so afraid?"

Nancy nodded.

"What's her real name?"

"She didn't say."

"Start at the beginning," Howser said.

"She found me at Skinhead Manor. Said she was looking for this high-class hustler boy with a big rep. Dustin Skye. Dustin is the roommate of Tania, the girl Lady Tomahawk killed at the Harvey. She didn't say why she's after him."

Howser recalled that the address on Tania's driver's license found at the Harvey had turned out to be incorrect. Tania's girlfriend Laverne, who'd been questioned by RHD just after the murder, had not been cooperative and refused to reveal where she and Tania had really been living.

"And?" Howser said.

"The boy lives in a pool house in Studio City. Karen knew where and pointed it out to me once, because the digs were so nice. The lady had me get into her truck and drove me up there so I could tell her where it was. I couldn't remember the exact spot but I pointed out the right street, or at least what I thought was the right street. She seemed satisfied. When she dropped me off back in Hollywood, she told me I work for her now. Said my clothes were too dirty for one of her girls, so here I am. The whole thing is weird."

Howser had his pen and notepad out. "Describe her in detail," he said. "And her truck."

Dustin stepped out of the steam shower. Now that he lived alone, he chose not to cover himself with a towel. He stopped at the base of the stairs.

A woman was in the pool house, sitting at the dining room table.

"Hello, Randy," she said.

Dustin let out a deep breath. "How did you find me?"

"Some entertainment reporter called the house in Willard. I happened to take the call. They said you were a secret consultant in Hollywood for a film about male prostitutes and that you were an expert because *you* were a prostitute. They wanted a comment from your family. I told Father and Mother that I was going to find you. I never told them about the call. I've still never ruined their image of their precious baby boy."

Allison stood up. The structure of her body had changed. She was so muscular now. Imposing. "You were going to tell them about us years ago," he said.

"Your hold on me was strong. I agreed to kill my baby because of you. Back then, I would have done anything to keep us together."

No one had called him Randy in years. It felt bizarre. "You loved something special about me. Something you got from me. There's a lot of people here in L.A. who like that special something they get from me."

Dustin walked up to his bedroom. He got dressed in a new pair of Ralph Lauren jeans and a silk Gucci shirt that one of his dates paid for on Rodeo Drive.

Allison stood in his doorway. "You were my brother."

"I still am. Have you been with any other men besides me?"

Allison said nothing.

Dustin laughed. "I didn't think so. You think you came here for revenge, baby. You really came because you want to get back together. But you also don't want to walk away from all that old time religion our parents taught us. Right?"

"It's been a long road for me."

Dustin pulled open the curtains. The sun flooded in. "Look at where I live. I drive a Ferrari and wear three-hundred-dollar sunglasses and a brand-new Rolex."

Allison took off her bag, reached in, and pulled out her tomahawk. "You want to buy your way out of this?"

Dustin searched for the right words. "I'm telling you that I've started to believe in God for the first time ever. I thought I had escaped the church, but it's still with me."

Allison looked suspicious.

"Things worked out for me since I left home. At first, I didn't think my success had anything to do with God. But I've slowly realized that was wrong. If I perform well for a new group of clients, I'll be intimately close to the men and women that father and mother look up to as leaders. These new clients are pursuing a higher agenda, a way to change the world for the better. What I will be doing can serve as a type of therapy for the Christian men who will lead the world soon. I need to satisfy them sexually because God wants me to."

Howser, sitting at his desk at Wilcox station, checked his watch. He had to leave soon.

At the desk next to him, La Rocca was on the phone. Except to take a few periodic hour-long naps on the cots here, they'd both been working continuously since they first came across Karen's body in the dumpster. So far, they'd been unable to tie the name Dustin Skye to a home anywhere in or near Studio City.

La Rocca hung up. "Winslow, Arizona PD says a woman who was questioned over a murder there is now also wanted for questioning for the theft of that same murder victim's white '73 Ford pickup. She's now a suspect in the murder."

"Murder of who?" Howser said.

"A local businessman with a long sheet for solicitation."

Howser sipped coffee. "They have a name on the woman?"

"Amy Grant," La Rocca said. "But they're almost positive it's a fake. The woman wouldn't show her I.D. and some patrolman kicked her too soon. Said at the time she seemed like a good Christian who wouldn't get involved in anything dirty. Also, Amy Grant's the name of a popular Christian singer. However, their description of her matches Lady Tomahawk. I just put out a local APB on the truck they're after."

"She killed a guy and is still driving around in his truck?"

La Rocca nodded. "She sounds crazy, but inexperienced."

"I wonder why she's after this hustler in Studio City. What does she want him so bad for?" Howser finished his coffee and stood.

"Where are you going?"

He put on his suit jacket. "I need a couple hours to pop in at this fancy cocktail party in Bel Air. Sue got me an invite."

Sue Schultz was Howser's agent. "Who all's gonna be there?"

Howser shrugged. "Buncha big shots. Sue's been riding me for not doing enough networking."

On my way out here to find you, I met a man in Winslow, Arizona," Allison still held the tomahawk. "He assumed I was a prostitute, like you. At first, I thought I would become one too. I thought I would just do what he wanted and take his money. But when he put his hands on me, a feeling overtook me. I imagined he was you. I remembered what you did to me. It just happened… and afterward, I saw that it was easy."

"I didn't make your choices," Dustin said. "Don't blame them on me."

Allison's eyes filled with rage. She ran forward and swung the tomahawk at Dustin's head. He ducked down before the blade rushed by, ran around her and out of the bedroom.

"Calm down," he said at the edge of the stairs.

Allison wound up. She threw the tomahawk. It sailed through the air, straight at him. Dustin ducked again. It cut into the wall. Plaster chips flew. Dustin ran.

Allison shrieked.

Dustin rushed out the front door, past the pool and around the side of the house. He ran past his Ferrari—he didn't have his keys—and out to the street. He ran between two other houses and kept on running.

By the time he'd made it down to Ventura, she was no longer behind him.

Allison found Randy's keys in his bedroom and tried each one on the back sliding door of the main house. She was able to unlock it and enter. It was a beautiful home and bigger than any house she'd ever been in. She saw framed pictures of a well-dressed black man and figured this must be her brother's manager.

Allison roamed through every room and imagined herself living here. She pictured herself being in charge of her brother, just like Ginny and Nancy.

In the master bedroom, she thought about Randy when he stepped out of the steam shower. Then she laid back on the bed and fully relinquished herself for the first time in years. After, she stood and looked out the bedroom window.

An LAPD patrol car was up the street. The officer had stepped out and was looking at the license plates of the pickup truck she'd stolen from the man she murdered back in Winslow.

Alone, La Rocca arrived at the location of the patrolman in Studio City. The stolen pickup was still on the street. *She* had to be close.

"I haven't seen anyone come near it," the patrolman said.

"Take off. If our suspect is here, it might spook her seeing a black and white parked out in the open. This case is media sensitive. The Higher Ups are expecting a drama-free conclusion. We want her to come in easily without an incident."

"Sure you don't need me close, around the block?"

La Rocca checked his watch. "No, my partner's busy for at least another half hour. I'll radio him and tell him to come meet me when he's done."

The officer nodded, got back into his car and drove off. La Rocca got into his parked Matador and watched the white pickup. The street was quiet. The only people he saw moving were a crew of Hispanic landscapers who finished their work on a house up the hill, gathered their equipment into a van and drove off.

He decided to knock on doors. He got out his radio, called Wilcox station and told the dispatcher to let Howser know where he was and to meet him here as soon as he was available.

At the first house, a Mexican housekeeper answered. She told La Rocca that the rest of the family wasn't home. La Rocca asked her a few questions, got nothing, and moved on. At the next house, no one answered. Same at the third.

At the fourth house, a young blonde woman in a white blouse and an ankle-length black skirt came to the door. Under the conservative clothes she looked muscular, like a bodybuilder.

La Rocca stayed calm.

He raised his detective's shield. "LAPD," he said.

"What can I do for you?" she said innocently.

"Are you a resident here, ma'am?"

"No. I'm just visiting my brother, who actually lives back in the pool house." She pointed behind her. "He's not home right now. Neither is his boss, the man this house belongs to."

"Are you the only one here?"

"Yes."

"What's your name?"

"Allison Mae Dummar." She pointed at the gold crucifix hanging around La Rocca's neck. "That's beautiful."

"My wife bought it for me," he said. She'd got it on their last trip to Rome.

The woman nodded.

Despite her build, she seemed far tamer than what he'd been imagining. He'd handled far more dangerous suspects on dozens of occasions. He developed a plan: plant some fear inside her through interrogation, let it grow, then order her to come in for questioning over the truck. If she resisted, he was armed. Subduing this woman without further violence would not be difficult. Also, Howser would be here shortly.

"Could I see some I.D.?" he said.

"It's inside. Would you like to come in while I get it?"

La Rocca nodded. Allison led him into the living room. On the way, La Rocca noticed a painting of a muscular black man in a thong flexing his biceps.

"My I.D.'s right in here," she said and reached into a green military bag on the floor.

La Rocca put his hand on his gun.

The woman turned toward him, already gripping a tomahawk and winding up to throw it.

"Lord Almighty," he said, his body frozen.

The tomahawk spun in perfect circles. It landed clean in La Rocca's skull. He dropped to his knees and flopped over. She'd hit him from twenty feet off.

Dustin wandered the streets. He didn't call Frank or anyone else to warn them about his sister being Lady Tomahawk. Night fell. He roamed and thought about his life. After it had been dark for a long time, he called his answering service from a payphone.

There was a message: *"Change of heart. Call the main house when you get this."*

He hung up and dialed Frank's.

"Hello?" Allison said.

"How'd you find the number for my answering service?"

"It was listed in your room in the pool house. I want you to come back. Please. I promise I'm not going to hurt you."

He got off the bus at a stop on Ventura. A bunch of LAPD squad cars roamed the area. He walked through them without drawing any attention. At the front door he knocked. Allison opened it.

She ran into his arms. She almost knocked him off his feet. They kissed, just like they used to. She locked the door behind them. He led her to the bedroom. She laid back on the bed.

Five

The curtains were open and shafts of dusty light shone across the walls of Frank's bedroom each time the headlights of cars went up or down the hill outside.

Allison rested her face on his chest. "How'd you turn out so good at what you do?"

"Mostly from movies. They have theaters that show older films in L.A. They're called revivals. They show foreign ones too. Mostly I would just copy the sexy European actors that are popular. Then I studied hard and got my massage license. Over time, I stopped being Randy."

"Dustin Skye," Allison said, testing it out.

"Now, characters in movies are based on me. Everyone in L.A. is trying to look as cool as Richard Gere did in *American Gigolo*."

Red lights from a police car flashed through the window. They both got up to look. Squad cars were lining up on the street.

"More cops," Dustin said. "I wonder what's going on."

"They're looking for the police officer."

"Who?"

"The one I killed."

He turned toward her.

"It was over the pickup truck I was driving. I took it from that man in Arizona." She shut the curtains. "I stuffed his body in the trunk of his car, drove it off and abandoned it, miles away. I abandoned that truck I've been using too, but miles in the other direction. Then I came back here and cleaned up all the blood. The cops might have gotten me this time if they had moved a little faster. But they weren't and I won't make any mistake twice."

Dustin looked at her as if for the first time.

"I do what your manager does now," she said. "Two girls work for me."

"Two?"

"I started because I needed money. But I also needed to understand you and how you thrive in this world." Her voice was peaceful. "I've already realized that I'm good at it. Now, I want you to work for me as well."

He stepped back. "What do you mean, work for you?"

"You said it yourself. God wants you to succeed at this sensitive, big-time deal that your current manager is wrecking. So I'll take his place and steer the deal on course. I'll be in charge of you and all the others who work for Frank. When you aren't working, we can be together like tonight. We can serve God in our own way, honoring how he truly made us."

A hard knock came at the front door.

"It's the cops," Dustin said, scared. "Has to be."

"We won't answer. They might suspect that something happened here, but they cannot prove it. We'll wait it out and when they're gone, we'll escape."

"Even if we do, Frank'll still be out there."

Allison rubbed her fingers through his hair. "Not for long."

The loud knock came again.

She hugged him tight. "Just wait for them to pass."

He was with a woman that knew who he really was and loved him anyway. She was the only woman he'd ever been with who really knew him. "I'm sorry for making you kill our baby," he said and began to cry.

Dustin waited in the parking lot of Glendale High beside his Ferrari. Frank's Continental appeared up the street on East Broadway and pulled into the lot. Frank stepped out in a wrinkled Armani power suit. It was a Sunday afternoon and they were the only people here.

Frank, usually so composed, was a mess. He looked sleep-deprived and twitchy, probably from cocaine. He'd driven straight from Palm Springs.

Dustin looked back at the school. "Did John Wayne really graduate here?"

"He went by his real name then. Marion Morrison."

"He became this iconic symbol of a great American and this hardly looks much different than the high school I went to in Ohio."

"Everybody starts somewhere."

Dustin said, "Lady Tomahawk is my sister."

"She's *what?*" Frank looked at Dustin's Ferrari and saw a figure in the back, covered in shadows. "Troubling development."

"We used to be close, but there was history. I didn't know until last night that she's running girls too. She killed Tania, Monroe, and others to get close to me. We've fixed our problems now. I called you here to tell you personally that I'm choosing her."

The Ferrari door opened. Allison stepped out, tomahawk in hand. Frank brought his arms above his head. She reached forward, removed Frank's holstered .38, and placed it on the hood of Dustin's car.

"I'm not happy about this," Dustin said. "But it's no different than how you treated Debussy. My sister caught up with me. So did God. I've got to serve someone, and that someone isn't going to be you."

"You're going to give me everything that's yours. I want it all, even the rich men you've been making this deal with. Right now, you have one thing you can control," Allison said.

"What's that?" Frank said.

"If you choose to make this smooth, I'll go easy on you."

It was in the middle of the night and the wind blew loud outside of the house in Encino. Hank saw that Dustin was awake and looked concerned.

"What is it, son?"

"I need your help with something."

"What?"

Dustin waited. "Frank isn't my manager anymore."

"What? Who is?"

"My sister."

Hank sat up. "Your sister?"

Dustin kissed Hank's cheek. "Frank mocked you all behind your back."

Hank said, "God is not mocked."

"My sister is a real Christian," he whispered.

Hank nodded. The wind outside continued to howl.

"She needs to meet with Milton."

Six

Allison walked into Chasen's at lunchtime. Business was slow. She spotted Milton where Dustin said he would be. He ate chili and drank a Perrier.

"I won't waste your time," she said, sitting across from him. "You've never wanted Frank. You want me."

Milton wiped the side of his mouth. "Because?"

The waitress walked up.

This booth was officially named the Ronald Reagan booth. Dustin told her Ronald and Nancy came here on their first date. They'd gotten engaged in these very seats. Chasen's had long been patronized by big-deal people who ate bowls of their famous chili. Allison was now among their company. She ordered a bowl for herself.

"Clark Debussy was obviously weak," she said. "So was Frank. From what I understand, you grew fond of him."

Milton coughed awkwardly. Frank's body had been discovered by hikers the day before in Griffith Park. He'd been hacked to death, dumped there, and picked apart by a mountain lion.

"I'll grant that I may have been partially manipulated," Milton said.

"His logic wasn't sound. More importantly, Frank wasn't saved."

"And you are?"

"Yes."

Milton nodded, impressed, as if he had just been introduced to an appealing new idea for the first time. "Interesting," he said.

"I know what good Christian men need."

"What about the others who worked for Frank, besides your brother?"

"They understand that I'm in charge now. They've agreed to follow me."

"Just like that?"

Allison nodded.

"I'll have to run this up the ladder."

"To the men who really run this country?"

Milton touched his glasses. "My recommendation carries weight."

"Good." Allison exhaled. "There's one other thing."

Milton waited.

"A cop is snooping around."

"LAPD?"

"Yes. I killed his partner. He's been digging deep and won't back down on his own."

Detective La Rocca, who was also found hacked to death and stuffed in the trunk of his Matador in Coldwater Canyon, had been national news.

Milton whispered, "Are you Lady Tomahawk?"

Allison just smiled. "I can make him disappear. But my methods may just attract more cops. Can you use your resources and make him go away quietly?"

"Isn't it early to be asking favors?"

"If I walk, I take my brother with me. I don't think Hank Shepherd and all of your other clients would be happy with that outcome."

"Yes," Milton said. "I'll see what I can do."

When Howser returned to the station, the desk sergeant said the captain wanted to see him. On his way back, Howser stopped at his desk, unlocked his bottom drawer, and took out a manila folder. The captain's door was open. Howser knocked gently and stepped in.

"What's up, Cap?" he said.

"You and Roberts were up in the rotation. He just showed up to the scene of the shooting at Coach and Horses tonight alone. Where were you?"

Roberts was Howser's new partner. They weren't getting along. Howser didn't answer the question.

"You were in Studio City again, weren't you?"

"All my manpower got pulled without clearances on any of the Lady Tomahawk killings. But last I heard, I was still assigned to those cases, which are still open. I was doing detective work. Anthony La Rocca was last seen by one of our guys on that street, about to go knocking on doors. He radioed and told me to meet him there right away."

"But you took four hours because you were jerking off at some Hollywood cocktail party, trying to sell another script."

Howser looked at the floor. He hadn't written a word in weeks. Moreover, he was now questioning his whole artistic outlook. Simple, escapist fare was not his wheelhouse anymore. After everything he'd seen recently, it now seemed appropriate that the pessimistic, ambiguous cinema of the seventies should go on forever. "Tony was killed inside one of those houses, then moved," he said. "Tony found the house Lady Tomahawk was in and she clipped him. I know which house it was."

Hudson let out a frustrated sigh.

"The former owner of the house, Frank Carson, was found dumped in Griffith Park. Tomahawk again. I'm now told that before his death he had been making payoffs to the LAPD for years, which is probably why he wasn't on our radar. I've been sitting on that house and I've witnessed known associates of former Governor Reagan just coming and going."

"Associates of *Reagan*?"

Howser opened the file and held up sheets with plate numbers. "I ran them at the DMV."

Hudson looked away.

"Something major is going on, Captain. Lady Tomahawk has an untold number of bodies on her at this point and she's just walking around, breathing free air."

Hudson leaned forward in his swivel chair. "It's still time to move on. That's the order I was given. Other cases get priority."

"What about Tony La Rocca? Someone high up the food chain suddenly doesn't want to cause drama and we just forget about him?"

"Nobody's forgetting about La Rocca. This comes from the Higher Ups. There's other bodies out there, other killers that need to be caught. Barring any fresh developments, the Lady Tomahawk cases go on the back burner. Roberts is your partner now. Catch up with him."

Allison was inside John Wayne's old house in Newport Beach. It had been loaned out to her tonight for a private party. She roamed in a Valentino dress, unapologetically showing off her biceps and shoulders. It was July 17th. This party was to celebrate the nomination of Ronald Reagan at the GOP convention being held in Detroit. A who's who of the L.A. GOP and major figures in Pentecostal Christianity were here and watching the broadcast on a TV that had actually belonged to John Wayne. Enthusiasm soared for Reagan's acceptance speech, scheduled to start soon. These men were politicians, preachers, and businessmen—a fellowship of like-minded Christians. None were supposed to be at a party like this.

On the TV screen, Allison saw a clip of Reverend Hank Shepherd and his wife. They'd gone to Detroit in person. They shook hands with George Bush, the vice-presidential nominee.

The rest of Frank's roster, his nine girls and six boys, all worked for Allison now. Each was here. So was a fancily dressed Ginny. But, as usual, the star of the show was Dustin Skye. His mustache was trimmed and he wore a brand-new electric white Dolce & Gabbana suit, an intentional standout from the other boys in black tuxedos. Dustin would smile and laugh in a masterfully playful way each time an old and flirty man made a quip. They all wanted him.

Allison was gripped with excitement. Ronald Reagan was about to meld Christianity with every facet of America. Roe vs. Wade would be overturned. There would be a meld of God and Hollywood, money, war—a meld of God and all things. Those who were truly Christian would thrive and others would fade. America was hurtling toward its glorious and perfect peak and she had a front row seat for the best part of the show.

A fly got unzipped. Allison turned and saw Ryan, one of her boys, take a pastor in his mouth. It was obvious to her that some of these men were just blatant hypocrites. God would punish them in time. But most were authentic in their hearts—believers like her, and also cursed with a weakness, like her. She was grateful to gift them a release.

Allison looked through the glass wall at a lit-up sailboat passing by on the water. She made a mental note to buy a sailboat for herself. She could afford sailboats now.

Back in the high-ceilinged master bedroom of her new mansion in Bel Air, Allison got into bed. Jane was resting by her feet, purring, and she drifted off.

Hours later, Dustin returned home, his blue eyes alive and tender in the darkness. He crawled into bed and wrapped his arms around his sister.

"We've traveled such a long road," he said.

"I'm grateful for all the difficulties God put us through."

"Do you think He'll ever cure us of our love for each other?"

"I hope not." She waited. "Did you catch Reagan's speech?"

Dustin had taken a prominent congressman up to John Wayne's old bedroom before the speech began. "I heard it on in the background."

"He's going to kill in the general."

In the morning, Allison went to the bathroom. She came out with a pregnancy test and held it out so Dustin could see. Jane chirped and tried to bat the test from Allison's hand, as if she wanted to remain the only child in the family forever. Dustin looked at the blue plus sign.

Allison smiled.

The Perpetrators:

ALEC CIZAK is a writer and filmmaker from Indiana. His books include *Down on the Street*, *Breaking Glass*, *Lake County Incidents*, and *Cool It Down*. He is also the editor of the fiction and pop culture digest, *Pulp Modern*. He has spent his life pissing off yuppies and hipsters and other foul iterations of Puritanical fascism.

Plaid in your polarized world: the work of **SCOTCH RUTHERFORD** is a sharp detour away from the open-hive mindedness and faux activism of the indie crime-lit mainstream. He is a fornicator and a heathen with a strong aversion to all organized religions (including the Republican and Democratic parties), and an independent screenwriter and author, whose work has appeared in *Pulp Modern*, *The EconoClash Review*, *Pulp Metal Magazine*, *Greasepaint &.45s*, *The Flash Fiction Offensive*, and *All Due Respect*. He is the unapologetic creator of the vulgar, no-limit crime fiction anthology, *Switchblade*. He lives in Los Angeles. This is his first novella.

ANDREW MILLER was born in Ohio. He lives in Los Angeles with his girlfriend Genevieve and their two cats, John Wayne and Calamity Jane. He writes crime fiction. His stories have appeared in *Close To The Bone*, *Pulp Modern*, *Switchblade*, *Broadswords and Blasters* and on *Medium.com*. His film work includes the music documentary *Soul Of Lincoln Heights*. Andrew is a member of the Independent Fiction Alliance, a network of authors, publishers and editors committed to combating censorship and promoting freedom of expression.

REX WEINER is an author, journalist, and screenwriter based in Los Angeles. His articles have been published in *Vanity Fair*, *The New Yorker*, *The Paris Review*, *Capital & Main*, and *Los Angeles Magazine* where he is a contributing writer. Screen credits include the TV series *Miami Vice*, *Forgotten Prisoners: The Amnesty Files*, and the cult classic *The Adventures of Ford Fairlane*, based on his original stories. His fiction has appeared in *Switchblade*, *Pulp Modern*, *Broadswords & Blasters*, and *Hoosier Noir*. He is the co-founder of the Todos Santos Writers Workshop where he will kick your ass.

An Indianapolis-based
Independent Publishing Mafia